NOAH

CARA DEE

Noah

Warning: This story contains scenes of an explicit, erotic nature and is intended for adults, 18+. Characters portrayed in sexual situations are 18 or older.

Edited by Silently Correcting Your Grammar, LLC.
Formatted and proofread by Rachel Lawrence.

To Lisa

For the adventures, the laughter when I needed them the most, and the memories I'll cherish forever. I still want to pour soy and water into a Diet Coke bottle and see your reaction.

PART I

CHAPTER 1

Noah Collins

I was usually exhausted after a day of traveling. I'd woken up in New York, flown to LA to pack some essentials at my place there, and now I was home. Mendocino. Northern California, where the summers were stunning enough to knock the air out of your lungs, where I was away from the Hollywood noise, and where I had my last name painted on an old-fashioned mailbox outside my house.

It was a different world, and tonight, I wasn't drained. It had been two long months without Emma. I was ready for a spectacular night—me and my girl.

We needed it.

I just had to wrap up the phone call with my sister first.

"Noah, are you even listening to me?" Mia asked.

"Yeah, sure." I got off the interstate, the roads empty in the small town. "You were saying something about jet lag."

Rookie.

My sister lived with her family in Berlin. With Emma and me in California, Mia in Germany, and our folks in Pittsburgh, we only got together—all of us—once a year. This time, we were heading for Disney in Florida. I couldn't give two shits about roller coasters, but it'd be nice for my niece and nephew.

They'd flown in from Germany today, meeting up with our parents in Philly where they'd spend the night, and then tomorrow everyone was flying down to Orlando.

Emma and I would join them in a couple days.

"You can complain when you travel as much as I do," I said.

Mia huffed. "You used to be nicer."

What the hell? "No, I didn't." I chuckled and adjusted my earpiece. "It's my job to annoy you." But I supposed I could play nice for one night. I was the one, after all, who had called her. "I wanted to check in."

"In the middle of the night?" she whined.

"When you sound like that, I forget you're forty-three," I noted.

"When I see your face, I forget you're forty," she mocked.

Was that an insult?

I checked the rearview mirror and drew a hand over my jaw. Sophie, one of my closest friends, had used the word *distinguished* last time I saw her. I kinda dug that.

"You know what might stop the whining?" I asked. "Moving back stateside. No more jet lag, and you wouldn't deprive your kids of seeing more of their favorite uncle."

"*Only* uncle," she snickered. "But speaking of, we've actually discussed moving back home." That was certainly good news. I knew our folks missed them like crazy, especially the kids. "Makes sense now that Julian's graduated from uni, and James can easily find a good position at the New York office. Or maybe the one in Philly."

"Jesus," I muttered. "Julian's that old already?"

He was James's son from his first marriage, and the kid couldn't have been more than sixteen last time I saw him. He was always too busy with school and friends to come to reunions.

"Twenty-three," my sister replied dryly. "One might think you'd know, or did you get some PA to send the card to him two weeks ago?"

I winced and made a turn to get onto my street. "There was a gift too, wasn't there?" But yeah, it was possible my assistant had taken care of it. Last month, I'd been balls deep in post-production.

"Money," she said. "We were hoping to throw him a graduation party in Orlando. We're so proud of him—two majors and all—but—"

"Wait up." I slowed down the car in front of my house, my eyes narrowing.

The driveway was full. Emma's Mercedes was in its place, but there was a brand-new lookin' truck, too. If she'd made another impulse buy, I'd be irritated as fuck.

"Looks like I have a fight to come home to," I told Mia. I killed the engine and sighed. We could catch up in a few days, and I'd see Julian then, too. No need to hear everything about him right now.

"Uh-oh." She chuckled. "What did she do this time?"

I grunted and got out of the rental. "She might've bought another car."

I was torn between anger and feeling like a prick. Emma didn't use to be materialistic, though something had changed this year. We'd argued more, and I'd been gone a lot… I wasn't sure. Then again, every time I asked her to come with me—hell, I'd even offered to take on fewer projects—she wouldn't have it.

Sometimes, it felt like she was picking fights as a way of punishing me, but she was a good person. And maybe I was reading too much into things.

"Uh, Noah?" My sister's voice was tinted with wariness. "You're a day early, aren't you?"

"Yeah, so?" I grabbed my bag from the back and slammed the trunk shut. "I told you—I got all this romantic shit planned. We gotta talk and solve our problems."

"Okay. Yes. Christ, let Sophie and Brooklyn be wrong." She sighed, and I was confused. I didn't know she was that close with my friends. "Just…call me if you need me, all right?"

"Uh, sure." I frowned, but I'd deal with confusion later. Right now, I had to take care of this. "I'll talk to you later, sis. Have a safe flight tomorrow, and we'll see you guys soon."

"Okay, love you…"

"Love you too." I disconnected the call and pocketed the earpiece.

Walking up the pathway to our house, I saw the additions Emma had made in the past two months. New shutters, a porch swing, lawn manicured and framed with new flower beds, and a fucking waterfall next to our lemon tree. Jesus Christ.

I dug out my keys and unlocked the door, and I was greeted by music playing in the living room.

I remembered when we'd just moved here. It was supposed to be our haven away from LA. A place for us to unwind. A studio for her costume design, a study for me when I read scripts. But it had been ages since I saw her passionate about work. Hell, it'd been ages since she worked, period.

"Emma?" I walked farther into the house, and something akin to dread crept up my spine. *Nah, fuck this.* I'd been exposed to too many trashy, clichéd movies. Two wineglasses on the counter meant nothing. "Emma!"

There was a thump coming from upstairs, and I dropped my bag on the floor. *No.* I was about to lose my shit over nothing.

"Noah?" That was Emma's voice, all right. From the stairs, it sounded like. She was breathless, and I hoped I had imagined the panic in her tone. "Is that you?"

I automatically steeled myself, jaw clenching. Fists, too. I prayed I was wrong, and I'd apologize to no end if I was, but…

"Yeah." I rounded a corner and took the steps two at a time. Reaching the landing, I came face-to-face with my girlfriend of four years, and I hadn't imagined the panic at all.

"Y-you're early," she stuttered. "This—this isn't what it looks—I mean…"

My pulse went through the roof.

"This isn't what it looks like? Is that what you're going with, Emma? Huh? Of all the lines in the book, you pick the worst one?"

My stomach churned and twisted. She was wrapped in a motherfucking sheet, and a trail of clothes led to the bedroom door that was closed. *Our* bedroom. Our fucking bed.

"Tell me you fucking didn't," I whispered through gritted

teeth.

Holy fuck, this hurt.

Her eyes grew wide and glassy. "I…I…" She had nothing.

Nausea built up, the pain near crippling, but the rage helped me keep my shit together. I pushed past her and ripped open the door, and there he was.

"Noah, please!" Emma cried out.

I didn't know him. Someone from town? Owner of a nice Ford, I bet. Pants on, shirt on the floor.

Jesus fuck.

Along with the image of his awkward fuckin' expression, I was assaulted with memories. All the goddamn hours Emma and I had spent in here. Every *I love you*, every morning kiss, the laughs, even the fights, and the promises and plans about our future.

"I-I'm sorry, Noah." Emma grabbed my arm, teary eyes pleading with me, but I barely saw her. I didn't recognize her.

"Don't touch me." I coughed into my fist, my throat all but closed up. Vision blurry. Fuck. *Fuck.* My mind was an utter fucking mess, but I managed to jerk my chin at the motherfucker who had screwed Emma in our bed. "Get the fuck out."

Emma was sobbing, and whatever she was talking about went unheard.

The guy scrambled to get his clothes on, and when he reached for—Jesus fucking Christ—a wedding ring on the nightstand, I lost it. My body buzzed with pent-up fury, and I couldn't keep it in.

As he stumbled past me, my arm shot out. I slammed him up against a wall and punched him twice in the jaw.

"Oh my God, stop!" Emma screamed.

"You shut the fuck up!" I shouted, glaring murderously at her.

She froze in place.

I took a step back, my chest heaving. She'd never seen me this way. Tough shit. I'd never seen her as a two-faced cunt.

I stared at her. Saw the sheets, the messy hair, the smeared lipstick. She'd gotten pretty for him. She'd done her hair and put on makeup for another man. But in that instant, she became so fucking ugly to me.

"Go before I put you in the hospital," I told the guy.

He didn't spare Emma a single glance as he raced downstairs, one hand cupping his face.

I looked away from her. Sickened.

Adrenaline, disgust, hurt, and anger rolled around like a brewing storm inside me. My head was fucking swimming. I couldn't see straight, and the memories wouldn't stop flooding in. Four years. She was the woman who'd made me wanna settle down. The only one. I'd enjoyed the life of a bachelor and no strings. No complications. Then she'd barged into my life and changed everything.

"Was it worth it?" I lifted my gaze to her again.

She wiped at her cheeks and stared at the floor. "You've… I… It was a mistake, but you're not innocent."

What the…?

I shook my head, wishing I'd heard that wrong. Though, it kinda helped. Rather than becoming unglued, something in me died. I grew numb and was able to look at her without either throwing up or getting violent.

A chuckle escaped me, 'cause this was surreal.

"You gotta be kidding me," I said.

She got angry. "No, I'm serious. You're never home, and—"

"One more word." I was in her personal space in an instant, a finger in her face. "One more *fucking* word about my job, and you'll regret it." Her fear satisfied me. It was evident in her eyes. "You gotta make up your damn mind, Emma. You bitch at me for never being at home, but who found my last project? It was you. Who promised me we'd be a team and try to get gigs on the same sets? Also you. But I can't even remember when you last worked. All you do is sit around the house and spend the money I make when I'm gone so much." I grinned darkly and took a step back. "My bad, I guess there's more you do. How long have you been spreading your legs for others?"

She dropped her jaw, looking like I'd slapped her.

It was only the beginning of the shitshow that would sum up my first night home in two months.

*

"You never listen to me!" she screamed.

"Oh, I listen, all right." I glared at her as she started throwing clothes in bags dramatically. "It's kinda impossible not to hear the shit you say; you're always yelling. I listened when you told me you wanted to be the industry's most desired costume designer. I listened when we visited Tennyson and Sophie and you said you wanted this—a nice house away from LA—"

"Ugh, fucking Tennyson and Sophie this, Tennyson and Sophie that!" she ranted. "Do you think I'm blind? You're always comparing us to them. They're your friends, not a relationship guide!"

"What the fuck is wrong with you?" I was getting heated again. "I've given you everything, and they have nothing to do with this!"

"You haven't given me you!"

"Bullshit! I don't make a single decision without your opinion, and…" I stopped there, thinking back.

Holy hell, I hadn't asked for her opinion when I'd had work out of town lined up. I'd asked for *permission.* For other reasons, that was worse. I'd always been my own man. Sharing my life with Emma had been eye-opening in the best ways, but at some point, I had started obeying instead of having a damn say myself.

And she had the balls to say I hadn't given her all of me?

*

After packing an overnight bag, she moved on to the living room downstairs, and I followed her.

"I've told you over and over what I want, Noah," she said angrily. She grabbed a couple photo albums from her childhood and tucked them into an empty bag. "I want us to settle down and raise a family—away from LA. But no matter how much you say you want me, you can't commit."

"Can you fucking blame me?" I asked incredulously. "You've bailed on everything we've talked about. What happened to traveling back and forth between our house here and the loft in LA? When did you become so caught up in spending my money?

Since when did you have to have the latest goddamn Mercedes? What happened to compromising? You didn't bring up children until I turned forty a few months ago, and it was right *after* you had told me to pursue my last project. A kid can't fix us, Emma. And you're outta your fuckin' mind if you think I'm gonna propose when we're having problems!"

I didn't know why we were still at it. There was no way I'd forgive her cheating ass. Looking at her made my skin crawl.

I was blown away by all of this. I knew we had shit to solve, but the thought of her stepping out on me…it was unbelievable.

"Am I not allowed to change my mind?" she spat out.

"Not every five minutes," I snapped. "You can't encourage me to go after my dream gigs when I'm at home and then call me when I'm on the road and complain about me not being here."

At that, she had nothing.

*

More bags of fancy brands piled up in the hallway. Clothes, keepsakes, a mountain of beauty products.

I was over the fight. Sitting down in the living room, I poured a whiskey and took swigs as she continued turning the house into a war zone.

What was she waiting for? Me to ask her to stay?

"Who's the guy?" I asked.

She cringed and took down a photo of us from the wall. "A mistake. I met him at the grocery store."

I grinned bitterly and poured another drink. "How long has it been going on?"

Turning to me, a glimpse of the old Emma appeared. She was in pain. It wasn't fake. However, her big, expressive eyes, freckled nose, and everything I'd once found pretty was just…ruined.

"I swear it was only a few weeks, Noah. I—"

"You can stop right there." I didn't need to hear more. I was oddly calm. The whiskey worked. "I hope it was worth it."

Standing up, I walked out to the hallway and grabbed her keys.

"It was a mistake!" She started crying for the umpteenth time. "What are you doing?"

"What does it look like?" I took the house key as well as the keys to her car and the loft in LA.

"I'm going, okay?" She snatched back what was left on her Dior key ring. "I'll drive down to my mother's in Sacramento, and then we can talk in a few days when we've cooled off. We'll work this out."

That was…the most ridiculous thing I'd heard in a long time.

"Work this out?" I smiled down at her. I had a feeling I'd be a mess for months to come, but right this moment, she was a stranger to me. Everything ours was mine again. I'd paid for it. "You should've thought about that before you fucked around on me. We're done, Emma."

"You can't mean that!" She gripped my arms, and the panic was back. "Are you just going to throw away four years?"

"*You* did that. When you hooked up with some bastard you met at the fucking store, you threw away four years." I opened the door and began tossing out her bags. "See, I knew we had some shit to talk about. That's why I'm off this summer, so we could work things out. It's what people do *before* they get hitched and bring kids into their lives."

She hiccupped on a sob and walked out of the house. "I-I believe we can get on the right track. I b-believe in *us*, Noah."

"I don't," I said bluntly. "I'd never be able to trust you. This is over."

She swallowed what she was about to say and fiddled with her keys. "I need the car key."

"You mean the nice car over there that's in my name? Tough shit."

I almost broke my resolve at the despair that flitted across her face, but all I needed was to remind myself of what she'd done. The mere idea of her *fucking* another man in the bed we slept in was a punch in the gut. Had she moaned his name? Had she sucked his cock after getting off the phone with me?

"I have nothing, Noah," she croaked.

I blinked back the emotions and grinned faintly. "I suggest

you get a job, then. And you can always call your new boyfriend if you need a ride."

After closing the door and locking it, I headed straight for the phone to cancel her credit cards. I knew she always carried some cash, and she had a couple cards in her own name, too. That was enough.

I was done.

Time for more whiskey.

CHAPTER 2

I woke up the next morning with the mother of headaches. And as expensive and huge as the couch was, sleeping on it wasn't recommended. I groaned and rubbed my neck, surveying the destruction in the living room.

There were Post-it notes on some furniture, a few of the pictures on the wall, and various knickknacks. It was fuzzy, but I was pretty sure I remembered deciding last night to get rid of the house. Everything marked was shit Emma could keep, and the rest would be donated.

I couldn't stay here.

"Fuck." I stood up, nausea and a new wave of fresh pain bolting through me. I felt fucking dirty. Not the kind a shower could fix, either. "That cunt." I scrubbed at my face. I despised her. She'd turned everything about this house into pain and ugliness.

Padding over to the kitchen, I got coffee started and then checked my phone. I squinted at the display. My inbox had blown up with messages from my sister, Sophie, Brooklyn, and even one from Tennyson—Sophie's husband and probably the guy I'd call my best friend.

My sister… Brooklyn… Sophie…

It jogged something in my memory. Mia had mentioned them

last night before I walked into this clusterfuck. *"Don't let Sophie and Brooklyn be right."* About what? Emma? How in the actual fuck…?

I wasn't sure it mattered, though I called Sophie. If I wasn't mistaken, Mia was in the air now.

"Finally, I've been so worried, Noah!" was Sophie's greeting. "Are you okay?"

"How…" That didn't work. Maybe I'd been a pussy and cried a bit last night. Maybe I'd emptied a bottle of whiskey. My throat was raw. "Emma's fucked around on me. Did you and Brook know?"

She cursed then sighed softly. "I'm so sorry, sweetie. I wanted to be wrong. It was just a theory."

I rubbed my eyes tiredly and grabbed a mug from the cupboard. Theory, she'd said. Nothing else made sense. We were tight. If she or anyone else in my group of buddies had known for sure, they would have told me.

"Mia called me before they got on their flight," she went on. "She filled me in about the truck outside the house. We've been trying to reach you all morning. Are you okay? So it's really true? She's been cheating on you? God, that bitch! I'll cut her!"

Painkillers. I needed them.

Blinking blearily, I headed for the medicine cabinet in the guest bath and swiped a bottle of Advil.

"I walked in on her and some motherfucker."

Sophie cursed up a storm and made promises that no cop should hear. I appreciated it, except I had no desire whatsoever to talk about Emma anymore. I assumed Sophie and Brooklyn had become friends with my sister at my birthday bash in February. Women talked, eh?

As I poured coffee and downed two painkillers, I listened to Sophie going on and on about what she wanted to do to Emma's body parts. It was…colorful. On a good day, I'd have gotten a laugh out of it.

I felt like a fucking idiot instead. It took a hit on my pride, not gonna lie. But I knew I didn't have to hide shit or be ashamed in front of my friends. They were good people. Sophie, despite being ten years younger than me, was a fierce li'l chick. Protective and loyal.

She'd learned the hard way by growing up in Hollywood. Child star gone diva, who got knocked down. Once off her high horse, she'd rebuilt her life. She'd earned her status as a real star, and even though she was the youngest in our group, she was the momma—no doubt.

"Noah? You still there?"

I took a swallow of my coffee and nodded to myself. "Yeah." The sun was shining outside, not really mirroring my mood. Wasn't it supposed to rain or some shit? "I'm selling the house. And getting my dick checked." I couldn't say I trusted Emma when she'd said it had only been going on a few weeks. I wasn't taking any risks.

Sophie choked a bit. "Uh, okay. Ha." She snorted a chuckle. "I'm delighted you told me that last part."

I smiled faintly at the floor and scratched my bicep. "I figured. I can't stay here, though. And there's no word to describe how much I don't wanna go to Florida now."

The thought of all the questions from my family…

Tennyson was one of the biggest directors in the world, and I'd been his assistant director a few times now. There was a reason why we clicked. He was simple like me, and we both enjoyed flying under the radar. But with all this…my family would give me every shade of attention I despised.

Sophie hummed. "Well…they're gonna be in Orlando for two weeks, right? So how about you come down to LA for a couple days? We'll chill out. You get your head straight and rest up. Then you can see your family when the wounds aren't as fresh."

Didn't sound half bad, though I suspected the wounds would be raw for some time.

"Staying at the loft sounds better than this hellhole," I admitted.

To my friends, Mendocino would remain a fairy-tale getaway. Tennyson and Sophie belonged up here and lived in what they called domesticated bliss when they weren't working in LA—or elsewhere. But I was done. I had a feeling I'd lose my mind if I didn't find any distractions, stat.

"Can you agree to something before I tell you what it is?" Sophie asked.

I grunted and took a sip of my coffee. "That's not my thing. I know you broads. That's how guys end up going to the salon or the mall to hold your purse."

She laughed. "I promise, no malls or salons. This is because we love you and want you here as soon as possible. Feel free to even call it selfish, but I'd sleep better tonight with you across the hall."

She'd just given it all away, and I couldn't bring myself to care. I'd always loved my loft in Pacific Palisades, and with Sophie and Tennyson as neighbors, I wouldn't have to go far to get distracted. Tennyson and I could catch a game, I could bring greasy food and watch movies with Sophie, or I could teach their kids shit Mommy and Daddy didn't approve of.

"Okay, call your pop, hon," I said.

Peter Pierce, former big shot in the film industry. He lived in nearby Fort Bragg these days and had a private jet on standby. His cottage-style house probably hadn't cost as much as it did to keep that jet fueled for a week.

"How did you know…? Never mind." She sighed, though there was a smile in her voice now. "Thanks, Noah. I know you don't like to take advantage of your Hollywood perks, so I appreciate it. Now, get your ass back down to LA, all right?"

I managed a chuckle. "Yes, ma'am."

*

Exhaustion kicked in halfway to LA. It offered a blanket of numbness, but the roller coaster of emotions was never far away. I had to do my best to think of anything other than Emma looking freshly fucked by someone else.

I failed most of the time, and that was what booze was for.

I'd left everything behind that reminded me of her. An hour was all I had needed to box up personal belongings from my childhood and the few awards and memorabilia items I'd collected from film sets throughout my career. The rest, I couldn't care less about.

Closing my eyes, I struggled to get comfortable in the luxurious leather chair. I tried to come up with shit I could distract myself with while I got over Emma. Work would probably suit me best. I'd been somewhat of a casual player before her, but women were the last thing I needed in my life at this point.

I was *single.*

Kinda difficult to comprehend. Four years wasn't that long in comparison to many, yet the fact remained: I'd thought I was done. Re-fucking-gardless of recent issues in our relationship, I'd considered myself off the market for life.

No, I would simply go back to being married to my job. Perhaps it was time to listen to Tennyson. He was only in his mid-forties, but he'd accomplished a fuckload, and he'd been a mentor to me in many ways. He liked to tell me I should get out of the shadow of being an AD and direct something on my own.

Directed by Noah Collins.

Maybe.

It could be the perfect time for me to step out of my comfort zone. A new challenge, a more time-consuming one. There'd be more publicity and pressure, though I'd deal.

I stood up and walked over to the liquor cabinet to pour myself a drink. It was five o'clock somewhere, right? Then I figured I could use social media as my next distraction. It was a plan. Moving from one distraction to the next. No stopping.

Sitting down again, I took a swig of my drink and punched in the WiFi password on my iPad. The pilot announced we'd be landing on time as I dicked around on Twitter a bit. There was a hashtag about some plane crash that was trending rapidly, so I muted that one. No need to fucking jinx myself.

Sophie, Daniel, his husband Zane, and Brooklyn weren't online as far as I could see, so I moved on to Facebook where I mostly had my family.

And Emma.

I rolled my eyes and ignored the stab in my chest at her juvenile change in her relationship status.

It's complicated?

Nah, I don't think so, toots.

I had half a mind to change mine to single, but it felt ridiculous. I moved on instead and was thankful when Brooklyn called me.

"Hey, gorgeous. I have no interest in talking about Emma, but anything else goes," I told her.

She didn't laugh, as I'd expected. She was married to Tennyson's brother, and I'd known her since she was a makeup artist to soap opera stars and I was a lowly PA. We'd come far in fifteen years, and I hoped she hadn't lost her sense of humor along the way.

"You're in the air, right?" she asked.

"Yeah." I didn't like the edge in her tone. As if she was hiding something upsetting. "What's up?"

One of the ladies in Peter's cabin crew joined me briefly to say we were about to land. I nodded in response.

Brooklyn cleared her throat. "Tennyson and Daniel are on their way to meet you at the airport—"

"I'm not a fucking child, hon." I got a bit impatient. I needed my friends to distract me and be there, not coddle me. "If something's happened, tell me right now, Brook. Don't assume what's best for me or whatever. Just spit it out."

She was mumbling something to someone else. I couldn't hear what it was, and I was getting more and more frustrated. The flight attendant came in again and smiled apologetically, saying they were shutting off the WiFi for landing.

"Sweetie," Brooklyn said, "I need you to turn on the news. And please wait for Tennyson and Daniel to get to you. Stay on the plane."

I frowned, confused, and I was out of time for now. It couldn't be so important that it couldn't wait until I got to the loft. With Emma's recent Facebook change, maybe she'd done something dramatic elsewhere on social media. Much like she'd grown fond of expensive things, she'd also developed a flare for diva antics. They were mild in comparison to what was out there, but for a laid-back Pittsburgh fucker, I disliked the smallest amount of drama.

"I'm about to land," I told Brooklyn. "We can talk later."

I disconnected the call and set my phone on airplane mode, then buckled my seat belt and spent the following twenty minutes nursing my drink. Vodka was my buddy, too.

*

After getting off the plane, I realized I'd clearly underestimated the power of alcohol. I needed to take a piss, so instead of going straight home to the loft, I grabbed my bag and headed into the lounge where other rich fuckers were waiting to board their private jets.

I nodded hello to some industry folk I knew and ducked into the bathrooms. I'd barely zipped up my jeans and moved over to wash my hands when my phone went off.

"What the fuck is wrong with everybody today?" I muttered. The phone went silent as I dried my hands, only to ring again two beats later. "Jesus Christ." I pulled the damn thing out and barked out a "What?" before I could even look at the Caller ID.

"Where are you?" It was Tennyson, and he sounded out of breath.

"I'm in the private lounge." I exited the men's room and looked around. "I'll order car service. See you soon—"

"We'll be there in five," he said quickly. "Stay there, man."

I was in no mood for this. There was no goddamn rush, was there? Then I saw the fancy bar some twenty feet away and figured I could keep working on my buzz while I waited.

Dropping my bag next to a stool, I sat down and ordered an Old Fashioned. The bar wasn't packed by any means, besides a few businessmen and one man who looked like a rapper without an entourage.

"Turn that up, please." One of the businessmen nodded at the flat screen behind the bar.

The bartender complied and then finished making my drink.

I removed the orange slice and threw half of it back, a nice burn sliding down my throat. The TV had nothing interesting to show. It appeared to be about whatever plane crash...

Wait.

I checked the headline scrolling past and felt bad for my folks. The plane had crashed near Orlando, so I could only imagine the delays they'd have down there.

Taking another swallow of my drink, I listened to the reporters and the experts they'd already called into the studio. No survivors—that sucked. The footage showed a massive area of destruction. Debris everywhere. Experts were ruling out causes based on how the plane had gone down and how much fire there was.

And I was having a bad day? I felt like an asshole. Bitching about getting cheated on when whole families were being shattered.

"Jesus," the suit nearest me said. "An associate of mine was supposed to be on that flight, but he was delayed. Didn't even make it to Philadelphia before the plane took off."

"What?" I frowned at the screen. Philly-Orlando? That had been the route?

I coughed as a sudden burst of nausea did a somersault on its way up my gut to my throat, but I swallowed it down and shook my head. That didn't mean anything. There were several flights going to the same destinations every day. School was just out for the year; families all over the country were heading to Disney.

I retrieved my phone to check the flight details from the text Ma sent me when they'd booked the tickets. I only remembered the airline, and now I didn't wanna check the news to see if it matched.

With the flight number going on a loop in my head, I steeled myself and looked at the flat screen. A helicopter was flying over the area littered with fires, smoke, and debris.

There were only two pieces of wreckage that were big enough to contain people, and they were destroyed by fire. Close-ups showed blackened seats, plastic melted—fuck. People. Or charcoal.

The anchor repeated that there were no survivors just as the flight number scrolled past on the screen again.

My stomach dropped.

The onslaught of emotions came so fast and fucked with my head so much that I chuckled first. My mind couldn't work it out. There was no way. No fucking way. Tears welled up in my eyes. I chugged the last of my drink and then laughed again.

This isn't happening.

One of the businessmen gave me a disapproving stare, and it pissed me off.

"Can I fucking help you?" I snapped.

A pounding headache settled in, and when I turned back to the screen, I had double vision. *Fuck.* No survivors, no survivors. Bile rose. My palms grew cold and sweaty.

Why does the flight number match?

"Jesus." I squeezed my eyes shut, feeling disoriented and sick. *It can't be.* This was the sort of thing you saw on the news, and you felt for the relatives of those lost.

My fingers shook as I searched my phone for numbers to my parents, sister, and brother-in-law. I could barely see the digits, and I swayed in my seat. Gripping the bartop, I pressed Call and placed the phone to my ear.

Mom would respond.

"Hi, this is Abigail Collins. I can't come to the phone right now…"

Fuck.

Next number.

I tried Mia and immediately got her chirpy voice saying something in German.

My brother-in-law's American number.

"You've reached James Hartley. Please leave a message or contact my assistant at…"

"Noah?"

I tried 'em all, over and over, but no one picked up the fucking phone. "Answer, goddammit!" I knocked back the stool and stumbled. My surroundings were blurry, and I heard voices, yet I couldn't decipher the words. Like a faint echo.

I started to hyperventilate.

My parents. My sister and James. Holy fuck, JJ, Linda, Julian…

"Noah!"

I turned toward that voice. I couldn't get my head straight, my vision still fucked and my skull pounding, but I knew that one.

Tennyson.

He knew. One look at his face, no matter how out-of-focus, made it clear this was why he'd insisted on meeting up with me. Daniel ran over too, not far behind. They both knew.

"I gotta call the airline," I rasped.

I needed to see the passenger list.

"Whatever you need, Noah." Tennyson squeezed my shoulder while Daniel grabbed my bag. "Come on, let's go home. Sophie and Brooklyn are at the loft, too."

"How did you all…?" I couldn't speak past the lump in my throat.

Tennyson hesitated but didn't hold back, thank fuck. "Sophie saw the news right after it happened, and she managed to track down your eldest nephew. Julian?"

"Oh." My insides twisted again. Okay, so Julian was at home. "It's not true, is it?"

This time, Tennyson didn't answer.

CHAPTER 3

Two weeks later

"Christ, not again," I whispered to myself. I wiped at my cheeks and headed for the living room. Felt like all I'd done lately was cry. I took a deep breath, waiting for some sense of relief, but it was nowhere to be found. The nightmare was true, and everything around me was real.

My parents' house just outside of Pittsburgh made it extremely difficult to believe the reality. The only thing that didn't fit was me—wearing a black fucking suit. My folks were blue-collar and casual. *Had* been.

Suits had no business in the house I'd grown up in. Family photos and Penguins memorabilia hung on the walls. Pop's chair stood in the corner, ratty and well-used. Ma had wanted to buy him a new one, and he'd always refused. Additions had been welcome, but no replacements.

"Don't fix what ain't broke, son."

I'd given him the universal remote and the surround sound system one Christmas. He'd immediately pulled out a VHS of the Stanley Cup final from '91 when the Penguins had won, and we'd watched the game together.

I brushed my hand over Lemieux's signed jersey that hung on the wall above the TV. Had Pop been here, he would've scolded me for going near it.

"Noah?" Sophie called from the kitchen. "Anything I can get you?"

"No thanks." I walked over to the window and stuck my hands down in my pockets.

The lawn needed mowing, a reminder that everything wasn't the way it was supposed to be. Pop always kept the yard groomed to perfection. Since he'd retired, it had been his pastime to make the backyard pretty for Ma.

She'd enjoyed bragging about her flower beds. At the time, I'd been bored to tears hearing about it, and now I'd give everything to hear it again.

The sun was out. Blue sky. No clouds in sight. The cherry tree would bear a lot of fruit this year.

I hung my head.

What a fucking waste of life.

They still weren't sure why the plane had gone down, but experts were speculating freely about several causes. I wasn't sure I cared. Good luck finding the black box in the Florida wetlands, anyway.

They had ruled out everything from terrorism to sabotage, leaving all the mechanical shit that could go wrong but usually didn't.

Regardless, my entire family was gone.

Not Julian, I reminded myself, but fuck that. I'd spoken to him over the phone once we'd gotten our fears confirmed, and then he'd gone off the grid. His father's assistant had visited their house in Berlin, and Julian had left it all in shambles.

It wasn't until yesterday he'd contacted me to say he'd be here for the memorial service today.

He'd sounded hungover as fuck, which…to be honest, I couldn't blame him for. I'd been on a bender since I pushed Emma out the door.

Inhaling deeply, I closed my eyes and took myself back in

time. The fragrance of home wasn't likely to go away anytime soon, and it worked like the most painful comfort now.

These walls bore scents of decades of Ma's cooking, her perfume, and flowers. Pop's cologne and the soap he used. The house was essentially a bottle of memories, and if I concentrated, I could see flickers of film rolling. Mia and I chasing each other around when we were kids. All the pranks. Prom dates, fights, bitching, Pop yelling at the TV, Ma crying when I went off to college, Ma crying even more when Mia moved to Berlin.

I wasn't ready to let go.

Returning to the kitchen, I leaned against a counter and stared at the floor. The third board creaked, which was good to know when you had the midnight munchies and wanted to get leftovers without waking up the 'rents upstairs.

Tennyson, Sophie, Daniel, and Zane were with me, and the "How are you doing?" question hung in the air, though no one ever asked me. For obvious reasons.

Everything was shit, and they knew it.

"We should head over to the church," Daniel said quietly. "We'll call when we've gotten rid of the reporters."

"Good luck with that," I muttered.

It bugged me to no end. Only because I was semifamous and linked to A-listers Sophie Pierce and Tennyson Wright, I'd found myself in the spotlight for this circus.

Sophie and I had both lashed out at the paps for following us, and it probably hadn't helped the matter.

Enter Daniel. He was Sophie's manager and knew how to work these situations, along with her publicist. Getting rid of reporters completely, though? Un-fucking-likely. They were vultures.

"Thanks, guys." I didn't look up from the floor, but I wouldn't be a complete dick. Without my friends, I wouldn't have gotten anything done. Sophie and Tennyson had been there every step of the way, taking charge and helping me plan the memorial, and Daniel and his man had joined us here in Pittsburgh this week.

"Don't mention it." Zane clapped me on the shoulder as they passed. "See you in a couple hours, okay?"

I inclined my head, having nothing else to say. They had it all covered, what to run past the priest again, check on the photos Sophie had helped me pick out, arranging of flowers and whatever.

"Let's have a drink." Tennyson pushed out the chair across from him at the table and refilled our glasses with bourbon. "Have a seat, my friend."

"You boys drink." Sophie stood up. "I'm gonna call Brooklyn and Asher and check in on the kids."

Tennyson snatched up her hand so she couldn't leave. "Give them my love." He kissed her knuckles before letting go, and she smiled and ran her fingers through his hair.

"Of course."

I envied them.

They deserved everything they had, and I was nowhere ready for something that heady, but I craved human contact. Being bear-hugged by li'l Sophie was nice and always welcome, yet it lacked the comfort I wanted.

Maybe because the people I wanted to hug were dead.

There wasn't even anything to bury.

I took a seat at the table and nodded in thanks as I got my drink. I had no desire to discuss my life, so that left me with two options where Tennyson was concerned. Film and family.

"You ready for Kayden to start first grade?" I asked.

He loosened his tie and took a sip. "Ready might be a stretch, but I'm not freaking out about it."

Like Sophie was, in other words. She wanted their kids to remain her babies.

"When're you heading up to Mendocino?" As far as I knew, that was where Kayden would go to school. Then Ivy, but she had a few years to go. She was only four.

Tennyson smiled ruefully. "We don't have to talk, you know."

The man knew me well.

We clinked our glasses together and then stayed quiet as we drank.

*

My sister and mother had loved twilight. Sun setting, rush hour ending, families reconnecting after a day of work or school, and the sky painted in stunning colors.

It was the main reason I'd picked a late service, and it seemed like the weather was working for us. I stood outside the church with my closest friends and greeted everyone who showed up, and the sky above us looked like fruit punch.

Every "I'm sorry for your loss" made me wanna vomit, but I pushed that shit down. This wasn't for me. The memorial service was for the others. The friends, the old coworkers, the distant family, and the community my folks had been part of.

James's parents were here, too. His mother could barely keep it together.

Some kids had shown up with their folks, coming all the way from Germany. Classmates and soccer friends of JJ and Linda.

That made the grief tighten its grip on my heart.

The church was filling up, and when there was a break in between arrivals, I checked my watch and wondered where the fuck Julian was. His whole family had died, too. It'd be nice if he could be here on time.

His biological mother had never been one to stick around. She'd come and gone over the years, so it hadn't taken long before Julian had begun relying on my sister. She was Mom to him. No one else.

"He'll be here." Daniel nodded firmly. "His flight was on time, and I sent someone to pick him up."

I grunted and pulled out a flask from my inner pocket.

That earned me a look from my buddy, though he was wise not to say anything.

I had to speak in front of all these people. It was my excuse for bringing a little something.

There was no denying I'd turned into a sad motherfucker, though. I could barely spell health anymore. I didn't know when I'd last worked out or eaten something that didn't come in a Styrofoam box. I drank every day. I hadn't shaved in two weeks. It was a chore to get in the shower.

"Could that be him?" Daniel asked.

I pocketed my flask again and looked to where he was watching. A young man was stepping out of a black car, and it could be him, yeah. It had been years, but I remembered that dark, curly hair he could never bother with. His skinny tie was crooked, his suit jacket thrown over his shoulder.

One piece of luggage.

"Yeah." I turned to another few latecomers and nodded politely. "Thanks for coming."

An old lady patted my hand. "I'm so very sorry for your loss, dear."

Forced smile.

Julian hurried over, his clothes wrinkled and his eyes probably as haunted as mine. He looked like shit. Like a kid in mourning.

I felt for him.

"Sorry I'm late." He fidgeted with the strap of his duffel, only pausing for a moment. Then he continued inside.

All right, then.

"You sure you guys are family?" Daniel quirked a wry smile.

I shrugged and rubbed the back of my neck. "It's been a while."

Besides, why talk to me when Julian could go over to his grandparents on James's side? We'd never been that close, anyway.

"Come on, I wanna get this over with," I muttered.

*

The pews on the first row were occupied by me, James's folks, a few of my aunts and uncles, their spouses, and Julian. I'd never been religious, so having my friends behind me was a relief when the priest droned on and on about God adding to his harem of angels. Maybe those weren't his words, but whatever.

There were breaks every now and then, and it was when those of us closest to the family shared stories and gave speeches.

Pop's brother fell apart at the podium, which shattered a bit more of me. I didn't think that was possible. But seeing these men—of that generation—get emotional was unheard of.

"Jesus, that bitch needs to give it a rest," I heard Sophie

whisper.

I frowned and looked over my shoulder, finding her glancing apologetically at those who had heard her.

"Sorry." She was mortified, and then she gave me a subtle look and a roll of her eyes. Holding up her phone, she showed me a missed call from Emma.

I shook my head and faced forward again. Sophie was right. Emma needed to give it a fucking rest. She'd been trying to reach all of us since the news broke about Noah Collins losing his family, and she was the last person I'd talk to right now. I had more important things to deal with.

Gerald, James's pop, spoke of his son with pride. Some about his successful career, but mainly about his fortune in finding my sister. He went on about my niece and nephew, choking up, and Daniel tapped me on the shoulder, indicating I was next.

It made me queasy. I didn't feel forty. I wanted to be seven again. I wanted to fucking hide. Or drink myself into a coma and never wake up.

It seemed like no time passed, and then I was the one standing up there. I blanched for a second, seeing all those faceless people. Maybe going unscripted had been a bad call, even though I'd never been good with written speeches.

I adjusted my tie and cleared my throat. It was hot in here, or perhaps it was just me.

Glancing behind me, I saw the photos we'd had enlarged and framed. Ma, Pop, Mia, James, JJ, Linda. Their smiling faces.

What the fuck did I say?

There was nothing left.

So that's what I went with.

"Life goes on, they say," I said, raising the mic a bit. "I just don't see how at this point. My family's always been there for me, even when we were separated by oceans. Each and every one of them played a huge part in my life, so I don't have a favorite memory. I have hundreds." I paused, staring unseeingly at the speech someone forgot earlier. "They're supposed to be here. And—" I had to clear my throat again. "And now that they're not, it's kinda like running out of purpose."

I was always so fucking excited to share something with my family. My passions were mine alone, but they supported me. Had. *Had, had, had.* With them being gone, I had no clue how to stay motivated.

"I guess it's selfish, needing them for me." I scratched the side of my head. "It is what it is, though. I'll miss the little things. JJ and Linda calling me on Skype to fill me in about soccer and dance classes, bitching with my sister about everything between heaven and earth, catching a game with Pop…" I smiled wistfully and dragged a hand over my face. "They made everything worth it, and I'll miss them more than I can say."

I released a breath and returned to my seat, ignoring everyone who tried to catch my eye. I was done with the attention. I was done with this suit and the tie that was suffocating me. I was done with responsibilities.

I was just done.

The priest shared something from the bible, and I closed my eyes and leaned forward, elbows on my knees. If I could get away with earplugs, I'd probably ask for them. I needed today to be over.

Thank fuck we were parting ways after this. There'd be dinner for the closest at my folks' house, but nothing big like this.

"Now, please, the stage is yours, Julian," the priest said, which confused the fuck outta me.

I looked behind me at Daniel, lifting a brow.

"I didn't tell you?" he whispered.

No, he damn well hadn't. I didn't mind, obviously. If Julian wanted to say something about our family, great—good for him. I'd just figured it wasn't his thing.

This was the kid who had spent the past two weeks trashing their home in Berlin, if James's assistant was correct. He hadn't returned any calls; he hadn't given a fuck.

Julian didn't go to the podium like the rest of us had done, though. He headed for the piano that stood to the side.

I straightened in my seat and folded my arms over my chest.

I recalled Mia telling me he'd had a double major. Maybe music was one of them.

Julian didn't say anything. He rolled up the sleeves of his

white shirt, and the moment his fingers gently hit the keys, I heard what song it was. *Mad World.* If he did this well, he'd fucking ruin me.

He sang quietly, with a hint of a British accent. If I wasn't mistaken, I'd teased him about his accent changing when they'd moved to Germany. Now, his voice was merely a punch in the gut. Quiet and soft, yet clear and raw. I hadn't expected any of this.

Songs like these…they triggered memories and emotions, and I was already near my breaking point. I didn't wanna be around people when I was pushed over the edge, which was inevitable.

He went on, a bit choked up, singing about drowning his sorrows and no tomorrows, and it made me wonder if he'd been pushed over the edge, too. 'Cause the first thing that came to mind was destroying things.

For a relatively short song, Julian seemed to go on forever. I sniffled and rubbed my eyes. He needed to fucking stop. He didn't only perform it well; he was gifted as hell. His fingers danced over the keys flawlessly, and his voice…Jesus Christ.

The kid was in pain.

I was going through purgatory, but damn. Despite how close I'd been with our family, he'd seen most of them every day. He was young, and he'd lost his mom and dad, his little brother and sister. Plus two grandparents.

Glancing over at James's parents, I wondered if they could be there for Julian. They were beside themselves with grief for their son, daughter-in-law, and two young grandchildren. Where was Julian off to after this? Back to Berlin?

I bet he had friends there, but what about family?

No matter how he'd acted before today, I kinda owed it to myself and my sister to talk to him.

CHAPTER 4

I was spent after the whole church ordeal was over, and when we got back to my parents' house, the first thing I did was pour a drink.

Fuck what the others thought. It was only James's parents, my friends, Julian, and Pop's two brothers with their wives. Luckily, though, no one seemed to think I'd turned into an alcoholic yet. While the women gathered in the kitchen to set up the food we'd had catered, the men ended up in the living room with glasses of whiskey.

"You did good, son," one of my uncles told me. "Organizing all this today…Abigail and Frank would'a been proud."

I strolled over to the window and emptied half my glass. "I didn't do much. Thank Sophie and Danny." It was dark outside, though I was sure I could see movement in the backyard. There was a porch swing attached to an ancient tree, and I was willing to bet it was Julian out there. He'd kept to himself on the way over to the house, not saying much.

We'd gotten lucky where the reporters were concerned. There had only been a couple waiting outside the church after the service. Easily dealt with, but maybe it had affected Julian negatively. I didn't know.

I loosened my tie and took it off.

If I never had to wear one again, I wouldn't complain.

My uncles told Tennyson and Daniel about my pop as a young guy, and my friends had a couple stories to share as well, about my birthday party where they'd met Pop the first time. I'd had it and needed some air, so it was a good time to play the uncle I was supposed to be and check in on Julian.

Shrugging out of my jacket, I opened the door to the terrace and stepped outside. It wasn't the heat of California I'd gotten used to; it was perfect. Fresh air. I unbuttoned the top button of my shirt too, and I could finally breathe.

I kicked a football that was in my path, alerting Julian to my presence.

"Food's almost ready if you're hungry." I sat down next to him with a grunt, the old swing creaking with age.

"I'm not, but thanks." He stared out at nothing. I couldn't see his features clearly, though his eyes shone from the light in the house.

I stared ahead too, enjoying the silence. I saw when Sophie and my uncle's wife came into the living room. Probably announcing that dinner was ready.

"You stayin' with Gerald and Trudy?" I asked.

He shrugged. "Yeah, for now."

And then what? We didn't know each other that well, but it didn't seem healthy for him to take off on his own. Even at twenty-three, he was very young. To go from having everything to nothing like that wasn't easy.

"Do you need me around for lawyers and whatnot?" he wondered. "I'm not sure I can deal with that."

I shook my head. "Not much to settle. Aside from the house, I'm signing over everything into your name."

Maybe the house would be his one day too, but for now, I wanted it to stay my parents'. It was too soon to go through everything, and I wasn't hurting for money. I'd have the furniture covered and hire someone to clean until I was ready.

"Let me know if you need help with your dad's will."

"Our family lawyer's already contacted me," he responded. "Grandpa said he could fix it for me. I don't care. I don't want anything."

He'd find it useful one day, when he felt better.

"I know we're not close," I told him, "but you can always come out and visit me in LA."

It was what I had to give. I couldn't stay in Pittsburgh much longer. The pain was too fucking much in this city, and I had no energy to go with him to Berlin—if that was where he wanted to stay.

Tennyson had not-so-subtly suggested I try therapy or grief counseling, and maybe it was a good idea. First, I needed to be on my own turf, and only my loft felt like home.

Julian didn't acknowledge my offer, which was fine with me. I didn't know his thoughts or his needs.

"Did you mean what you said at the service?" he asked softly after a while. "About not knowing how to go on."

I nodded slowly, my mind already fuzzy. I remembered most of what I'd said, but since it hadn't been rehearsed, it wasn't all there. I knew I'd meant every word, though.

"Yeah."

He swallowed audibly. "I don't know, either."

As the adult, so to speak, I reckoned this was where I was supposed to have some golden advice. I had absolute shit.

Part of me wanted to get buried in work, though there was no way I'd pull through. I wouldn't be able to deliver and stay committed. There was no motivation or inspiration.

"Well, my offer stands, kid." I gave his leg a pat as I stood up. "Come out whenever you want. I probably won't be the best company, but I have plenty of room and LA is full of distractions."

I began walking back to the house; then I remembered something I wanted to tell him, so I stopped and turned.

"Julian, did you major in music?"

He lifted his head as if it weighed a ton. "And art. Why?"

"I could tell. You were great today."

"Oh. Thank you." He looked down again. "I wasn't sure I should do it. Dad wasn't stoked about me going with not one, but two directions where it's not easy to get a job."

My mouth twisted up, if only a little. Sure sounded like something James would say. "That's what parents do. You think my folks were thrilled when I said I wanted to study film?" But much like mine, Julian's mom and dad were...*had been*...good people. "You know what my pop did when I landed my first big project, though? He took me out for a beer and was happy to admit he'd been wrong. James would have done the same thing."

He bobbed his head slowly. "Okay."

I watched him, wondering if there was a protocol I didn't know about. Was I supposed to press? What would I even say in that case? I was at a loss and figured it was probably best to give him space. Either he believed me or he didn't. Or he needed to digest, fuck if I knew.

He had my number, my address, and my email. If he wanted help or whatever, he could contact me whenever.

With that thought, I headed back inside to force some food into me. I'd rather go straight for the bottle, but that could wait until I was alone.

*

Tennyson and Sophie flew back to LA the following day, and the day after that, it was Daniel and Zane's turn. They went home to New York, though not before Danny insisted I needed a PA. I definitely didn't, but I guessed it couldn't hurt to have someone come over with food that didn't come from takeout places.

The morning after, it was my turn to leave Pittsburgh.

Completely drained and anxious, I boarded the flight and checked my emails while the plane filled up. I confirmed payments for the gardener and housecleaning I'd ordered for my folks' place, I checked in with James's parents, and I fired off a quick email to Sophie to say when I was landing.

I had a few minutes to spare, so I wrote Julian a text, too. I hadn't heard from him since the night of the memorial, and something told me to pay attention to him.

Off to LA now. Take care of yourself, kid. Don't hesitate

to call if you need anything. —Noah

The rest of my blown-up inbox could wait. I was giving myself a month to be a selfish dickbag and drink my sorrows away. After that, maybe I'd return to the land of the living. Possibly.

I looked out the window as the plane taxied down the runway, and there was a tremor of unease and irrational fear. But perhaps I traveled too much to let the accident get to me. The statistics were a comfort, and it ensured that flying remained…slightly tedious and a whole lot boring.

*

The plane crash was old news in LA, and I was back to being only semifamous. Industry people knew me well, but otherwise, I was only interesting to paps if I was out with Sophie or I was at a premiere.

I took a cab from LAX and switched on my phone on the way. A shipping company had sent an update on the two boxes of photo albums I was having sent from Pittsburgh, and I had a message from Sophie, as well.

The only bad thing about our building is that we don't have a doorman. Someone buzzed Emma in, and she won't leave. Let me know if you want me to deal with her.

I groaned quietly and pinched the bridge of my nose. She was right. Having a doorman wouldn't have hurt. Too bad I'd never been the type of man to want a mansion. I loved my loft, the New York factory feel, the high ceilings, and open space. What I didn't love was having my ex camped outside my door.

Might as well get it over with, though. Our spectacular breakup had ended abruptly, and I'd known I would see her again. Despite that she hadn't been to the loft in ages, she had shit of hers there.

About a year after we'd gotten together, my roommates had moved to their own places, so with them leaving and now Emma taking her stuff, I wouldn't have much left, I reckoned.

No fucks to give.

When we finally reached my street, I was both relieved and

anxious. Once I'd dealt with Emma, I would be alone. At fucking last. I couldn't wait to shut everyone out and be miserable. At the same time, I was dreading it 'cause I knew it was gonna get ugly. As difficult as it was to hold myself together—somewhat—for the sake of others, it also kept me from knowing how deep I'd fall once I let go.

I paid the fare and got out of the cab, and I wasn't too surprised to see Tennyson waiting outside our building. He had his daughter and their new puppy with him.

"Uncle Noah!" Ivy waved madly, almost dropping the leash.

"Hey, sunshine." I smiled, a genuine one, and walked over to them. "How many dogs do you guys have now?"

Tennyson and his brother ran a charity organization for rescue dogs, including a massive rehabilitation ranch in San Diego. He and Sophie had at least four of them up at their house in Mendocino. Someone lived there 24/7 just to take care of the dogs.

"Not enough," she said cheekily. "Right, Daddy?"

Tennyson chuckled and ruffled her hair. "If you say so, baby." As if he didn't agree. His grin faded a bit as he turned to me. "She's waiting outside your door." He spoke of Emma. "Sophie tried to get her to leave, but unless we involve the authorities, there isn't much we can do."

I shook my head grimly. "I'll deal with her. Might as well get it over with. I want her outta my life."

"I figured." He inclined his head and opened the door. "I took the liberty of ordering a truck for her belongings, and Sophie stacked a bunch of moving boxes in the hallway. Emma was quite adamant about talking to you, but her excuse for not budging was her 'right' to get her things."

Yeah, that sounded like Emma. She knew persistence.

"I appreciate it, man." I passed him, and we rode up to the third floor together. "Can I expect movers soon, or…?"

"In a couple hours," he replied with a nod. "Sophie's taking the kids to Asher's, but I'll be around if you need any help."

"We gonna play in the pool," Ivy supplied.

I patted her head. "I bet you'll have fun."

The elevator doors opened, and part of me wanted to veer left to hide out in Tennyson and Sophie's loft, but… I exchanged a look with him and a nod, and then I headed right to the second and last loft on the floor. Mine. Not *hers*. There she was, and she stood up fast when she saw me.

"Noah," Emma breathed out. Her eyes welled up, and she smoothed a hand over her hair.

I said nothing as I dug out my keys and waited for Tennyson and Ivy to disappear into their place.

It hurt to see her, I had to admit. She was still fucking ugly for what she'd done, except my heart wasn't about to erase the last four years as fast as my mind had.

I entered the loft and dumped my bag in the hall.

Emma followed me inside and closed the door.

"How are you?" she asked carefully.

"Peachy," I drawled. I surveyed the large, open living room. The couch was mine, though I didn't want it anymore. The flat screen, I was keeping. "You know where the boxes are. I'll help you pack."

Heading to the kitchen, I kept looking around me. Maybe waiting for the loft to not feel like home, either. But that feeling didn't come, thankfully. I knew why, too. We'd barely spent time here together.

In the beginning of our relationship, we were mostly at her place. Then, around the same time my roommates had moved out, we'd bought the house in northern California.

As I opened the fridge, finding it pathetically empty, I texted Daniel and grabbed the last bottle of water.

You got me. The PA is a good idea. What's his/her number?

I needed groceries, booze, and a website of a furniture store that delivered within twenty-four hours. Not necessarily in that order.

Emma appeared with a few empty boxes and a sad expression.

"You said you wanted to talk." I grabbed one of the boxes. For now, I was numb, though that could change in a heartbeat. Not wanting to waste any time, I started opening cupboards.

"I'm not—what're you—ugh." She was frustrated. "Can we

please sit down and talk like adults? You're acting like everything I've touched is tainted."

Spot on. I'd learned that my dick wasn't tainted, but I didn't know about the rest, and why risk it?

"That's kinda how it feels." I shrugged and dumped a drawer of silverware into the box. "Listen." I paused and faced her fully. "Almost my entire family is gone. How I deal with that is my business, and if getting your shit out of my home helps, then that's what I'm gonna do. Are we clear on that?"

She averted her gaze and wiped away a tear rolling down her cheek. "I'm so sorry, Noah," she whispered. "I want to be here for you. I'm not a bad person, and I *know* you."

My phone buzzed with Daniel's response as I answered Emma. "I never said you were a bad person, but what you did?" I shook my head. "I wasn't built to forgive that kind of betrayal."

Daniel told me he was sending a guy over from an agency right away, so I thanked him and then continued packing.

Emma was quiet as she took over packing in the kitchen. Not wanting to be too close to her, I moved on to the dining area. I grabbed my toolbox and began dissembling the dining room table.

I'd fucked her on that once.

As the boxes piled up, I knew it wasn't about getting rid of the shit she'd bought. It was about getting rid of anything that came with memories of her.

"I still love you," she said, sniffling.

By now, I'd moved on to decorations and photos on the walls. "It'll pass in time." Christ, I fucking hoped it would. "There's no room for this in my life now. I need you to get that through your skull. I wanna be alone."

She started crying.

The more emotional and pleading she got, the more detached I became.

It made it easier to breathe. Fuck emotions.

*

Twenty minutes before the movers were due to arrive, we'd

gotten a lot accomplished, and I'd done a decent job of not thinking too much about my family. Actually, Emma had made it easy because she made everything about her.

My new PA, Nicky, had stopped by to introduce himself and get the list of items I wanted, and I'd given him the keys to my truck before he'd left again. I'd been where he was. PAs made a shit salary—on film sets, it was sometimes nothing—so I reckoned free transportation would go a long way.

"Do you want the bed?" Emma asked dully.

She'd finally given up on me taking her back.

"No." I wiped some sweat off my forehead and looked out over the emptied living room. The hall outside the loft was packed, and only a few shelves with my stuff remained.

I wasn't stupid. By the time Emma had understood I wasn't changing my mind, she'd gotten greedier. There was plenty of shit she'd probably sell, 'cause God forbid she get a goddamn job. I didn't care. She could take it and shove it up her ass.

"You don't know how hard this has been for me," she said.

I chuckled darkly, and I wasn't touching that one.

"I'm serious," she cried. "I'm thirty-seven and back to living with my *mother*. It's humiliating."

"I don't think it's wise we discuss what's humiliating," I warned her with a pointed look. "Are you honestly whining about living with your mother right after I've lost mine?"

She paled, realizing the situation, though she pushed on with her own agenda. "You can't hold that against me. I'm very sorry you lost your family, but that doesn't make my problems any smaller. It's unfair that I'm the only bad guy here—"

"Stop talking, Emma." The movers were here, and I walked over to the door to buzz them in. "I never claimed to be perfect. I've probably made plenty of mistakes, but I would never fucking step out on you. A relationship is sacred to me, and to learn four years later that you don't feel the same… It makes any other issue useless to argue. 'Cause, no matter what, I didn't push you to betray me." I leveled her with a look that said I was fucking through. "We're done for good. I mean it."

She clenched her jaw. "You're heartless."

Fuck you.

I opened the door for her. “Goodbye, Emma.”

CHAPTER 5

Two weeks later

I stared at the remote.

I was on the mattress in front of the flat screen in the living room.

The remote was on the floor.

I couldn't reach it.

Maybe I didn't need to change the channel.

A knock on the door made me throw the covers over my head.

Go away.

"Noah?" It was Sophie. No surprise. "I know you're in there."

Well, of course I was. Where else would I be? I hadn't left my loft in ages. No one judged me for being a fucking coward here. No side-eyeing for every bottle I drained. Although, I could imagine the looks my family would give me.

I flinched and closed my eyes.

Too fucking bad you're all dead.

After a week of hiding, I'd tried to get up and live. I had

showered, shaved, used deodorant, and put on clothes to go out and buy groceries on my own for once. Then I'd checked my phone and saw they'd found out why the plane had gone down.

They'd located and dug out the flight data recorder and learned the pilots had been dealing with a mechanical error.

By the time they'd started the decline, they hadn't fixed it yet, and then they'd flown into a thunderstorm, counting on backup systems to guide them safely to the ground.

It had been one hell of a drop. And I had retreated to my bed and the nearest bottle.

I had nightmares of JJ and Linda screaming. The plane had been filled with families.

"We're hitting the road, sweetie," Sophie said. "Please let me know you're at least breathing."

Hit with guilt, I pushed away the covers and reached for my phone. A text would have to suffice 'cause I looked like shit and hadn't showered in…way too long.

I'm fine, just exhausted. Enjoy the holiday. Give the kids a smooch from me.

I heard the chirp of Sophie's phone and could imagine her sigh that followed.

"You have the keys to our place," she said. "There are leftovers in the freezer. I don't know what it is Nicky drops off, but I doubt it's good for you."

Nicky—what a godsend. I tipped him well for bringing me microwave dinners and alcohol a couple times a week.

He'd also arranged for my new bed to be delivered. All that was missing was a bed frame, and I didn't care enough to pick one out. I'd just placed it where the couch used to be, and it was my haven.

I didn't like leaving it.

Rolling over to bury my face in the pillow, I came to the reluctant conclusion I wouldn't have a choice but to leave it soon. The pillowcase reeked, and if I could smell it while living in the filth, it had to be bad.

*

It took me hours to talk myself into getting outta bed. But eventually, I got up and threw the sheets and pillowcases in the washer. Then I suffered through a shower, brushed my teeth, said *fuck it* to shaving, and pulled on a pair of sweats and a T-shirt.

In the living room, I opened a window and threw away some paper plates and plastic forks and knives. I'd have to buy some fucking silverware at some point.

I killed some time playing ridiculous games on my phone that Linda had liked to compete with me at, and then I tossed the laundry into the dryer. In forty minutes, I'd be back under the covers.

"Food," I muttered.

I was running low on microwaveables, and the real groceries Nicky had bought the first day were going bad. I had milk and cereal, so I went with that.

Happy fuckin' Fourth of July.

Technically, it wasn't for another three days, but I didn't see anything changing in that time.

When the doorbell rang, I frowned. Tennyson and Sophie had packed up the kids and their youngest pup and were probably nearing San Francisco at this point, and Daniel and Zane lived in New York.

Brooklyn, maybe?

While Tennyson and Sophie wanted a road trip along the coast and quality time with the family, Brooklyn and Asher were flying up with their two daughters. They all owned a beach house in Vancouver with Tennyson and Asher's folks. I'd been there, and I'd been invited this year too, but spending that day with people who were happy and in love…? Fuck no.

I'd ruin their whole vacation with my misery.

I shoved a spoonful of milk and Froot Loops into my mouth and headed for the hallway. The spoon was still in my mouth when I looked through the peephole, shocked to see Julian standing there. Opening the door, I raised my brows and let him in.

I removed the spoon. "This is a surprise, kid."

A good one, it felt like.

He passed me, head down, and dropped a bag and a guitar

case on the hallway floor. "It wouldn't have been a surprise if you'd checked your email. I called you three times last week, too."

Fuck. I was failing at this uncle gig.

"Then I called Daniel yesterday." He cleared his throat and fidgeted with a loose thread in his ratty hoodie. "He and Sophie gave me their numbers after the memorial service, so…" Sounded like something they'd do. Both of them were caregivers. "He suggested I fly out and kick your door in. I don't think he was joking."

I snorted and jerked my chin for him to follow me. "No, they're all a bunch of worriers. How did you get into the building?"

"Someone was leaving when I arrived." He shrugged and took in the empty loft. When I said empty, I meant there was nothing in the large space aside from the bed, the flat screen on the wall, and a couple boxes of photo albums. "Did you just move in?"

"No." I set the bowl in the sink and then turned around, hopping up to sit on the counter. "I broke up with my girlfriend and wanted to get rid of everything." I rubbed the back of my neck, a bit embarrassed. With Julian here, my failure at being an adult shone brighter than the sun.

"A fresh start." He nodded, avoiding eye contact. "Kind of why I'm here, I guess. If you don't mind. I mean, I'll look for my own place, but I can't stay with Grandma and Grandpa anymore, and I don't want to go home."

"Stay as long as you want, Julian." It was honest. I had to get my shit together, and maybe if I had someone with me, like back when I had roommates, I wouldn't be a walking train wreck anymore. "Pick a room. The one farthest down the hall is my new study, which is a nice way of putting it. It's more of a room I just threw my personal shit in." I had some awards, my college diploma, photos, and framed scripts of projects I'd been involved with that I treasured. "Anyway, there are two other rooms—both emptier than California's water supply."

Which reminded me, now I really had to get some furniture. The energy to do it remained completely fucking dead, but a sense of responsibility rose in me. I was a pathetic motherfucker these days, though if I could succeed at being an uncle, it could lead to more. Like eating better, going back to work…

"Where do you sleep?" he asked, a crease forming in his forehead.

I nodded at the bed.

"Ah."

Yeah…

This was probably not what he'd expected.

"Pick a room and leave your stuff there," I told him, getting down from the counter again. "I'll change the sheets, and then we can order some shit you'll need."

He nodded and disappeared down the hall.

Looking down in the sink, I cringed before I followed him to get to the laundry room. Frat kids lived better. So… No more reusing Styrofoam bowls from Panera. No more *sporks*.

After making my bed smell fresh and clean again, I picked up my laptop from the floor and sat down. Julian joined me and sat down too, and I didn't like how cautious he seemed to be around me. I was the *fun* uncle, goddammit. Linda and JJ had always gotten a kick outta the crap I taught them.

Julian didn't know me very well.

Hell, right now, *I* didn't know me very well.

I was getting a headache. I'd accomplished so little in the past couple of weeks that doing laundry, showering, and exchanging a few words with my nephew exhausted me.

"You want a drink?" I asked as the idea struck me. Because, fucking hell, I needed one. "You find a site—actually, Danny's got a deal with Pottery Barn. They'll deliver first thing in the morning if we go through him."

"Um, all right."

He took the laptop, and I stalked to the kitchen. Once there, I was hit with regret. Booze had been my go-to for too long now, and encouraging Julian to chug whiskey the way I'd been doing probably wasn't wise.

I hung my head. I wasn't ready to be around people, despite the fact that I usually thrived in social settings.

I had to, though. Nobody was gonna make me climb out of this hellhole. I had to force myself, and now was the time.

My fridge lacked a lot of things, but Nicky had done well when buying alcohol, and I had ingredients to make drinks that didn't scream of grief and depression.

Keeping it simple, I poured ice into two Solo cups and mixed us some 7 and 7. I topped them off with lime and then returned to Julian. I could do this. I could shoulder responsibility and be there.

"What's this?" He sniffed his drink before taking a sip. "Okay, this will work." He kinda smiled a bit there.

Thank fuck. I did something right.

"All right, so go nuts," I told him and grabbed my wallet. "I don't care what you pick. You're actually doing me a favor."

"How so?" He scrolled down a page with mattresses.

I went with honesty. That way, he wouldn't be too surprised when I fucked up.

"I don't have my life together." I placed a credit card next to him. "I'm glad you're here, and I'll do my best to make sure you feel at home, but most of the time, I'm the living dead. I channel surf, get wasted, go through photos, and pass out. Rinse and repeat. Decorating my home isn't exactly a priority."

Felt good getting that off my chest.

"I'm not looking for a parent," he responded quietly. "The reason I came here is because I think…I think you might understand." He kept staring at the screen, though I doubted he was perusing right now. "Grandma cries whenever she sees me, and Grandpa's got enough on his plate with her and dealing with Dad's work stuff."

Damn. I remembered wondering if James's parents could really be there for Julian now, and I guessed they couldn't.

"I figured, with me being here…" He cleared his throat and clicked on a bed. "I won't have to pretend everything's okay."

Fuck no, he didn't.

"No pretending," I agreed. "And no pity looks, since we're going through the same shit."

"Exactly." He released a breath, meeting my gaze briefly, and I detected relief there. "So I can stay?"

"Long as you like," I promised.

*

"Just press the damn button, Julian."

"It's an awful lot of money…"

"Jesus Christ." I finished my drink and then leaned over to complete the purchase myself. "Money's the only thing I don't have to worry about. There. The loft will soon look like a real home again."

We'd set my credit card on fire, and in between whiskey drinks and adding things to the cart, I'd learned a bit about Julian. He was methodical and picked items after great consideration, and rushed decisions seemed to make him fret. It was sweet.

Our pseudo family roles to each other made him the kid, though there was no denying he was a smart young man. It wouldn't surprise me if he was smarter than me.

"What about tonight?" He glanced apprehensively at the bed we sat on. "Do…do we share?"

I smirked wryly.

"Have you never fallen asleep on a couch with a buddy?" I stood up to refill our drinks. "I don't bite and it's a big bed. One night won't kill us."

I was tired as fuck—Christ, nowadays I woke up exhausted—but the alcohol and the company had improved my day. And it was nice that we didn't have to pretend. It kinda made Julian the optimal roommate for me. Because even though I didn't have to hide my grief from my buddies, nobody liked the one who was always down in the dumps.

Or the one aiming straight for alcoholism.

Despite the two-week bender Julian had evidently been on after the crash, I had a hunch he didn't really drink. He seemed inexperienced around it, so I decided it was time to introduce him to a favorite of mine. Jameson, ginger ale, and a lime wedge. I licked some juice off my thumb and carried the cups over to the bed, handing him his.

"Mia was the bartender in the family, but I think you'll like this."

He sniffed it as usual and raised a brow. "Mom worked in

bars?"

"It was how she put herself through college." I dipped my chin and went for the laptop. "I did it briefly when I first moved out here, but she was a natural."

He sipped it slowly then nodded to himself, approving. "Don't you get hungry?"

Oh, right. Food.

Cooking used to be a passion. That had disappeared, too.

"Top drawer next to the fridge," I said as I went to Best Buy's website. "It's where I keep all the takeout menus. Order whatever you want and get me something vegetarian. I'm not picky."

Julian had done a good job of ordering furniture, kitchenware, bathroom stuff, and even some decorative crap like pillows, blankets, and drapes. I was useless in that department, but I knew gadgets.

"You're a vegetarian?" Julian scrunched his nose, and he sounded adorably British there. The faint accent he'd picked up among international scholars in Germany shone through here and there.

I chuckled. "A fake one. I eat seafood and poultry on occasion." I side-eyed him, wondering what world he lived in. "You didn't know? I was the butt of every dinner-related joke at reunions. My pop thought it was hilarious." Not to mention ridiculous, but it was all in good fun.

It was a health choice. I used to be somewhat of a fitness freak, and avoiding steaks and burgers tended to lead to healthier meals. Unfortunately, alcohol was vegetarian.

It bothered me, my new drinking habit, and I wasn't ready to give it up. Then again, when was anyone ever?

Julian ended up ordering us pizza while I shopped for tech. He would need a flat screen in his room, I wanted a desktop computer in my study, a couple gaming consoles would be cool, a Blu-Ray player, upgrading my surround sound system…

"Damn, you're buying a lot." He shifted a bit closer, intrigued. "It's strange having money. I bought a guitar last week and felt bad."

"Why?" I frowned at him.

He shrugged with one shoulder. "I didn't work for it."

Understandable. "Did you have a job back home?"

"Part time, since I was in school. I worked at a movie theater, and sometimes I ran errands for Dad."

I smiled to myself. Jobs like that took me back to when life was both harder and easier. When you worked for your next meal and the ability to pay for gas and electric. I could borrow from my folks if it got really bad, but they'd always encouraged both me and Mia to pursue our dreams on our own. Those were simple times.

A care package from Ma with cookies, a new shirt, and aftershave meant the world. Sometimes she'd sent us quarters, which had been a hint to get our asses to the nearest payphone and call home more often. Sometimes there were printouts of simple recipes.

The cookies were my favorite, though.

I swallowed down the stab of pain and the emotions rising and tried to focus on…gadgets. Which, fuck, felt empty and worthless now. Memories were cunty. They could change my mood in a second.

*

I didn't touch my pizza, and Julian could undoubtedly sense that I was done talking for the evening. I poured a cup of vodka and sipped it while staring at the TV. No idea what movie he'd picked. I didn't care.

It was a good thing I'd told him I probably wouldn't be the best company if he came out here.

Around three in the morning, I was ready to pass out. Julian was still awake, but he looked tired.

"We should get some sleep." I grunted as I rose from the bed, and a wave of dizziness took over.

"Right." He sat up. "Do you mind if we move the bed into your room first?"

"Why?" I could barely stand up. Heavy lifting could get me injured.

"Because when the furniture gets delivered tomorrow, I can

get started without waking you up."

That…that was a solid idea. I didn't think I'd sleep that long, but if he could handle the delivery without me, that'd be awesome. I didn't have a single polite smile left in me, so I wanted to avoid people.

"Yeah, okay." I rubbed my eyes and tried to clear my head. "Which room is mine?"

"I picked the middle one across the hall, but I can change."

I shook my head. The middle used to be mine, so it was a relief he'd gone with that.

*

I woke up the next morning to my phone going off. The sun was fucking brutal, and memories came flooding back from yesterday. Julian was here. We'd moved the bed into my new bedroom, which meant I got the morning sun.

My mouth tasted like death, and I groaned as I rolled over to reach my phone. I blinked blearily at the screen as a headache settled in.

Four missed calls from Sophie.

"Jesus," I whispered hoarsely.

I pressed Call and ended up on my back. Julian was probably in the living room. I could hear someone moving around, so maybe the furniture had been delivered.

"Oh, good! You haven't forgotten how to use the phone," Sophie said as she answered.

I held my forehead, wincing. "Too early for humor. What's up?"

"Nothing much. Just my daily check-in to see if you're alive. And two in the afternoon isn't early for those of us who don't live on booze."

Ouch. That one hurt, but I supposed I needed to hear it. This couldn't go on. I'd slept away half the day.

"I'm alive," I muttered groggily. "I should go help Julian with the furniture."

She hummed then stopped abruptly. "Wait, Julian's staying

with you?"

"Yeah." I dragged myself up, my feet thudding against the floorboards. "He got here yesterday. Looks like he's sticking around a while, so we ordered a bunch of shit."

"That's great!" she gushed. "Holy hell, you have no idea how relieved I am to hear that." It sounded like she was getting emotional. "I was worried about him at the service. I'm glad he turned to you. I think you can be good together. You're going through the same pain, so maybe you can, like, help each other heal and move on?"

Her rambling was cute, but it wasn't helping my headache. Or my conscience. I had to be the shittiest friend in history. My buddies cared a lot for me, and I was doing absolutely nothing to show my appreciation.

"Yeah, it might be good," I said to appease her. "Focus on your vacation, hon. We'll be fine."

After wrapping up the call, I stumbled to the bathroom across the hall. I downed a couple painkillers and cringed at my reflection. Looked like I'd shower today too, as if I were a normal, functioning human being. 'Cause I couldn't show myself to anyone looking like death warmed over.

I turned on the shower and took a leak while waiting for the water to heat up.

My skin was sensitive, another symptom of bad habits I needed to shake. Everything hurt. My mood shifted too fucking fast. I was determined one second, then ready to throw in the towel in the next. And as I showered, I warred with myself, 'cause it all boiled down to the goddamn alcohol. I had to get rid of it completely, at least for a while, and I had to do it while my mood allowed it.

It had been my crutch for a month now. Enough was enough. Quitting was already gonna be painful, so the last thing I needed was to drag it out.

Turning off the water, I stepped out and wrapped a towel around my hips. The bed called, but I wouldn't cave that fast. An uphill battle was supposed to burn, so let it begin.

I brushed my teeth and hoped most of last night's bender was gone. I knew what whiskey smelled like the day after. Applying some deodorant and aftershave—even though I hadn't shaved—I left the bathroom and walked down the hall, only to come to a stop when I reached the living room.

Jesus Christ.

I didn't recognize the place. Julian must've had help. Maybe he'd checked the box for having the delivery guys help assemble everything. A few dressers and shelves were still stacked in the hallway, though the living room looked perfect to me.

"Morning." I passed the seating area first. New couch, two chairs, a low coffee table. Even a rug. I'd missed that. Old met new, mismatched colors that still fit. "I didn't know you were an interior designer."

Julian popped up from the floor where he'd been putting together the last of the dining room chairs. "I'm not. This is literally taken straight off two pages in their online catalogue."

I let out a low laugh and glanced around me. "All right, but Pottery Barn ain't getting my thanks. This is all you, kid."

An ancient-looking wooden chest had been placed behind the couch. The lid was open, and I saw Julian had put the photo albums from Pittsburgh in there. Good place for memories.

Julian shrugged, ducked his head, and pushed in the chair at the table. "We didn't wake you up, did we? The movers left a little while ago."

"No." I couldn't stop taking it all in. It was a bit overwhelming 'cause…goddamn, he'd turned my loft into a home. I had to step up my game. "This is fucking incredible, Julian."

He flashed a quick grin. "I'm glad you like it, but you have to tell me if I've overstepped any boundaries."

"No overstepping whatsoever." I had an urge to hug him, but I pushed that aside for now. I didn't wanna make shit awkward. "Let me get dressed and then I'll order us some food." I was starving, having not eaten much yesterday, and I had an idea I wanted to run by him.

It was sometimes easier to help others than to help yourself, and my gut told me he'd be good for me. I wanted to return the favor, so whatever he told me he needed help with, hopefully, I could come through for him.

CHAPTER 6

It would take some serious adjusting in order to help Julian. I'd ordered bagels and cream cheese and juice for breakfast, and he had quietly spoken up about his hopes and plans while I had resisted the temptation of pouring vodka into my OJ.

Right after, I promised I'd do my best to assist him, but even now, a couple hours later, I still didn't have a fucking clue.

I stood in the kitchen and reluctantly poured all the alcohol I had down the drain. He was sorting through silverware, glasses, plates, utensils, and appliances, not-so-subtly side-eyeing me every now and then.

Of course, I admired him for what he wanted, but it didn't make it easy for me. He'd told me he wanted to pay rent; that was easily taken care of, I guessed. Not necessary at all in my opinion, though I knew where he was coming from.

Next, he wanted a job. He wasn't quite ready yet—understandable—but he hoped to be soon. And when he was, I wasn't allowed to use my connections. Not even to get him into some PA agency or have him pour coffee at a studio. Again, I understood where he was coming from.

Lastly, he needed a car, but he was gonna give public transportation a try first…

In fucking LA.

He was gonna regret that—fast.

All in all, my so-called *help* would come from sitting by, twiddling my goddamn thumbs.

It wasn't what I called help.

As I emptied a bottle of the finest Irish whiskey into the sink, I added stubborn and admirable to the list of Julian's traits.

"Are you addicted?"

Though I had half expected his question, his soft, apprehensive tone still packed a punch.

"No…" I grabbed the last bottle, phrasing myself carefully. "It's too soon, I think. But my mind's adapted fast enough, and it's my first escape route. Soon as anything's wrong, slightest mood change, or if memories hit too hard, I seek out a bottle."

"I understand." He carefully placed a stack of new plates in a cupboard. "I'm on medication, but if I hadn't been, perhaps I wouldn't have stopped at emptying Dad's liquor cabinet. I don't know."

I furrowed my brow. "What kinda meds are you on?"

"Antidepressants."

"Because of the plane crash?"

He shook his head and moved on to wineglasses. "It's been about a year, but I did see a grief counselor in Pittsburgh. He said I should continue taking them, and he prescribed me a mild sleeping pill, too."

My mind spun. He'd done the right thing, obviously, going to a shrink for professional help. I'd failed at that, too. What baffled me was the antidepressants he'd been on for a *year.*

How come I didn't know? Mia would've told me. Despite our mutual love for riling each other up and driving one another bonkers, we could still talk. I calmed her down. She explained shit to me. It was what we did.

Had done.

*

When the Fourth of July rolled around a couple days later, I used the morning to set up the last furniture in my study. I hooked up the computer and then threw my lazy ass on the couch. Julian was borrowing my car to run some errands, and he was picking up lunch on the way home.

I wanted a drink.

Instead, I watched movies and dicked around on my phone.

Julian was a musician, and I wanted to encourage him. Since he didn't want me to help him with a job or a car, I'd pull a sneaky move and place a baby grand in the corner behind the dining area. He could suck it.

Before noon, I'd received texts from my friends wishing us a good holiday, and it wasn't long after that Julian returned. And he wasn't alone. I was surprised to see Nicky with him.

"Hope you don't mind I let him in," Julian said. He headed to the kitchen with a bag from a local sandwich place.

"Of course not." I looked over the back of the couch where I was sprawled. "You not spending the holiday with family?" I asked Nicky. I didn't get up from the couch 'cause…well, I was the new me. I did everything half-assed, it seemed.

"No, but I'm going to a barbecue later with some friends." He walked over with a thick, familiar envelope. "Tennyson Wright overnighted this to me. He wants you to read it."

A script.

Persistent fucker. Tennyson thought he could get me back to work by throwing scripts my way?

"I like what you've done with the place, Mr. Collins."

I waved a hand and flipped open the script. "Julian's work. And I thought I told you to call me Noah." There was a note from Tennyson on the first page.

You're the only one I trust to direct my first production.

My brow rose.

A Tennyson Wright Production, huh? He'd produced before, but a creative producer was a step above that, and they were a rare breed these days because of the risks. They went in with only their own money and ran the entire show, from casting to final say in edits. Too much could go wrong, and someone with an underdeveloped idea was more likely to sink the whole ship than to make it float.

If he was doing this, and he wanted me to direct it, it was a huge fucking deal.

After everything he'd done for me and my career, I couldn't ignore this.

That asshole.

I tossed the script onto the coffee table and scowled.

"He knows I gotta read it now—" I cut myself off when I glanced over to the kitchen. Well, hey. Nicky was working my nephew. Flirting and whatnot.

Julian had his back to me as he unpacked groceries, so I couldn't see his face. Was the flirting appreciated? Reciprocated? Was he even gay? Fuck if I knew—or cared. But he and Nicky were around the same age, and if they hit it off, then great.

A rock of unease settled in my gut, though. He hadn't even been here a week yet, and he seemed to be doing much better. I was the one whining like a fucking kid. Maybe the script had arrived with perfect timing.

Ten minutes later, Nicky left, and I lured Julian over to the couch with chips, dip, our lunch, and beer.

"Are you sure the beer is okay?" he asked.

"Hell yeah." I straightened up a bit and found a music channel that actually played music. "Not enough alcohol in beer to get me wasted before I piss it all out again."

He chuckled and got more comfortable.

"So did Nicky ask you out?" I'd never been one to beat around the bush.

Julian's earlier smile vanished, and he grabbed his beer. "I'm not gay."

Oh…so that's what's up.

Way too defensive.

"There's nothing wrong with it, you know." I frowned, wondering why he kept that hidden. Sure, there was a chance he was telling the truth, but his reaction to my question raised some serious doubts. "I've had my fair share of fun, so no prejudice here." It wasn't necessary to mention my friendship with Daniel and Zane.

Julian took a long swig from his bottle and did his internal battling for a while. I was learning his tells, and he always waited with the questions until he'd gone back and forth a bit first.

Then he shrugged and averted his gaze. "I'm not gay, is all. Those who are…I don't care. S'just not me."

Uh-huh.

There was clearly something he struggled with there, though I wasn't gonna pressure him. Living in LA would loosen him up eventually.

No pun intended.

I grinned, unable to help it. Maybe my crass—sometimes fucking juvenile—sense of humor was returning.

Turning back to the TV, I ate my sandwich and watched a few music videos, and the tunes were brightening my mood a bit. Julian seemed busy with his phone, and I felt like being useful for once. We didn't have anything planned for today, and neither of us wanted to go out, but a nice meal couldn't hurt.

"I'm gonna start on dinner." I stood up and brought my beer to the kitchen where I opened the fridge to see what he'd bought.

"We just ate! Wait…you cook?" he asked from the couch.

"Well, the old me did." I scanned the fridge and started pulling out vegetables. "The new me can't be assed to do much of anything, but I reckon it's time I get back to who I used to be." At least, as far as I could take it.

I was pretty sure I was changed permanently in some ways. Trauma did that, but I had to live.

As I grabbed a box of pasta sheets, Julian joined me and hopped up to sit on the kitchen island. "I didn't really know the old you."

"Someone was always too cool to show up at reunions." I shot him a smirk over my shoulder and then got cracking. My vegetarian lasagna was fucking stellar; even my pops had loved it. Starting now would make it even more delicious. It'd be a while before we got hungry, and that meant more time for the flavors to soak in properly.

"I wasn't too cool," he argued. "I…had m-my reasons."

"How cryptic." I finished washing the vegetables. "I can't

imagine what those reasons would be, but if you don't wanna say, so be it. At least it couldn't have been my fault you didn't show up. Otherwise, you wouldn't have flown all the way out here to move in with me."

Come to think of it, it was a shame we didn't know each other better. I remembered him as a gangly kid back in the day. He'd adored his little brother, though he'd had a soft spot for Linda.

Julian didn't answer, and I got lost in making my sauce. More garlic, definitely. Salt, pepper, olive oil.

It didn't take long before the kitchen was smelling like good old times.

"I know *some* things about you," he said after a while. "Mr. Life of the Party."

I grinned and took a swig of my beer. "No arguing there."

I'd always been popular for getting a party started. I was great to have around for casual fun, in and out of the bedroom. It was for the heartfelt stuff I was known for bailing. Red carpets, interviews, even being chased by the paparazzi when I was out with Sophie—shoot. No issues. Then when shit got serious, I didn't like attention at all.

Fuck being vulnerable. It had always made me uncomfortable to the extreme. And, of course, opening myself up and getting into a genuine relationship with Emma had worked out so well…

I added a layer of basil and sliced mozzarella in the pan, followed by pasta and some butter.

"Noah, what did you mean earlier when you said you'd had your fair share of fun?"

"Hmm?" I poured some sauce on next and then turned to Julian. "You mean…ah. I meant with men."

"Oh." He looked away and tugged on a lock of his hair. "I figured you were straight."

I shrugged and bent over a little, getting closer to the cutting board to make sure the slices of eggplant and zucchini came out perfect and thin the way I liked them. "I'm not really into labels, kid. It restricts my fun. I suppose I'm straight, yeah; I never felt anything deep for a dude. Doesn't mean I'll turn down a threesome with a hot couple, though. And it sure as hell didn't stop me from having fun with my buddies in college."

After finishing all the layers and dumping a shit-ton of cheese on top, the lasagna was ready to go in the oven, and I was itching for another beer.

I was a bit rusty without the same enthusiasm I once had, but I could get into this again. Cooking. I still had it in me, the passion. Buried somewhere.

*

Dinner was a hit, and no bullshit, I was smug when Julian collapsed on the couch afterward in a food coma. Darkness had fallen, fireworks were going off in the distance, and I clung to my good mood.

Nothing stronger than beer, I kept telling myself.

We didn't have any liquor at home anymore, though that didn't mean there wasn't a bar or two nearby. I'd deal. It wasn't a painful struggle. I just had to readjust a bit in my noggin'. It was all in the head.

While watching a movie, Julian got into asking me about the actors I'd worked with. He was slightly starstruck when I told him some of my favorite memories from film sets. I doubted he was into gossip, yet he did get a good laugh from hearing some actors' diva antics.

"Does the big Sophie Pierce have any outrageous demands when she works?" he asked.

I shook my head. "Not really, unless you count bigger trailers. She and Tennyson sync their schedules so they don't have to spend more than a week apart. So when one works, the other is usually nearby with the kids."

"That sounds nice." Julian quirked a grin. "Are they really the American Sweetheart couple the press has us believing?"

I snorted. "You read gossip rags? You should know better."

"Some things can't be avoided," he argued in his defense.

True, unfortunately. Running mouths in LA were loud.

"They're pretty fucking perfect, yeah," I conceded. "They fight and fuck up like any couple, but they're in the same league as your parents and mine. They come out stronger, and unlike my lovely ex-girlfriend, they remain loyal."

Had Emma been right to say I always compared us to Tennyson and Sophie?

Always was a strong word, but maybe my expectations had been too high. Then again, who wouldn't want what my friends had? I supposed I was all-or-nothing in that respect. Fuck settling. Fuck her for stepping out on me.

Julian's forehead creased, and he hesitated a beat before asking. "She cheated on you?"

Right. I hadn't told him why Emma and I broke up.

"Yeah. I walked in on her and some guy she'd picked up at the store." I reached for my beer and drained half of it. "This was the day before the plane crash."

"Jesus." Julian flinched. "I'm sorry."

It was what it was. Thinking about Emma didn't hurt as much as it had a few weeks ago. With everything else going on, her betrayal paled in comparison, and it made it easier to move past.

*

That night, it was difficult to sleep.

Boredom had kicked in, which I supposed was a good thing, and I tossed and turned until I gave up. Putting on a pair of sweats, I headed for the living room to watch TV.

I'd bought a flat screen for Julian. I didn't want one in my room.

The script was still on the coffee table.

Fuck it.

I got up to make some coffee and read the script, but the moment I reached the kitchen, I heard a strangled cry coming from down the hall. Julian had told me he had nightmares every now and then.

Changing direction, I walked down the hall and listened through his door.

"Stop laughing, Lin," I heard him mumble. "I'm serious. Don't go on that flight."

"Shit," I whispered. He was dreaming about his sister, and was…what, trying to warn her? That couldn't end well.

Julian cursed viciously, and there was a thump coming from his room that made me reach for the doorknob. Then I waited. It was quiet for a while, but eventually I heard him moving around.

I gave the door a couple knocks before I opened it. Worry shot through me when I realized he was crying, but instead of giving comfort a go, I was struck mute and immobile. I guessed my impression of Julian wasn't everything. Half-shy and cautious, I knew. But wearing only pajama bottoms revealed tattoos along his ribcage, one nipple pierced, and the little shit was smoking a cigarette out the window.

I ignored the smoking for now, though.

Staring at him, it was easy to see his battle. Trying to keep his hurt to himself but failing. He stared back, apprehensive; then he sorta gave up. He hung his head and rubbed at his eyes, tears rolling down freely.

"I hate losing them over and over," he croaked. "It's the same almost every night."

I closed the door behind me and approached the window. It was dark, though the streetlamps from outside provided enough light to see he was a fucking mess.

As I leaned back against the wall and folded my arms over my chest, he took a pull from the smoke and then threw it out.

"Sorry about that," he muttered.

"It's okay." It wasn't the smell that bothered me. It was the temptation. Despite it being a habit I'd kicked twenty years ago, I tended to go for vices in rough times. "Tell me about your dream."

He shuddered and wiped his cheeks. "They're always fine. Laughing and joking around. I drop them off at the airport knowing what's going to happen, and they don't listen to me. I guess, in my dream, the plane crashes on the way from Germany."

Fuck, that had to be hell. My dreams usually revolved around childhood memories, and there was the occasional nightmare where I relived the day I found out about the crash on the news.

Whatever thoughts were running through Julian's mind became too much for him. He buried his face in his hands, shoulders trembling from silent cries.

"It hurts too fucking much, Noah."

I yanked him in for a hug, acting on instinct. The pain in his raw voice made me choke up, too. "I know it's not much, but I'm here for you, Julian." I'd thought he was doing better. Maybe he was, but I'd been a fool to believe he wasn't still in pain. "You don't have to hide any of this for me. Remember we said no pretending?"

He nodded jerkily, hugging me back, and I tightened my hold. It was a fucking relief. Human contact. I'd missed it beyond words. Touch gave me energy. I was a physical man, and without affection, the world was bleaker.

"We'll get through this together, yeah?" I stroked his back, my mind trying to come up with ways that could help. Activity had always worked for me. Exercise, healthy eating, staying occupied.

Julian shivered and nodded again. "Thank you."

"I'm just as thankful," I murmured. "Easier finding purpose with you here, kid."

And, goddammit, we were starting tomorrow. I was done hiding at home.

CHAPTER 7

Two weeks later

"Rise and shine, ya little fucker!" I banged on Julian's door and then proceeded to the kitchen. A bunch of fruit, some protein powder, and ginger went into the blender, and as usual, he didn't wake up from the noise. Or, rather, the kid ignored it.

It'd been a week of this now, so I was getting used to it.

Julian Hartley was not a morning person.

After placing our breakfast shakes in the fridge, I went back to wake him up. I tightened the drawstrings on my sweats and scrolled down on my phone to find today's playlist.

"Julian!" I pushed his door open and headed straight for his closet.

"Get out," he said groggily into his pillow. "Enough of this hell."

"Did you get any sleep?" I found a T-shirt and a pair of shorts and threw them at him.

"Some. No nightmares."

"That's because you're staying active," I told him.

Exercise couldn't cure depression all on its own, and he'd had a handful of bad dreams these past two weeks, but it was a good start.

"Like I have a damn choice." He sat up, eyes filled with sleep, hair messier than ever, and reluctantly pulled on the shirt. "The sun hasn't even come up, Noah."

"Quit whining." I smirked as I attached my phone to the elastic band around my arm. "You think I'm enjoying this? I'm fucking suffering. But I know it's good for us, and as soon as it becomes a routine, we'll be moping if we *don't* get to run first thing in the morning."

"I highly doubt that," he muttered and slipped into his shorts. "And stop calling it morning. I *like* mornings. This isn't it."

I rolled my eyes.

*

As had become normal once I'd found out Julian smoked, he lit one up as soon as we came out of our building. And this morning, I wasn't having it. I grabbed it and stubbed it out.

He scowled.

"You said you'd been tryin' to quit," I reminded him.

"Yeah, and then my family died."

I didn't reply as I stuck one of the earbuds into my ear. He had a point, and I hadn't been a saint, but we had to move on, yeah? So if I could at least help him smoke less, it was good enough for now.

"Come on." I jerked my chin, and then we were jogging down the street toward the beach. It would be an uphill battle on the way home, and I was planning to make it a race.

Julian kept a few paces behind me, a fan of complaining, which I just thought was fun. He'd be sold soon enough.

Once we were warmed up, I went a bit faster, enjoying the burn in my legs. I didn't know I'd missed it until this week. Getting the blood pumping, heart racing. I felt more energetic with each day that passed, and I was getting ready for more. Namely, work.

I'd read Tennyson's script. Of fucking course, it was brilliant. He wouldn't have decided to back an entire project for anything less.

They were coming home today, too. They'd spent a week in Vancouver, all of them, and then Tennyson and Sophie had taken their two runts on a vacation to Hawaii. Tonight we were having dinner with them, and I was looking forward to getting Tennyson's thoughts on the script.

It was the kind of project you went all in for, and it was supposed to take place in Paris. For authenticity, it made sense to film it there too, though that required a lot of fucking green.

Like I'd already mentioned, this was a huge deal. I'd been comfortable in my role as the assistant director. But I'd be a liar if I said I didn't wanna go for it. Several buddies in the industry, Tennyson among them, had told me to try.

"No more detours, man," Julian panted. "Let's hit the beach."

Looking over my shoulder, I saw he was sweating and struggling to keep up. *Fair enough.* I made a turn in the next cross section, and it only took us a few minutes to reach the running path.

The sky above the mountains was glowing orange and purple.

As we approached the gym farther down the beach, I slowed and checked my watch. We were good on time. Juiceheads wouldn't be arriving until much later. After that, the beach gyms were useless.

"I need to lie down," Julian gasped.

"That's fine." I didn't stop until I reached the bars where I could do chin-ups. "We're racing home today, so you rest while I exhaust myself."

He'd already collapsed on a bench. "That's one way of saying I'm ridiculously out of shape."

I chuckled and pulled off my T-shirt, using it to wipe off sweat from my hands and forehead. And with the shirt and my phone on the ground next to the bars, I grabbed on and grunted as I pulled myself up.

Julian eyed me before quickly looking away. "So why are we racing?"

One.

"Because there's a prize."

Two.

Another thing I'd learned about Julian was that he had the Collins pride. We may not be related by blood, but dammit if he hadn't inherited some of our traits anyway.

I would have to be blind not to notice how much he wanted to use the baby grand piano that had arrived last week, but evidently it was getting in the way of his frugal life.

He was already paying rent, and he didn't borrow my car without filling the tank afterward. He pitched in for food and whatnot, and if he couldn't imagine a college student affording something, then he'd do his best to stay away from that.

He took the *bus* occasionally.

"Do I even wanna know?" he drawled.

I huffed out a heavy breath. *Nine.* My arms shook on the last one. *Ten.* Then I hopped down and bent over, hands supporting me on my thighs. "It's about the piano." I swallowed dryly, my heart pounding. "You're supposed to play it."

"This again?"

I chuckled, out of breath, and checked my watch to set a rest for another twenty seconds. "That's where the race comes in." I straightened up and wiped away some more sweat. "If I win, you play."

"You're faster than I am!" he argued.

"Why the fuck do you think I'm working out now while you're resting?"

Apparently, that was the wrong approach. When my twenty seconds were up, I started over with my next ten chin-ups, and I tried something new on Julian.

"Never mind," I grunted. "Not every well-rested young man can take on a fucking spent forty-year-old who can barely breathe."

He flipped me off at that, and I winked at him.

"Asshole." He fought a smile. "You never mentioned what I get if I win."

Six.

"Pick whatever you want."

That turned out to be the right approach. Noted for next time.

His eyes lit up, and I could practically hear the wheels turning.

"Okay, if I win..." He paused, pursing his lips. "Drum roll."

I jumped down one chin-up too early 'cause I had to laugh. He was a sweet fucking guy, and his good mood was infectious. I really dug having him around.

"If I win, you let me get a pet."

I cocked a brow. "A pet?"

"Yeah." He shrugged and looked out over the ocean. "We had a cat in Berlin."

I remembered. And I fucking hated cats.

Luckily, I was gonna win.

"Deal, kid. You win, you can get a pet."

*

I was almost there.

We only had the hill left, and then we were home.

Julian was all but dead on his feet, yet he kept pushing. He ran some ten feet ahead of me. I was running on fumes, but challenges were my crack and I could go faster.

"You ready to go down?" I called, panting.

He gasped for air as he laughed. "Thanks, but you're not my type!"

I grinned and narrowed my eyes. We were halfway up the hill, so I reckoned it was time to show him who was boss.

Every part of me burned and protested. I fucking loved it. It made me feel alive.

The sun was climbing higher.

Julian growled in frustration when he noticed I was coming up next to him.

As I passed, I couldn't help myself. "I'm everyone's type."

I gave it my all and sprinted the last distance, seriously doubting I'd be able to stand up in the shower later. But fuck it. Sweat poured down my chest, the shirt in my hand was soaked, and my eyes stung.

I reached the door a couple seconds before Julian did, and he—hell, both of us—were too spent to dish out digs.

My legs were turning into jelly, so I opened the door and got into the elevator. In another moment or two, I'd need to sit down, regardless of where I was.

"The young oughta carry the old." I threw an arm around Julian's shoulders and leaned back against the wall. The elevator was kinda slow, so it let me catch my breath a bit more.

"You're heavy. And sweaty as hell."

"No shit?" I chuckled.

I tilted my head, smiling down at him. He looked healthy with flushed cheeks and bright eyes. Blue, I noted. Bluish, grayish. His curly hair was darker than usual with sweat.

"You did good today." I wanted him to know that.

He nodded and looked down, but I could still see his smile. "Thanks."

*

Two of my old roommates were brothers and had shared the master bedroom because it was bigger. I had lived in the room Julian was in today, and my third roommate had lived in my new study. And since the master bedroom was still new to me, I wasn't used to having my own bathroom, so I tended to use the one in the hall. Which, of course, Julian liked to point out as stupid.

As I stood under the spray, eyes closed, shivers of contentment running through me, he knocked on the door and told me to hurry up.

Like I'd done the past few days, I told him to use my shower instead. He'd declined the other times, but I guessed he'd had enough. I heard him stomping into my room.

I grinned to myself for no apparent reason and started soaping up. It was so fucking good. My legs felt weak, but I'd live. Hanging my head, I pressed and rubbed lazily, my chest, my neck, my arms. I washed my cock and gave it a slow stroke. It had been understandably dead for a while, though there was some sexual frustration buried somewhere.

The thought of dating or even hooking up for a night didn't even exist. I wanted to be alone, and I didn't mind building up a nice porn stash.

My stomach growled and twisted in hunger, though. Jacking off could wait.

I turned off the water and stepped out, wrapping a towel around my hips. I'd actually grown to like my beard, so I let it be and just applied some deodorant before I left the bathroom.

Once in my bedroom, I opened my closet and removed my towel to run it over my head. At the same time, Julian emerged with a cloud of steam from the shower.

"Breakfast's in the fridge," I told him, in case he was too hungry to wait.

"A-All right," he stammered as he dropped a sneaker on the floor. He was quick to pick it up, his arms full, which reminded me I'd left my workout clothes in the bathroom. Julian adjusted his towel and darted out, still flushed from our run.

Drying my junk, I picked out a pair of boxer briefs and a pair of jeans. A T-shirt would suffice for now, and then when we had dinner tonight, I could change into a button-down depending on whether we'd go out or stay in at Tennyson and Sophie's.

*

"I need a nap." Julian yawned and threw himself on the couch after breakfast. "I'll admit that the exercise is helping in some ways, but don't you get tired once the adrenaline has settled?"

"Sometimes." I nodded and sat down on the other end. "Nothing wrong with a nap here and there, though." He could sleep while I took some notes on the script. "I'll wake you if you sleep talk about your brother and sister again."

It had become an unspoken rule. He napped on the couch when he hadn't had a good night's sleep, and he seemed to appreciate it when I stayed close. To be honest, I liked it, too.

"You're taking up too much space." He gave his feet a pointed look, indicating he couldn't stretch his legs out.

Weird. The day before yesterday, he'd had no issue planting his feet on my lap while I watched a movie. But then, I hadn't been working.

I eyed him pensively. "You could always sleep in your bed,

you know." This couch was extremely comfy, but the one time I'd fallen asleep here, I'd woken up the next morning with a sore neck. "I can sit at your desk and do this. I don't mind."

Knowing that Julian found it difficult to ask for things and sometimes worried he was in the way, I didn't give him a choice. I stood up with the script and my notebook and told him to follow.

Unlike me, who could sleep with bright lights, music, the TV, and so on, Julian needed darkness and silence. So I drew the blinds and only let the lamp on his desk stay on.

He was quiet as he stripped down to boxers and a T-shirt, and then he slipped under the covers and scooted closer to the wall, his back to the room.

Hopefully, he'd get some rest.

Taking a seat at the desk, I adjusted the chair and flipped open the script. I liked the title, *Catching Stars*, and I hoped it wouldn't change. It fit the story too well.

I assumed Tennyson envisioned Sophie playing the leading role, 'cause that's who I pictured. Solid story, sweet but gut-wrenching, about a young woman's hard work and tragic fate. She was on a quest to leave a legacy behind, and some of the lines jumped off the pages. She was mentally ill, so I'd have to do my own research to get a better insight.

There was one scene I could see as a set piece. Done right, it could be in the trailer and sell the whole film.

"Smash cut," I wrote down and marked off two scenes I wanted connected. *"From Dutch to medium with R. lighting? See how it develops."*

I tapped the marker against a word that bothered me. According to the script, they were in a cottage, yet it took place in Paris. I'd never seen any cabins or cottages in that city. Instead, I jotted down *"Attic/loft."*

"I can't sleep."

I swiveled the chair and looked over at Julian. "Anything I can do?"

He shrugged. Lying on his back, he had his hands planted under his head, and he stared up at the ceiling. "Maybe I need a girlfriend or something."

I snorted a chuckle and rocked back a bit in the chair. A girlfriend wouldn't do much for him. It was the little things I'd noticed. And *he* noticed men when we were out, not women.

Nicky had been miffed when I'd canceled his grocery shopping for us the other day. I was done acting like a fucking child, so Julian and I had gone to the store instead. In fifteen minutes, he had checked out half a dozen asses, and none belonged to a woman.

"Or something," I murmured in response. "How come you thought of that now?" I smirked. "You need me to leave so you can get your rocks off?"

"What, no!" he spluttered, seemingly appalled I'd say something like that.

The kid cracked me up.

I wondered if it was just around me he acted kinda…prudish. He did strike me as a careful type of guy, but something didn't add up. Not with the piercing, the rather extensive tattoos, and even the smoking, to a degree. Part of me believed he was only putting up a front because he and I were still new to one another. As if he were testing the waters first to see where he had me.

Julian scowled up at the ceiling again. "Jesus Christ, I was talking about cuddling—intimacy like that. Why do you think I want to get a pet? To stare at it all day?"

I smiled widely, finding him endearing as fuck. And I hoped I wouldn't freak him out 'cause he was about to learn I didn't care much for social boundaries.

Turning off the light, I capped my marker and left the desk behind for the bed.

"All right, I'm not a hot broad," I chuckled and sat down on the bed, "nor am I a pet, but…" I leaned back against the headboard and used the corner of his duvet to bunch up a pillow for him on my thigh. "There. Use me as your pillow. I'll play Scrabble on my phone." He was about to prattle off some lame protest, so I stopped him. "Don't give me any of that shit. Wanting comfort ain't fucking reserved for women and children, and it's barely been two months since we lost everyone."

He closed his mouth at that, and he swallowed hard as he

lowered his gaze. A moment later, his head followed, carefully coming to a rest on my thigh.

"There we go." I instinctually drew my fingers through his hair. It was soft as hell, all silky and not unlike what women paid too much money to accomplish. Or maybe that had just been Emma.

It didn't take long for Julian to doze off this time.

CHAPTER 8

That night, we went over to Tennyson and Sophie's for dinner. They were tired and said they'd rather stay in, and when I suggested we do it tomorrow, Sophie got huffy. So Julian and I headed across the hall at around seven, and she ordered Thai from our favorite place.

Sophie and Julian could probably sense Tennyson and I wanted to discuss the script, so she happily dragged Julian into the kitchen. I felt for the guy. He was about to face an inquisition.

In the meantime, Tennyson and I sat down in the living room with the script, my notes, and two sleepy kids. Ivy was on my lap, dead on her feet and cuddly.

Kayden clung on his dad's back while watching cartoons on the flat screen.

"I'm really pleased you wanna do this, Noah." Tennyson scanned my notes, occasionally nodding to himself. "Asher sent the script to me, but when I read it, I didn't see the story. I tried, mind you. I tried for a goddamn week because it's spectacular."

I agreed and drank some beer. Ivy asked if she could have some, to which I grinned and said when she turned eighteen.

"So what did you see?" I asked him.

He hummed, still reading. "You and a small crew. Digital

shooting to save time and money.”

Digital shooting was common practice today, but Tennyson was old school. Even though he was only in his late forties, his preferences made him archaic. He liked watching the dailies at the end of the day on set, going through the film, and sitting in his trailer and making notes and marks.

He looked up at me. “I think you could do a lot with a little.”

I smirked wryly and threw a common industry quote at him. “‘We can do it good, we can do it cheap, we can do it fast. Any two, but not all three.’“

“Smartass.” He chuckled warmly and shook his head. “I’m well aware, thank you. But regardless, you can do it cheaper than I ever could. Your technique differs vastly from mine.”

True. Because, digital era.

“Any locations you have in mind?” I wondered.

He inclined his head. “Paris and LA.”

Fantastic.

“Inserts and flyovers in Paris or more than that?”

“Everything that takes place outside the…” He flipped a page in the script and smiled. “Loft or attic. And I agree. The writer might be brilliant, but this is Paris, not the English countryside.” He faced me again. “The only thing I need to know as soon as possible is your schedule.”

“Wide open here,” I replied. “What does Sophie’s schedule look like?”

He grinned. “You see her, too. I was hoping you would.”

I chuckled and took another swig of my beer. “Seemed to me the part was practically written for her.” Aside from age. The character was twenty-five, but Sophie hadn’t turned thirty yet, and she looked young. It wasn’t an issue.

“There is one thing,” Tennyson said, sounding hesitant now. “Sophie wants to cast Kayden as the son, and I’m on the fence. He fits the description, but this is more than cherry-picking a child off the streets. We compromised, and I told her he could read for the part.”

I reached over to Kayden and poked his side. “You wanna be an actor like Mommy, huh?”

He smiled and shrugged.

Tennyson gave me a pointed look.

Fair enough.

*

During dinner, Sophie wanted to know everything there was to know about Julian's love for music. Instruments he played, genres he enjoyed, aspirations, experience, studies, and so on. It was good. Evidently I only knew half of it, so I learned something new, too.

The kids had already eaten, according to their folks, so they remained on the couch to watch a movie while the rest of us devoured our meals at the dining room table. Sophie knew me well, plenty of vegetarian options, and I shot Julian a smug look every time he opted for those instead of meat.

"Will you give it a rest?" he bitched quietly, though he sucked at containing his mirth. "I never said vegetarian food was gross."

I was just fucking with him. I'd stuffed my face with shrimp minutes ago, and I was hardly one to convert people.

"You're such a shit stirrer, Noah," Sophie told me.

I frowned with a mouth full of food. "That's nothing new, babe. You can do better."

Sophie pointed a fork at me while addressing Julian. "How do you put up with that? I adore the man—he's one of my best friends—but to *live* with him? Sweet Jesus."

I blew her a kiss as Tennyson and Julian had fun at my expense.

It was a safe choice, though, playfully picking on someone in the group to relax the newcomer. I sent Sophie a brief glance of gratitude, and she winked.

"So, Julian." It was Tennyson's turn, I guessed. "Do you write your own music, too?"

"Sometimes, yes." Julian nodded. "Noah's been trying to get me to use his new baby grand."

"Well, since this morning, you're actually obligated," I drawled.

He rolled his eyes, and fuck that. Learning that he wrote original stuff made me wanna hear him play again even more. The memorial service didn't count.

"You bought a piano?" Sophie cocked her head, her gaze flicking between me and Julian. "You don't play…do you? No, I would have known."

"*He* plays." I emptied half a container of rice on my plate. "He's worked better for me than Xanax or whatever else a head-fucker would've prescribed me, so it was the least I could do."

Sophie appeared torn between giggles and amusement. "That's…one of the sweetest and weirdest things I've ever heard from you."

"That's me. Sweet and weird." I grinned and sat back, draping an arm along the back of Julian's chair. "So enough about us. How was vacation?"

*

It'd been great catching up with my friends, and I was glad Julian seemed to fit in well, but the day caught up with me fairly early. When we'd returned to the loft, my mood had crashed, and I'd retired for the night. And now I was staring at nothing, unable to sleep.

I wasn't restless, though. I was tired as fuck, my mind all but groggy and slow, yet something was up. My gut twisted with unease, and I hoped I wouldn't have a night of bad dreams to look forward to.

The sound of soft piano music made me sit straight up in the darkness. It was faint, but I heard it. I collapsed down against the mattress again and reached for my phone to check the time.

Almost midnight.

I had a text from Sophie, too.

I'm so happy for you, Noah. We're always here, don't forget that, but I think this is amazing. You've both come far since the memorial, and it was super great to see how close you've become. Love you bunches.

I smiled faintly and brushed my thumb over the screen. Were

Julian and I that close? Maybe. I hadn't really thought about it. She could be right, though. I didn't even wanna imagine what my life would look like if Julian hadn't come here. Jesus fucking Christ, I'd most likely still be living at the bottom of a bottle.

I appreciate it, you mush cake. Thanks for tonight, good to have you home. What do you mean by me and Julian being close?

He and I hadn't interacted that much, hence my question. It'd mainly been Sophie who had quizzed him.

Putting aside my phone again, I closed my eyes and concentrated on whatever Julian was playing in the living room. It was somber, tinged with something I could only describe as pain. Akin to hopelessness or a sense of being dragged down. Every now and then, he went off on a lighter tangent.

He was good.

My phone vibrated on the nightstand, so I guessed Sophie was still awake. Having traveled all day, she should've fallen asleep at dinner.

I can't put my finger on it. You're just very aware of each other, and I can tell you're protective of him. It's sweet. I'm off to bed, but we'll have to catch up more soon! Mwah!

Protective, huh? All right, then.

As I got comfortable on my back again, Julian's music was lulling me closer to sleep. I scratched my chest absently.

Maybe we'd take a day off from running tomorrow. A lazy Saturday morning in bed didn't sound half bad. I could get bagels from the coffee shop down the street. I'd force the kid to play more of his music while I continued studying the script.

I sighed.

Fuck it if I wasn't getting attached to him, and it was different from loving my niece and nephew. JJ and Linda had been kids. Actual kids. Julian was grown-up, and we had more in common. We were equals, which I supposed played a big role.

Eventually, the music faded to a close. I didn't hear him pad closer on the hardwood floor, but I waited for the sound of his door opening and shutting.

The unease was back in my stomach. I had no fucking clue

why.

It'd been a good day.

Moments later, it was my door that opened.

A floorboard creaked, and then the bed dipped with his weight, and yeah, this was strangely right. The unease faded like his music had, and I stretched out my arm.

"I'm glad you played," I murmured sleepily.

"I'm obligated." There was a grin in his voice, and I smirked to myself as he settled in. His pillow ended up on top of my arm, and he scooted as close as he dared.

"Stand-in pet reporting for duty." I yawned and drew him closer so I could put an arm over his middle. His T-shirt was threadbare and soft, and I was thankful for the barrier. With my luck and the way I sometimes tossed and turned, I'd tear off his nipple piercing in my sleep if he slept bare-chested like I did.

He laughed softly, his breath hitting my sternum, and burrowed his arms and hands into my chest. They were fucking freezing.

"The piano made of ice?" I grumbled.

"Yes."

"I can tell." I smiled into his hair, ignoring the faint warning bells going off. I wasn't stupid; I knew this wasn't normal, but our lives weren't fucking normal. Not anymore. "Sleep. No workout tomorrow."

"Thank fuck," he whispered. "Good night."

"Night, icicle."

*

It became somewhat of a routine. Whenever we needed closeness to ward off nightmares and anxiety, we sought each other out and shared a bed. It was indescribably comforting not to be alone, and it worked, too. Maybe too well.

I was decent at ignoring those warning bells, before it came back to bite me in the ass.

One night was anything but peaceful. Around three AM, I bolted out of bed with my heart pounding, a ringing noise in my ears, and horror coursing through me.

"Take it." I pushed my cock in and out of his tight ass, and he moaned, caught between me and a wall. "Fuck, so perfect."

He begged for more. I covered his mouth with my hand so the others wouldn't hear us.

Bile rose in my throat, and I rushed to the bathroom across the hallway. Nothing came up, yet I heaved over and over.

New nightmare. A vivid one. I couldn't get the images out of my head.

"Please let me come," he moaned as I reached around to stroke him. He was hard and smooth in my hand, and I wanted to taste. "Oh God, Noah…"

"Shhh, be quiet," I whispered. Our family was downstairs, for chrissakes. "Can't fucking get enough."

I shuddered and spat into the toilet before standing up. My heart wouldn't fucking calm down. I felt sick to my stomach with revulsion.

What's wrong with me?

I fisted my hair and squeezed my eyes shut.

Even I had limits.

Going to the living room, I ended up pacing for ages. I'd never been good at stewing in my own shit, though. I needed to bounce off ideas and interact. I needed someone to tell me I wasn't a goddamn head case.

I felt bad; however, after about an hour or so, I was only working myself up more. I'd make it up to him, but I needed to talk.

The nausea came back as I snuck into my room to grab a pair of basketball shorts and a T-shirt. Julian slept peacefully on my pillow. If only he knew what I'd dreamed.

I promptly left and grabbed my phone on the way.

Once outside the loft, I scrolled down my phone to Tennyson's number and called him.

Come on, man.

He answered on the third ring. "Noah?"

"Yeah, sorry to wake you up." I was a fucking tool. "Mind coming out and talking to me for a minute?"

There was some rustling in the background as he got out of

bed. "Uh, yeah. Of course. Be right there." He hung up, and I returned to pacing.

I was assaulted with more memories from the dream, and it made my skin crawl.

I kissed him, groaning in pleasure. My hands couldn't stay away. I'd never needed someone this desperately in my goddamn life.

Tennyson opened the door and stumbled out, rubbing his eyes from sleep. "What's wrong?"

"*I* am," I replied. I ran a hand through my hair and blew out a breath, frustrated with myself. Disgusted. "Sorry again for waking you up."

He waved it off and yawned. "When I say you can call me anytime, I actually mean it. So what's bothering you? Nightmares?"

You can say that.

"Background story," I said. "Julian and I sleep together. Sleep-sleep. We've ended up sharing a bed lately 'cause it's easier not being alone, and we're there for each other when we have nightmares."

Tennyson nodded slowly, not appearing to see any issue. "A bit unusual, perhaps, but if it works for you, then great."

"Right, except tonight I dreamed about fucking him."

I almost dry-heaved right then and there.

My chest constricted and my stomach rolled as the images flashed by me once more. They were glimpses I hoped my brain could block out soon. Until there was nothing left.

Tennyson looked at me with concern. "That doesn't have to mean anything, Noah."

"He's my nephew," I spat out. "It's fucking disgusting."

I pressed my palms against my eyes and flinched. Fuck, I could see us. In the dream, our family had been alive, too. At a reunion, Julian and I had snuck into my old room, and the next thing I remembered, I was fucking him up the ass.

"I'm not sure it matters what I say here," Tennyson told me. "It's not like you've forgotten the fact that you're not actually related."

"Semantics," I said dismissively.

"Is it, though?" He tilted his head. "I have a feeling you'd view Julian as a family member more if you'd been closer before the accident. Family has little to do with blood, my friend. Say JJ had been adopted, or even your sister. You would've seen them as family regardless, because you had that relationship. You never did with Julian, as far as I'm concerned."

I got what he was saying; it just didn't help.

"Do you see him as your nephew?" he asked.

I stared at him, frowning. "He is my nephew."

"Not what I asked." He cocked a brow.

I sighed heavily and looked down. Did it really matter how I saw Julian? Major boundaries had been crossed. The woman he'd called Mom was my sister. Forget the fact that I wasn't even gay; it was still wrong on so many levels. And that feeling was real. It *felt* fucked up. Even more so because I'd enjoyed it in the dream.

Heave.

I'd unleashed a monster within me I hoped wasn't real, and he'd begged for more.

"Jesus." I bent over and tried to breathe. "He's just a kid."

At that, Tennyson snorted. "He's twenty-three. Need I remind you that my wife is seventeen years younger than me? She was twenty-one when we met. Surely you remember. You were there, for heaven's sake."

Yeah, but it had been fun when it wasn't me. And no family ties had been involved.

"You call him kid like I used to call you kid," he went on. He wasn't bothered at all, which was fucked. "You were well into your thirties when that nickname kind of died out. It doesn't mean anything."

It meant something to *me.*

I cared about Julian more than I could say. That was clear. But maybe our attachment to one another had grown unhealthy. We couldn't rely on each other all the time, so sleeping alone might be a better idea.

CHAPTER 9

Two weeks later

"I'm on my way home now," I said. Well, I was supposed to be on my way home. In reality, I was stuck in traffic and going absolutely nowhere. As one tended to do in LA. "Is Zane flying out with you? Been a while since we all got together."

Daniel hummed on the other end, always working these days. When I met him, he'd been Sophie's PA. Now, he ran his own management business and had employees in both New York and LA. Not too shabby for a guy under forty.

"No, he's wrapping up his last shoot," he replied. "He's looking forward to ex-model life." I could hear him typing quickly on his computer in the background. "After this year, I'm gonna slow down a bit, too. Did Sophie tell you we're adopting?"

I grinned tiredly and scrubbed a hand over my face. "She did. We've kinda been waiting for it."

He chuckled. "Yeah, Asher mentioned a damn bet." It was our thing. "Anyway, the reason I called you. Tennyson wants recommendations for a PA agency for *Catching Stars*. If you're happy with Nicky, I'll go with the one he's at. Less paperwork, and you just have to sign him over to another payroll."

"I honestly don't need a PA yet—or anymore, I guess." I yawned and went for my coffee. Fuck, lukewarm. "Is he on a contract?"

Technically, we were in pre-production at this point, but it was mostly Tennyson making calls. We had a location scout working too, and I was doing rewrites and storyboarding. Either way, no assistant needed.

"He's not, no, so I'll give him a call and thank him for his time." Daniel paused. "You sound tired as hell, man. Are you all right?"

No. "Sure," I answered. "Feels good to be back at work."

In truth, though, I was feeling depressed. Frustrated, stifled, rattled, and depressed.

I barely slept. I got two or three hours a night and spent the rest of the time talking to myself. That fucking dream… I'd had it on a few more occasions, and it shook me every time. Realistically, I knew I dreamed about Julian more because I was obsessing. If I'd been able to let it fucking go, maybe it wouldn't be an issue.

Maybe I wouldn't wake up hard as a rock for all the wrong reasons.

"Did you forget you're not the actor in our group of misfits?" Daniel asked dryly.

"Don't mother me, buddy," I chuckled. "I get enough of that from Sophie and Brook."

Tennyson was a man of his word. He hadn't told Sophie about my…fucked-up state…but that didn't mean she was blind. She could tell I was more tired than usual, quieter—or what she called broodier.

"I hear ya. Still, you know we're here," Daniel said. "Same goes for Julian. How's he doing?"

Same as me, which was worse. I hadn't wanted him to be hurt by me pulling away for no apparent reason, so I had been honest with him. *Kinda honest.* I'd told him about my concerns of codependency and how relying on each other too much could ultimately keep us from moving on.

From that moment on, we had both *pretended.* Everything was *fine.* Forced smiles, conversation too casual, insignificant topics. We remained close, but another type of distance had been wedged in between us. And that was on me.

"He's playing a lot," I told Daniel, which was true. Julian did play. Every night, I heard him on the baby grand. His sheet music and scribbled notes were all over the loft. I dug that. "I think he's formed some strange friendship with Tennyson, too."

It wasn't *strange* in that sense; I'd just figured he'd connect more with Sophie, for some reason. But Tennyson and Julian appeared to enjoy discussing film and music together.

"How's that strange?"

I shrugged even though he couldn't see me. "I don't know. Maybe the age? Julian should be interested in finding friends his own age. Sophie and Zane are the only ones who come close in our group."

Daniel laughed. "Right, but the rest of us are fun-loving cradle robbers. How could he resist?" Rather than finding him funny, I couldn't help but cringe. Cradle robbing hit too close to home today. "I can't believe I'm telling *you* this," he went on, "but unclench, Noah. We don't always find what we want in our own age categories."

No, that was becoming painfully fucking clear.

*

When I came home and parked in the garage, I saw my truck in its spot. It meant Nicky was here, or he had returned the truck. Grabbing my stuff, I headed for the elevator and went up to our floor.

As soon as the doors opened, I was hit by bass from loud music and the smell of both cigarettes and weed.

There was no way Tennyson and Sophie were home. They would've noticed and called me. I hoped.

I dug out my keys and unlocked the door, torn between being irritated and worried. I found Julian in the middle of the couch. He lit up a joint as hard-core porn played on the flat screen.

Jesus fucking Christ.

Slamming the door shut got me his attention, though he was too stoned to be shocked. He had no expression whatsoever. He calmly lowered the volume on the stereo, and instead of turning off the porno, he poured a glass of vodka and soda.

He'd bought alcohol. Fucker.

"Welcome home," he said lazily. "How did your meetings go?"

I didn't answer, too fucking pissed. The worry didn't go anywhere, 'cause this wasn't him.

"What the fuck're you doing, Julian?"

He smirked. "I'm having some courage. Want some? We have the liquid variety, and Nicky hooked me up with the marijuana variety. He also gave me a bowl, but I don't know how to smoke it."

I stared at him, debating internally, then sighed and set my bag and poster tubes on the floor.

"Have you ever gotten high before, kid?" I asked.

He scowled as I joined him on the couch. "You need to stop that crap, *Uncle*. I know you think I'm all innocent and sweet, but we have weed in Germany, too." He shrugged and leaned back.

I shook my head and looked at the coffee table. A bag of weed, tobacco, two packs of cigarettes, rolling papers… One bottle of vodka, one bottle of my favorite mainstream whiskey, mixers all over…

"Just how much courage do you need?" I wondered.

He leaned forward again and placed a glass in front of me. "It's for you, too. So you don't get mad." He scooped a spoonful of crushed ice into my glass and recreated the Jameson and ginger I taught him weeks ago. "There's something I need to tell you, and I was nervous as hell about it. Then Nicky showed up."

Funny how quickly that broke my resolve. What the *fuck* made him so nervous? And why did that make me nervous, too? He better not be fucking leaving. Who knew what else Nicky had hooked him up with. Friends? A better uncle?

I winced.

All right, bring on the drinks.

My mouth watered, and the two first sips went down

smoothly, spreading warmth on the way down.

"What's with the porn?" I unbuttoned the top button of my shirt and got comfortable on the couch. "Doesn't really seem like your taste."

"You don't know my taste."

I chuckled and chugged more of my drink. "You're into S&M?"

Two women were being brutally topped by a guy in leather. He wielded one hell of a whip and made the girls sob before they crawled to suck his cock.

Julian appeared transfixed, and it didn't add up.

One glance at his crotch told me it didn't have a physical reaction on him.

Fuck.

I tore away and drained my glass.

"I've never done that," Julian said quietly.

I frowned. "Done what?"

"Given oral. I've received, been fucked, and topped, but never given oral."

And so the gay cat was out of the bag.

It struck me pretty fast he didn't know what he'd confessed, though.

My second drink went down in one go. I had a feeling I'd need it if sex was the topic. I poured a third, and then Julian extended a joint to me.

It'd been years…

Even in the City of Weed, it wasn't too common in my circles.

I accepted the joint and took a small puff, testing the potency. He hadn't blended it with a lot of tobacco, and it was some quality shit. Sweet, strong. Immediate effect.

Fuck…yeah…

I leaned back, closed my eyes, and took another drag. This was better than alcohol. My age had gotten in the way of fun. Back in the day, I smoked a lot of weed. Then I'd grown up.

"How are you feeling?" he asked.

"Better than I have in a couple weeks," I admitted. Cracking one eye open, I found him watching me. "This ain't becoming a fucking habit."

He grinned, his eyes a little glazed.

I liked seeing him happy.

The shadows under his eyes were back, though. My damn fault. I closed my eyes again and took a pull from the joint, and I held it. I held it until troubles faded and my nightmare was plain desire.

"Nicky asked me out."

Of course he did. Julian was a good-looking guy.

I turned to him, and yeah, he really did look good. I hadn't paid attention to his appearance before. Not a lot, anyway.

I took a final drag before leaning forward to put it out. "What did you say to him?"

"That…that I'd think about it."

I side-eyed him. No more bullshit. "Why have you been hiding that you're gay?"

Despite being high as a kite and halfway to Drunkville, he looked worried and ashamed. "Can we talk about that another time? I'm feeling all right for the first time in ages."

Fair enough.

I wanted to know eventually, though.

"I'll be right back," I said. I wanted to change into sweats and a T-shirt, and I needed to clear my head.

Julian returned to watching porn, and I escaped to my room. But nothing worked. The images from the dreams I'd had about him were back, and now there was nothing repulsive about them.

I washed my face and stared at my reflection.

Dating Nicky… Yeah. A guy his age. It was perfect. But fuck if it didn't irritate me. I missed Julian. I wanted just a little bit more—a bit closer. As if squeezing him to me could bring relief. It was fucked, though it was how I felt.

"I'm screwed," I muttered to myself. I stripped down, took a leak, and then I turned on the shower. If I didn't sober up, I'd go too far, and I needed to let this go. Maybe find a woman. Someone I could fuck, hold, and take comfort from. It didn't sit well with me, but it seemed like that was the best option.

Except…not.

I showered quickly, the water cold, and it worked a little. Unfortunately, my thoughts were as fucked as ever. Sobriety didn't change the fact that I ached to get the aforementioned comfort from Julian. Whichever woman I put in that position would be a replacement.

As I yanked on a pair of sweats, I warred with myself. I'd become a masochist for it. Logic told me space was good. Logic told me I was just deprived of touch, and my desires would change if I got what I needed elsewhere. My heart didn't agree. Julian wasn't a mere convenience.

Lastly, my body… What my body ached for was fucking obvious, and for better or worse, I had a past of listening to it. Even when I shouldn't. Perhaps especially then.

I threw the towel in the laundry basket and left my room.

Julian was still on the couch watching porn, but the movie was new, and I couldn't say he didn't have a physical reaction anymore. He was leaning forward and shielding his crotch, and his face was flushed. He couldn't look away from the two dudes fucking on the screen. Well, he did glance over at me once, making me question my choice not to wear a shirt.

"Isn't this something you should watch in private?" I asked, resigned.

Like I'd said, I was screwed. I would fuck shit up sooner or later.

"Most likely," Julian replied. "You can always tell me to shut it off."

Nice try, kid.

He was not throwing a goddamn challenge in my face, thinking he'd get away with it. Whatever reaction he wanted, I wouldn't give. We both knew when push came to shove, my balls were bigger. I didn't need weed or alcohol to speak my mind.

No, you only need it to numb out your entire life.

"I don't give a fuck." I tossed the notion of sobriety out the window and poured another drink. "You can watch whatever you want."

And he did. He'd hooked up his laptop to the flat screen, and he tended to pick videos with a lot of blow jobs. I hoped it wasn't for educational purposes, 'cause in porn, "good" head was all choking and facials.

In the meantime, I nursed a drink and reminisced about the times when I was fun. Noah Collins, always there for a good time. No complications, no internal wars, no attachments.

I missed those days.

Now I had an ex who had stomped all over my heart—though, perhaps I wasn't as torn up about it as one would think—and I had a pseudo-nephew who I fucked on occasion in my dreams.

Wonderful.

"Give me some of that." I jerked my chin at his joint.

He scooted closer to hand it over, and I was soon back in the blissful land of No Fucks To Give.

It was nice.

It allowed me to enjoy shit.

"Do you like this?" I asked, gesturing to the video. Two guys were completely wrapped up in each other, all hands and mouths. It wasn't hard-core at all, but it hit me more. *All hands.* All that touching and grabbing.

"Yeah," Julian rasped.

I watched him from the corner of my eye as he sat back. His hands covered his groin, and he was close enough to me now that I could smell his aftershave. And weed. We reeked of weed, and it was seductive.

Fuck.

After finishing the joint and my drink, I had a perfect buzz going on. I was relaxed, there were no worries, and I even got going on the gay porn. Without troubles clouding my vision, I could feel the charge in the room.

"You wanna fuck Nicky?" I lolled my head against the back of the couch and looked at him. "I reckon he's a sure thing."

Julian shrugged and rested his head on my shoulder. "I don't know. It's been a while, and I would feel like I'm using him."

That made me chuckle. "Eh. As long you're both on the same terms."

He hummed. "I think he's mad at you."

I swallowed dryly, admittedly turned on by the video now. "What the fuck for?" I became harder, and I brushed my thumb absently up and down the underside as my cock grew.

There was a hitch in Julian's breath. "Because…because he expected more work."

I shrugged with the shoulder he wasn't using as a pillow. "My first PA gig, I didn't even see my employer. All I did was guard his parking spot."

We forgot about talking as one of the men lubed up his cock and positioned himself to fuck the other. He kneeled behind the bottom, and the camera zoomed in. Perfect angle, perfect view. The top pushed in slowly, inch by inch.

Julian shuddered next to me, and I stopped using my brain completely. On instinct, I pressed a kiss to the top of his head, lingering. We used the same shampoo and body wash, so he smelled like me.

"Turn off the music," I murmured. "I wanna hear them."

Julian cursed and quickly reached for the remote. His fingers trembled, but he managed to lower the volume some more. Whatever rock music he'd been playing faded into the background, and the sound of skin slapping and two men groaning took over.

When Julian got settled again, he was closer than before, and he faced me head on with enough lust in his eyes to send a shiver down my spine.

"I think I know why you don't want to be close to me anymore."

Fucking hell.

I stared blankly, unable to bring forth any of the panic that rattled in the back of my head. What he said was packed with irony, though, because *close*? We were only a few inches away from each other now.

"That's what I wanted to tell you." He went on. "I heard you one night… Please don't get mad."

I clenched my jaw. "Don't read too much into that." Given how vivid those dreams were, I wasn't exactly stunned to learn I'd sleep talked. But I did wish he didn't know.

"I'm not," he was quick to say. "I know you don't want

it…like that—or me, in reality…but…"

In reality? My hard-on for him seemed too fucking real to me.

"But what?" I gripped his chin when he tried to look away. "Wrong time to be shy, Julian." Leaning in a bit, I grazed my nose along his jaw. "Speak up."

He shuddered through a breath. "I want to take advantage."

I groaned quietly and gave his skin a sharp nip. "You little fucker. You set this up." Not needing his answer, I grabbed his jaw and kissed him.

No going back now.

CHAPTER 10

It was a rush, how he melted into me as I took control. I kissed him slowly a few times, testing for my own sake. His lips were soft and tasted of cherries from his drink and weed.

With a swipe of my tongue, I parted his lips, and it woke him up. He kissed me back hard, after which I pushed him down to lie on his back. I followed and covered his body with mine. The relief, the one I'd said I ached for, was fucking everywhere. Like tiny explosions inside me, they fueled me to push harder and want even more.

"My bed," I growled. "Now."

I hauled him up and nudged him toward the hallway. He panted and glanced over his shoulder, and then he turned, and I was there to press him up against the nearest wall.

"Harder," he demanded. "I fucking need it, Noah."

No more than I did. "Lose the shirt." I pressed my cock against his lower abs and deepened the kiss. It was intoxicating, and for thinking this was brief—something to get out of my system—I grabbed at him as if I wanted to mark him indelibly.

As he got rid of his T-shirt, I moved us farther down the hall toward my room. I bit into his neck then licked the spot. In response, he bucked into me, groaned, and palmed my crotch.

"Holy fuck," he breathed out. "I-I want you in my mouth."

A rush of possessiveness bolted through me, and I lifted my head from his neck. I could barely see past the haze of lust. He stroked me outside my sweats and licked his bottom lip.

I cupped his jaw and forced my thumb between his lips.

My cock would be the first one he'd suck.

Fuck, yeah.

I liked that more than I should.

Withdrawing my thumb, I slid in three fingers instead and pushed down his bottoms. "Suck my fingers as hard as you can." I looked down between us, seeing his stiff cock. "Take more." My mouth went dry as pre-come pulsed out of him. "More, Julian."

He moaned and closed his eyes, and I rewarded him by squeezing his tight sac gently in my hand. I was glad he didn't shave. He wasn't smooth everywhere. He was a man. Though, I appreciated the softness about him, too. His chest was mostly free from hair.

"I'll have you spread out for me," I told him.

He nodded rapidly, and I removed my fingers. Then I turned him toward my room and slapped his ass.

"Go—now. I want you on your back in the middle of the bed."

I followed him, getting rid of my sweats as I went, and reached my bed at the same time as he got settled. Completely naked, he looked more vulnerable, and to me, it was the perfect fucking sight. So much to touch and hold.

"You have no idea how much I need this." I crawled over him, pausing to flick his nipple ring with my tongue.

He hissed and tried to pull me down on him. "For not being gay, you're kind of awesome at it."

"Kind of?" I lifted a brow.

"Out of this world," he amended, brushing a finger over my beard. "Can I just ask if it's me you want—even for the moment—or simply sex?"

"You." That was an easy one. The easiest question he could ask, actually. It was him. It was fucking comforting, sexy, freeing—it was like I could breathe again. I didn't understand it. I only knew

I'd needed this for weeks now, and it had to be him. "I gotta feel you."

Make sure you're real.

I dipped down and coaxed him into a slow, drugging kiss.

"Everywhere," he mumbled.

His fingers raked over my back, and we both moaned when I lowered myself to him. I covered him completely, and it brought more of that relief. Didn't matter the sexual frustration was building up; I was reveling. No fucking rush here.

He slid his hands across my chest as I stroked his neck and shoulders. The kiss never really broke, and it wouldn't be difficult to get addicted to his taste. Fuck, I'd missed this. Kissing, rolling around, just feeling.

I had to admit it carried more meaning with Julian. I didn't know why, but I assumed it had to do with the fact that, in one way, we were all we had left.

At some point, he ended up on top, and the sexual tension grew thicker. He felt fucking amazing wherever I touched him. He was needy, greedy, and instinctive. Sitting up, I cupped his ass in my hands and pulled him close so our cocks slid together.

"Oh, fuck, fuck…" He thrust forward as I kissed his neck and sternum. I looked down and saw pre-come connecting us, and it caused heat to flush to the surface of my skin.

"Jesus Christ," I whispered. It was sexy as hell. I hadn't expected that. "Julian…" I snuck a hand between us and rubbed our cocks, spreading the fluids. I stroked and squeezed, and I earned a whimper from Julian. "Open your mouth for me." I showed him two slick fingers, and he sucked them into his mouth like a starving man.

This time, I didn't let him suck for long. I drew back right away and yanked him in for a deep kiss, 'cause fuck if I didn't wanna taste, too.

A growl emanated from my chest, and I flipped him over, consumed by primal desire. The salt lingered on my tongue. It triggered me to go rougher, wanting more.

"*Christ*, Noah…I want to suck you off," he moaned breathlessly. "You're clean, right? I don't want anything in the way."

"I'm clean." I dragged my teeth along his bottom lip before I pushed my tongue into his mouth. My head swam. I wouldn't have been this easy to convince to go without protection if it weren't for him and the goddamn high I was on. "I want your ass."

It was something I'd always gotten off on. Anal sex, finger-fucking, tongue-fucking—I was definitely an ass man. And I'd been denied for too damn long. Emma didn't want it, and at the time, it hadn't bothered me too much. Now I was coming back from all that bullshit, and I wanted his ass spread and ready.

"I'll go get lube," he said, but I stopped him by shaking my head.

"No, I want something else. Get on all fours." I sat back on my heels and stroked my cock. "If you give me what I want, I'll let you suck me off until your jaw hurts and then some."

"Fuck yes, what do you want from me? Name it."

I bit my lip, eye-fucking his tight ass. "Sounds. Every genuine reaction to what I do. Don't hold back." I brushed my hand over his left ass cheek softly at first. He shivered and nodded. "Perfect," I said quietly. "Stroke yourself at the same time and follow my pace."

"I can do that… Are you sure I shouldn't get lube, though? It makes finger-fucking easier."

I chuckled, and for a second, I felt perverted and twisted. Leaning over him, I pressed my cock against his hole and kissed his neck. "Don't worry," I murmured. "Lube isn't necessary for a good tongue-fucking from your uncle."

"Jesus!" Julian choked on a breath and then whimpered, and it was the sweetest fucking sound.

It didn't feel as disturbing as I thought it would, though—the uncle part. And I realized it was because we'd never really lived those roles or had that relationship. Tennyson was right. Julian was my equal. We shared a family bond but no history. It helped to get rid of that taboo, and there was relief there, too.

"Oh my God, I want it," he panted. "I love it dirty. Role-play and stuff. I've never done that."

I didn't need inspiration, for chrissakes. It'd open the

floodgates.

I kissed my way down his spine and stroked his sides, over his ink and past his hips. Next, I palmed his ass cheeks and licked the smooth crease to his opening.

"Fuck…" I groaned at the taste. Goddamn amazing. The only thing that bummed me out slightly was that he'd probably showered right before I got home. I would have wanted more of his natural body scent.

Julian sucked in a breath as I swiped my tongue softly over his hole. The protruding skin tightened, which sent more blood to my cock. I'd force my way in.

"Please," he croaked.

I nuzzled the pale fuzz around his opening and then applied more pressure with my tongue. In response, Julian gave me exactly what I wanted. While I licked, sucked, probed, and kissed, he moaned and told me what my actions did to him.

Like me, he produced a lot of pre-come, and I used it to slick him up further. And to taste. It was a fucking turn-on. I loved a good mess.

Goose bumps rose on the skin of his back, and by the time he was relaxed enough for fingers, his skin glistened with a light sheen of sweat. Sucking two fingers into my mouth, I watched him stroke himself for a moment, until he was begging more persistently.

"Ass whore," I whispered.

"*Yes…*" He let out a drawn-out groan as I slowly pushed two digits inside him. "There!"

I paused. "That was easy." Twisting my fingers, I brushed them over his prostate. It milked him from the inside, and a string of come seeped out of his cock.

"I can't," he whimpered. "Oh hell, more…" He started rambling as I set a steady pace, altering between prostate massage, long strokes that fucked him, and soft teasing with my tongue. "Noah—fuck, Noah!"

I cursed, loving hearing him moaning my name. He was beside himself. I was doing that to him.

"Are you always this responsive?" I asked.

He heaved a breath, trembling. "Not everyone fucks like you.

Jesus. I-I need to come."

I grinned.

"Get on your back," I told him and withdrew my fingers. "Can you hold your knees to your chest and spread 'em?"

He nodded and complied, and I waited until I had him all on display for me. Arms hooked under his knees, ass spread, cock leaking, abs tensing. Holy fuck, he was a sight.

I wanted to fuck him something fierce, but it didn't feel right. He deserved better, and that thought made me recognize I was coming down from my high. Shifting closer, I hovered over him and kissed him deeply. There were words I wanted to say, but I refrained.

A few more kisses, and then I crawled farther down and tongued his ass. Since he was holding up his legs, I fisted his cock too, and stroked him firmly but slowly.

"Please, please, fuck, please," he groaned breathlessly. He tossed his head from side to side and tried to buck his hips, but I kept him in place. "I'm fucking close, Noah."

I tightened my grip on his cock, though I didn't jerk him faster. I wanted to milk him properly and make his orgasm last. But to bring him even closer, and eventually push him over the edge, I rubbed his prostate in quick little circles.

When he lost his vocabulary and began shaking more violently, I knew he was there. Seconds later, the first string of come shot from his cock and onto his chest. I kept the same pace, and he cried out and released his legs.

This image of him, completely rigid and coming, would be etched into my mind for-fucking-ever.

It turned me into a savage, and I barely let him catch his breath. In one long stroke, I slid my tongue up his torso. I tasted him, fresh sweat and come, and growled in need.

"Your sweet mouth on my cock—*now*."

He gasped, incapable of words, and hauled me down for a kiss first. I moaned into his mouth and fed him his own arousal, which seemed to renew his hunger for more. With a firm push, he had me on my back.

"Finally," he breathed.

There was no caution or apprehension this time. He dove for my cock and had half of me in his mouth before my head had even hit the pillows.

I hissed and pushed myself up on my elbows to see better. He licked, suckled at the slit, and sucked me like he was worshiping.

An out-of-breath chuckle slipped through my lips, and I winced a bit when he got too eager. "Watch the teeth, baby."

He spared me a quick apology, cheeks flushed and eyes filled with hunger. It was kinda like I wasn't here. All his focus was on my cock. Christ, he was perfect. Perfectly him, exactly what I wanted.

"There's so much I wanna do," he mumbled in between licks. His eyes met mine briefly, so maybe I did exist, after all. "I have all these fantasies…"

"Fuck," I whispered. "That's it, get me wet." Threading my fingers through his curls, I guided him slowly over my erection, encouraging him to take a bit more of me. "What kinda fantasies?"

I shouldn't have asked. I knew I'd regret it.

He closed his eyes and hummed around my cock, and every now and then, he paused to reveal his desires. "Some of the normal stuff, I suppose." He jerked me as he dipped down to tongue my balls. "Uni professor and student, boss and employee, doctor and patient…"

I clenched my jaw, countless scenarios swimming in my head.

My head lolled back, and I got completely fucking lost in the moment. Between his sucking and his fantasy sharing, it wouldn't be long until I exploded.

His mouth was goddamn stellar. There was no finesse or technique, but he sucked me like he loved it. He gagged a few times but was insistent on taking all of me. It didn't work, though he kept trying. And his tongue… His fucking lips.

I didn't even register that I'd started thrusting a little. It was his moaning that alerted me to something new exciting him, so I lay down flat on my back and moved both hands to his head. Fisting his hair, I began fucking his mouth.

"I'm almost there, Julian." I lifted my head briefly to get another look. "Goddammit, you feel so good." Saliva and pre-come trickled down my shaft, my breathing morphed into panting, my muscles strained, and…shit. I paused, as much as it killed me. "You wanna try swallowing? I don't care, just pick before I blow."

He answered by taking as much of me as he could, and I couldn't hold back another fucking second. I came hard. The air was squeezed out of my lungs, and I tensed up.

Julian choked on a groan, lapping and sucking at me. Pulse after pulse landed in his mouth.

I felt like I'd run a marathon. No ability to move whatsoever. I melted into the mattress, panting and swallowing against the dryness in my throat.

A warm body nestled into my side, and I mustered the strength to wrap my arms around him. The A/C was hitting us pretty hard, so I yanked the covers over us, too.

"Jesus fuck," I coughed.

Julian laughed softly and kissed my neck. "You're so intense."

That was a new one. "What do you mean?" I yawned and found a good spot on the pillow where I could breathe him in and kiss him on the forehead.

"I can't explain it. It's…passion, I suppose?" He lifted his head to look me in the eye. "Uninhibited. Even with men… Or me, anyway. Has it always been like that when you fuck guys?"

I chuckled drowsily and rubbed my eyes. "I'm not in the habit of having sex with men. I just don't rule it out. Call me an opportunist." I stroked his cheek. "I love sex, Julian. Always have. I go all in if it feels right." It had felt *too* right with him, though. "With you…" I had to find the words that wouldn't hurt him. "In a way, it was almost about survival. I can't remember the last time I actually *needed* to be with someone. I've had nightmares about it for weeks."

"I know." He smiled ruefully. "It's the family thing, right?"

"Not a small thing," I murmured. "But yeah."

Imagine if our family knew? That broke my fucking heart.

"I understand. Really." He lay down and looked up at the ceiling. "It's been sort of the same for me, though…with some minor differences. But anyway, it was like when I lost Linda at the park once. When we found her again, I didn't leave her side for a week. I hugged her until she got sick of me, and I sometimes set the alarm to check in on her while she slept."

Those were the exact words I needed to hear, and I didn't even know. It described this—all of this—perfectly. "You did it to assure yourself she was still there."

"Yes." He tilted his head my way, pensive. A bit of the apprehension was back. "So I get it, Noah—I do. But I'm still gay, and I've had a fucked-up crush on you since I was sixteen."

I blanched while his cheeks burned red. It was a cold-shower moment, although not entirely uncomfortable. Shocking as hell, though.

"That's fucking weird, kid," I said, fighting a smile. Okay, I was kinda flattered. It *was* weird—beyond weird—but that didn't make my pride swell any less.

He laughed. "You say that right after you had your tongue in my ass." *Touché.* His expression softened, and he blew out a breath. "It was a relief getting that off my chest."

That killed the humor, and I kissed him chastely. "I had no idea."

"Of course you didn't. I was freaked out—so much so that I didn't show up at reunions." Ah…so that answered *that.* Damn. He sighed and looked up again. "It's different now. You don't have to feel bad about telling me this was a one-time thing. I already knew that."

I frowned, mulling shit over. "What do you mean by different?"

"I guess…we all have infatuations? It's different because of everything." He seemed to struggle with his words. "I'm a mess. So are you." Painfully true. "Before, you were barely real. You were this so-called uncle who lived and worked in Hollywood and partied with movie stars. Mom was always bragging about you, and when I saw you—before I figured out I was gay—you were intimidating. There was a constant spotlight over your head at reunions. You were accompanied by a loud buzz."

The life of the party.

"People are drawn to you," he added thoughtfully. "And now…"

I cocked half a smile. "Now I'm real?"

He nodded and shifted closer again. "Very." He kissed my chest. "There's life to consider. Everything we've been through… I doubt it's healthy for us to rely too much on each other. But because I'm so attracted to you, it needs to be a clean break." He peered up at me. "I wouldn't want to live anywhere else, but I need to find my own friends and social life, which…" He made a face there. "I'm not very social to begin with, but closing myself in would probably do more harm than good."

I squeezed him to me, 'cause time was evidently running out. "I get it." And the irony wasn't lost on me. I'd felt like I was the one who would put a stop to things, and maybe I kinda had, yet I couldn't shake the feeling of being dumped. Not in a harsh way, fucking clearly.

He was right. We both were. Getting attached and building something based on grief and loneliness could only lead to disaster. I was thrilled he wasn't moving anywhere else, but having our separate social lives would probably help.

"So…does this fresh start begin with you dating Nicky?" I asked.

Julian snorted quietly and nipped at my collarbone. "I'm not ready for anything, any more than you are."

That was…strangely relieving.

"I'll go to a party with him, though," he said. "Maybe I'll make some friends."

Of course he would. Julian was a terrific guy. Who wouldn't want him? To be buddies with him, I meant.

No, this was good.

It was.

Hopefully, it wouldn't take too long before it *felt* as right as I knew it was.

*   *   *

PART II

CHAPTER 11

Nine months later

"I don't give a shit. Make it happen." I placed the phone between my shoulder and cheek as I parked my car. I knew it was illegal—sue me. "I thought money talked."

"You sound like a diva," Daniel chuckled wryly.

I cringed then got out of the car and slammed the door shut. *Deep breath.* I pinched the bridge of my nose. "Fuck you, for that," I replied slowly, "but you're right. I just want his birthday to be good."

Julian turned twenty-four in a couple weeks, and with me being in the middle of filming, I had forgotten all about it. Sophie had reminded me yesterday, thank fuck.

"I get it, Noah." Daniel got serious again. "Unfortunately, I can't force a restaurant to host the dinner only because Julian likes the food there. Trust me, I have bribed and tried to convince them, but evidently, they want to be the only restaurant in LA that doesn't attract big crowds or publicity."

I sighed and locked the car, and then I walked toward my shrink's practice. "I guess we could do something at home."

"It does sound like a party Julian would enjoy more," he reasoned. "He's not you, man. Less is more in this case."

He was right. I scratched my head with the key, thinking of what to do. I was strapped for time, so having the party elsewhere had made sense to me. Then again, if we had it at home, I wasn't *late*. I didn't need to book my own loft weeks in advance.

"You know a good party planner who can do low-key?" I asked.

"What a dumb question. Of course I do."

*

"Only ten minutes late this time," Dr. Kendall said with a smirk. "I'm impressed." She gestured for me to sit down, and I was too stressed out to give a fuck about sheepishness. I'd already apologized. I was a living, breathing apology. "Tell me how you've been since our last session."

I blew out a breath and racked my brain for something to say. "It's been…good. I traded in button-downs for T-shirts." Which meant pre-production and kissing up to suits were over. We were finally filming, and I didn't have to deal with any more producers—only Tennyson. It was his show. He was the only link between the film set and everything behind the scenes.

I didn't envy him.

"You're far away from the studio lots," the doc noted. "Are you off today?"

Only a couple studios *had* permanent lots these days, but whatever. "We're not with a studio, and no, I just took a few hours." I checked my watch. "I hope to be back before three."

In the meantime, my assistant director and director of photography prepared for the next scene. I'd gotten lucky to end up with an AD and DP I actually enjoyed working with. So far, they seemed to share my exact vision.

"So work is good, then?" Dr. Kendall jotted down a note on her tablet. "Any bad stressors? You mentioned having more nightmares around the same time you were busy with casting."

I shook my head. "Nah, it's been weeks since I had a

nightmare. I live for being on set, so work is all good now."

In fact, I'd been feeling a lot better lately, and I was hoping today could be the last head-fucking appointment. I was glad I'd come here, though. Also something I wouldn't have done if it weren't for Julian.

He'd started going last summer after he and I…had shared our night. His progress showed, and so I had manned up and gotten an appointment earlier this year. But it was enough now. I'd been seeing Dr. Kendall every other week since February, and with May just around the corner, I was satisfied.

It had gotten to the point where venting had started feeling like dwelling, and that meant it was time to move on. There was no damn diagnosis. It was plain grief, and it had lessened.

"That's great, Noah." Doc smiled at me and then moved on to the next topic. "Last time, you told me you were getting ready to sell your parents' house in Pittsburgh. Any more thoughts on that?"

Not really. I shrugged. "We've hired a Realtor."

It was time. A few months ago, Julian and I had gone our separate ways for a week. He had flown to Germany with his grandparents to gather all the belongings they wanted to keep, and I had done the same with Ma and Pop's house. Some trinkets and photos had been added to our loft, some things ended up in storage, and the rest was donated. Only the houses remained.

Well, my sister's house in Berlin already had a family renting it now. My folks' house was to be sold off.

"How does it make you feel?" Doc asked.

I shot her a look, 'cause we'd been over this before.

She chuckled. "I know you dislike the phrase, but it's the only way I can cover all bases. I can tell by your behavior from last session and this one that you wish to be done, and I understand that. It's been a rough year." She paused, scrolling a little on her iPad. "How did your date go after last time?"

I flinched internally. "*That* was a fucking disaster."

Last winter, Julian confessed he and Nicky were dating. I hadn't reacted very well. He had no clue, but I'd taken it pretty hard, which had infuriated me. He was doing the right thing, and I had tried, too.

By getting wasted and banging a new woman every weekend. For a few months, I'd woken up every Sunday morning in a strange bed before doing the walk of shame. The shame was new. I'd never cared before. Shit had changed.

I stopped eventually because it made me sick, and Kendall suggested going on an actual date. Try to get to know someone.

"How so?" She put aside her tablet for this one, ready to listen and analyze. "You said she seemed different."

"Sure, at the bar." My *date* in question was supposed to have been another hookup. Instead, I'd asked her out. Big mistake. "Halfway through our dinner, it was the same old shit. It felt wrong."

I had felt wrong. Summer was perfectly nice; something had been off with *me*.

"Something that was said, or…?" Doc prodded.

I frowned and rubbed at the back of my neck. "No, I just wasn't feeling it anymore. I zoned out and couldn't pay attention. No interest." And at the end of the date while we waited for her cab, I'd kissed her and *nothing*.

She hummed. "When you zoned out, where did your thoughts take you? Do you remember?"

I blew out a breath and stretched out my legs, thinking back. "Probably work." The second my mind turned to work, I was a happy motherfucker. I believed in our script, and I loved being in the director's chair for once. "Around the time of our date…" It hit me, and I straightened in my seat. "I think it was the day after Julian had finally let me hear one of his original songs." *Brilliant*, that kid. Jesus fucking Christ, he played and sang to rip out hearts. "It's way too soon to think about the score for the film, but I remember having that song on a loop in my head. I want it in the film."

I hadn't told Julian yet. He was dead set on making it on his own, but I'd get my way somehow. The song was perfect for one of the heavier scenes in the movie.

"That's interesting," the doc noted. "So work- and Julian-related. We've already established you're quite the workaholic." She sent me a pointed look, being the shrink she was. She probably saw *unhealthy behavior* everywhere. Fucking welcome to the industry. "Sounds like you're simply not in the right headspace for a new relationship."

No shit.

She lifted a brow. "This does not mean I recommend you go back to your previous coping methods."

Obviously. I preferred not being nauseated.

"I'll date my hand." I shrugged.

Porn worked all right; it provided me with visuals. I didn't need to think then. I couldn't risk jacking off away from a TV or laptop. My mind wandered, and I didn't always like where my fantasies headed. Or rather, I liked them too much.

"How is Julian doing?"

"You probably know more than I do."

After all, we saw the same shrink.

Kendall smiled ruefully. "I'm not asking about his feelings or personal opinions, Noah." She made a sweeping motion with her finger on the tablet. "You've told me he's barely home. Is that still true?"

I was willing to bet she knew the answer to that, too. If I wasn't mistaken, he was here a few days ago.

"He's a busy kid." I could admit I wasn't the easiest patient.

Had my pop been alive, he would've chuckled and shaken his head at his boy going to therapy. I wasn't created from the same stock, though maybe I had a foot in the door of the old school, too. Opening up like this wasn't my forte. But…being open about Julian? Even worse. I clammed up like a nerd in front of the prom queen.

I had a good excuse, though. 'Cause she *knew*. Julian had asked for permission months ago to tell the doc about our night, and as reluctant as I had been for that to get out, I would never stand in the way of his recovery, whatever that entailed. So she knew, and she often tried to get me to talk about it. I hadn't told her much, only that I'd felt this otherworldly need to…all but consume him, I guessed I could describe it as.

Clearing my throat, I leaned forward a bit and tapped my foot restlessly.

Kendall waited. Patiently staring.

"What?" I furrowed my brow.

She raised one. "Surely you can say more than that."

"I don't know what you want me to say." I got a bit defensive. I leaned back once more and folded my arms over my chest. "What I said is true. He's busy. If he's not working, he's out with his boyfriend or playing."

He didn't touch the baby grand, though. He'd bought a used keyboard that he kept in his room. I still heard him, only it came with the door closed now.

I didn't know how two guys managed to stay close and yet be a world apart, but we were kings at it. Talk was easy, there were no issues, sometimes we watched a movie together at home, we met up with Tennyson and Sophie for dinner often enough, and we showed interest in each other's passions—music and film. Still, there was something missing.

I could be reading too much into it, maybe. During the day, he ran errands for some big shot at *Variety*. Long hours, hardly any pay. During the weekends, he went out with Nicky and other friends he'd made at work. Combined with the hours I worked…no fucking surprise it was like something was missing.

"Noah." The doc clasped her hands on the desk. "I'm fully aware it's a sensitive topic for you, but we shouldn't skirt around it."

I clenched my jaw.

Don't ask.

She went on. "Are you still attracted to him?"

Narrowing my eyes, I saw my loophole. I was glad she'd phrased herself that way. "He's a good-looking guy. Attraction doesn't mean anything."

I'd had maybe…one or two months where I thought I was done obsessing. It had been a huge relief. Then, slowly but surely, a longing had begun growing inside me. It was one of the reasons I'd agreed to the doc's suggestion about the date with Summer.

"Mmhmm, I'm sure." She made a note, and I was officially irritated. "Don't worry, I'll leave it there." Then she glanced up again, her expression softening. "You're approaching the one-year anniversary of your family's death."

"I'm aware," I drawled.

I was lucky the anniversary coincided with the week we were off to Paris. I hoped to be so busy with work that I missed the date.

Doc inclined her head. "That is why I would suggest we have at least one more session after today. I think you're doing well with moving forward, but anniversaries can be difficult."

There was no way I wanted to go; however, I had someone else to consider, too. Depending on how Julian took that day, it could be useful to have someone to ask for advice and whatever.

"All right, one more session," I conceded. "I'll call in and make an appointment."

She didn't seem satisfied with that, maybe wondering if I'd really do it, though she didn't push. For which I was glad.

"I hope you will, but in the event that you don't…" She took on a gentle expression and smiled patiently. "Noah, over the past few months, you've told me a lot about your family. They seemed like wonderful people, and I think they'd want you to be happy. Every family has arguments and bridges to cross, but what it comes down to in the end is happiness. However and wherever they find it."

I nodded, agreeing. "I keep telling Julian that. He struggles sometimes because James had hopes he'd go another direction than music. But I knew James. He was just protective." I paused. "At least Julian's open about his sexuality now. That's good. I hope he'll tell his grandparents soon."

The doc pursed her lips then grinned a little. "You care about Julian a lot."

"Well, yeah." I frowned.

"I'm only putting it out there. He's often the first person you have in mind. I wasn't talking about him in this case, however. I was talking about you. Your family's approval never seemed to be everything to you, but it certainly mattered." She waited for me to object, though she was right. "So please keep that in mind when it's about *your* happiness. Your family would have wanted it for you."

"All right…" I didn't do well with hints, and I had no time to decipher anything. My phone was going off, and I had been away from the set too long. "Yeah, sure, of course." I quickly scanned the text from my DP, seeing a series of photos for the next scene. It was a new set, and I'd asked for pictures of lighting positions before I returned, though the lighting for the rehearsal wasn't my issue. "Listen, Doc—"

"I get it, Mr. Workaholic." She nodded and held out a hand toward the door. "Class dismissed, I suppose."

I chuckled and stood up, already calling my DP. "I'll get back to you. Have a good one." I left the office and headed down the hall toward the exit, and I couldn't say I was pleased with the photos. I'd kinda fallen for April, Sophie's character, and I wanted to do her justice.

"I was expecting your call, boss," Shawn said. "What's missing?"

"Street," I replied, pushing the door open. I slid on my shades and crossed the parking lot. "April puts her life story on canvas with graffiti. Skip that frilly lamp by her bed, and have someone take down the fucking posters. She doesn't read *Seventeen*. Have the art department start knocking everything down. I'm on my way back, so see you in an hour or so." Hanging up the phone, I unlocked the car and got in.

Back to work. The one part of my life where I always brought my A-game.

CHAPTER 12

When I came home late that night, I was exhausted, my neck hurt, and I was fucking starving. The loft was quiet and dark, so either Julian had gone to bed, or he was out.

With Nicky.

I opened the fridge and sniffed around the takeout containers. One had vegetarian chili from a place I ordered from a lot, and it didn't smell bad.

I plated it and put it in the microwave, and then I went through my mail as I waited for it to heat up.

"Noah?"

"Oh." I leaned over the kitchen island, seeing a sleepy Julian padding closer. "Sorry, did the microwave wake you?"

He shook his head sleepily and yawned. His flannels clung low on his hips, and he wasn't wearing a T-shirt. He usually did.

"I couldn't sleep," he grumbled. "Nicky snores."

I said nothing and waited for the jealousy to pass. It was completely irrational.

They'd never spent the night here before. It was easier to ignore when they were at Nicky's place.

The loft was my sanctuary, so I hadn't brought any women here. But Julian and Nicky were together. Of course they'd be here, too.

"Should I give him a talk about his intentions?" I gave him a wry smile. "You've been together a while now."

Julian snorted and grabbed a bottle of water from the fridge. "Are you my father now?"

"Jesus. Uncle's bad enough."

He took it as I'd intended and chuckled. "Hmm, I don't know…Daddy's got a ring to it."

I barked out a laugh. "Fuck you, kid."

"You had your chance and blew it."

Someone was feisty tonight.

The microwave pinged, and I retrieved a spoon from the drawer and found some bread in the cabinet to dip in the chili. I didn't want the moment to be over yet, so I hopped up to sit on the kitchen island.

Julian did the same on the counter, snatching an apple from the bowl by the coffeemaker. "How was work?"

"It was good. We wrapped the scenes with the kid and moved the kitchen set." Sophie had been a little peeved when we hadn't been able to cast Kayden, but the boy just wasn't interested enough. "April's art studio and bedroom are ready. We're starting there tomorrow." I shoveled some grub into my mouth and reached for a napkin. "What about you? How're the vultures down at *Variety*?"

"They fired me," he said dryly.

"What the fuck?" I blurted with my mouth full. "What happened?"

He shrugged and took a bite from the apple. "My boss wanted me to gossip about Sophie."

That…yeah, that part of Hollywood sucked ass. "I'm sorry. Unfortunately, there's always gonna be someone wanting to take advantage in this town. But they didn't fire you for saying no, did they?"

"No." He quirked a sly grin. "They fired me because I *accidentally* fucked up a scoop about some singer."

I grinned. He was doing just fine in LA.

"That's what they get for wanting me to betray my friends,"

he said with another shrug. "So anyway, I'll start a new job search tomorrow."

Goddammit.

"Julian," I sighed.

"What?"

I pressed my mouth into a tight line. He *knew* what. We could always use him on set, and I'd even need a new PA for when we went to Paris. My current on-set one couldn't travel 'cause he was a single dad.

"Nothing." I rolled my eyes and swiped up some chili on a piece of bread. "I just think you're taking this independence thing a bit too far." While I chewed, he opened his mouth to argue, so I shook my head and held up my hand. "Not like that. I get it—I get why you're doing it. But where do you draw the line? Because when I'd made some connections in this town, I was quick to use them. It's how LA works." I demonstrated the ladder with my fork held horizontally. "Connections, money, talent. It's fucked, but it's how it is." I paused. "Okay, sometimes money comes first, too. Either way, it's not talent."

"No, no, I understand that," he said. "But I haven't earned you as a connection. You're family. Had I made connections at *Variety*, of course I would've used them."

Fuck that noise. I understood him, and he had a point, but he assumed I'd give him a job based on only nepotism or something. He also assumed he'd get off easy. That didn't fly with me.

"Do you trust me, Julian?"

His brows knitted together. "Of course I do."

I smiled, 'cause that shit warmed my heart. "Okay. If I said you had a talent I wanted to employ, would you believe me?"

"My coffee's not that awesome."

I threw the last of my bread at him. "Smart-mouthed little prick."

He laughed, dodging it.

"I'm serious," I told him. And I might as well come clean about the score for the film. "Fuck running errands and making coffee. You have a song I want."

That shut him up. He looked surprised, not to mention

confused.

I went on to describe my vision for the song, how I wanted it for a scene—coincidentally, the one we were shooting tomorrow—and then how I wanted the piano woven into the main score.

It got me going, and before I knew it, I was pacing in the kitchen, gesturing like a fucking idiot as if I could paint him the entire scene. This was the sorta shit that had bored Emma half to death, so I wasn't counting on Julian to stick around for long.

"And there's this part where Sophie—April," I corrected, "kinda bends at the waist a bit, fists her hair, and screams at the top of her lungs—"

"I read the script, you know." Julian smirked at me.

Oh. I didn't know that. "Okay, so you know." That felt extremely good, for some reason. "Well, that's the spot. And in your song, there's this crescendo or whatever, and I want it right fucking *there*. I can't get that outta my head. It's a set piece, one I want everyone to remember."

Julian nodded and hopped down from the counter, and then he walked over to the piano. "I think I know which one you're talking about."

As he eased into the song, I followed him over and stood next to the bench. He played flawlessly, the soft notes teasing my ears and slowly building up. I pinched my bottom lip, seeing the scene in front of me, and I nodded to myself, 'cause this was fucking it.

When Julian finished, he sat back and fidgeted with his fingers. Then he glanced up and pushed some hair away from his eyes. "Tennyson called that scene your baby."

I grinned faintly. "Sounds about right." Wanting to seal this deal, I sat down next to him and bumped my shoulder to his. "I want you to be part of this project when we reach post-production, Julian. And trust me when I say it's your talent, not who you are."

Fuck me if he didn't blush. It was sweet as hell.

"That's overwhelming," he admitted.

"It kinda started at the memorial service," I murmured. "I don't think anyone remembers the speeches, but your playing is unforgettable."

His smile was half proud, half shy. Perfectly him. He knew he was good.

"I thought connections and money came before talent." He bumped my shoulder this time, and I laughed quietly. "I don't know, Noah. I mean…I'd be a damn fool turning this down, so I won't." Sweet mother of relief. "But I don't feel like I'm done with the menial work, if that makes sense. I want to work hard for any success I may or may not get."

"I can make you work," I chuckled. "Trust, kid. I can make you suffer, even."

He looked dubious. "What do you mean?"

I might be pushing it, but fuck it. I had to try. "I need a new PA for Paris."

That earned me a *look*. "Are we really going to have that conversation again?"

"No, 'cause you seem to be under the impression that I'm doing you a favor," I retorted. "You'll regret it. But, hey, if you don't have what it takes, no sweat."

He narrowed his eyes. "That doesn't work on me."

"Are you sure?"

"Well, how hard can it be?" He huffed. "Being a Hollywood director's PA in Paris doesn't exactly scream of menial work and suffering."

He really had no clue. There was no happy medium for a PA in the industry. When they were out of work, they were frantically looking for their next way in. When they did have work, they were either bored out of their minds or so stressed out they wanted to kill themselves.

"Only one way to find out." I gave his leg a squeeze, which I shouldn't have done. I always wanted more than one touch, and since I, for some reason, had no interest in touching others anymore, I was shit out of luck. "But so you know, it wouldn't be a favor to you." I withdrew my hand and stood up. "I want you to come with me, but you're not the type of guy to accept a ticket and take the time off."

Julian was mulling things over, eyes down, and I needed to go to bed. I had to be on set in five hours.

"Talk shit over with your man," I suggested. "And come to

the set tomorrow. It's gonna be a closed one, but I want your music brain there. Maybe you'll be inspired to write more for the film."

Julian frowned, confused. "I don't need his permission. We're not exclusive."

That was news to me, and I wasn't entirely sure what this meant. Then when I noticed he wouldn't look at me, I got worried.

"Are you okay?"

He nodded and gave me a placating smile. "I'm fine. Go to bed."

"Fuck that, we said no pretending," I told him.

Which made me a hypocrite since I hadn't been completely honest.

"Fine," he clipped, "I don't feel a hundred percent, but I will talk to Dr. Kendall about it next week."

Fair enough. Wasn't a whole lot I could argue there.

"Okay," I replied slowly. "Just…you know where to find me if you wanna talk. I may be busy as fuck, but I've always got time for you, kid."

His smile was small, but at least it was genuine this time. "I appreciate it, Noah. Now, go to bed. I'll be there tomorrow."

*

Julian was late.

The sealed-off street was packed with trailers, crew, picnic tables, and now a couple food trucks, but I would've known if he was here. Unless security had let him pass without ID and he'd wandered into the empty building where we were shooting.

I doubted it.

"Thanks, doll." I accepted my lunch from Lucia, my feisty little AD, and got back to my discussion with Shawn. "I want all three cameras on Sophie for this, and I want Paul to Dutch his at the end. Nothing shaky, and we'll start off with the tilt after the smash." I spoke of Shawn's main operator and an angle one should be careful not to overuse, but I had to get my vision out. "So, she goes from here—" I pointed at her line in the script and took a bite of my sub "—to here. We'll do a one-er, and then pickups in case we'll need them later."

The option was several takes, except knowing Sophie was best right off the gate for emotional scenes, I preferred doing several cameras instead.

Shawn brought out his printouts of photos of the set, making notes and floor marks, and I saw one of the crewmembers walking by with a big bucket. It reminded me that it was Five Dollar Friday, so I dug out a couple bills and dropped them in the bucket as he passed.

Old tradition. At the end of the day, one lucky crewmember would be a few hundred bucks richer.

"That's from me and Sophie," I told him. She was having lunch on set to stay in character, so I didn't want anyone to bother her. She'd even kicked Tennyson out earlier, which had been a comical sight.

"Noah!"

I looked up and saw Julian waiting by security. I nodded for the guard to let him in.

"I'll go talk to Paul," Shawn said. "We should be ready within ten. Rembrandt lighting's done, and it's just the grip for the Dutch that needs adjusting."

"Cheers, man—wait." I chewed the last of my sub. "The Rembrandt is for the next shot."

"Oh! Highlight on the dust particles?"

I pointed at him. "That's the one." Julian reached my table by then, and I took a swig of my soda. "Took you long enough. We're about to begin."

"Then I'm not late." He smiled and sat down next to me, so I introduced him to Lucia and two PAs sitting with us. "Nice to meet you all," Julian said politely. "I've heard great things about you."

I threw an arm around Lucia and gave her cheek a smooch. "She's gonna marry me one day. She just doesn't know it yet."

She laughed and slapped my arm. "I think my husband would object."

"As long as *you* don't object." I winked at her and then stood up. "All right, lemme show you the set, kid."

I licked some sauce off my fingers and jerked my chin for him to follow me inside the building. It was old as hell, though it had obviously passed inspection, so the run-down look was mostly external.

"I thought film sets were more glamorous," Julian said. "What is this place?"

"Old factory." I gestured toward the freight elevator, and we got in with a couple other crewmembers. "Our location scout found it last minute. Once you see the top floor, though… It's perfect." We hadn't needed to knock much down. It already looked rustic and vintage. We'd added new, smaller windows and a vaulted ceiling to turn it into a real attic. That was about it. And it left plenty of space for the crew and all the gear.

My phone rang, and speak of the devil, it was the location scout.

"Hey, Tiff," I answered. "How's Paris?"

"French," she quipped. "And I'm done. I've found an amazing street in the Fifth Quarter where we can shoot, and the front of one building looks exactly like the one where April's is supposed to be in the Eighteenth. Mr. Wright and I are working on the permits as we speak."

"That's great." As the elevator came to a stop, I put my free hand on Julian's lower back and ushered him out of the cart. "You get the view for April's apartment, too?"

We'd had another location scout from the start. Luckily, Tennyson had fired him when he'd suggested a "lovely view of the Eiffel Tower."

Because a starving painter could afford that…

"Yes, sir, all stock-photo ready and sent back to LA."

"Terrific," I replied. "I'll see you soon, then."

Pocketing my phone, I side-eyed Julian and found him wearing a weird little smile.

"What's with the smirk, kid?"

His smile grew. "I like this." He looked out over the large, open space. Cameras, dollies, lighting—everything pointed toward the attic apartment we'd set up in a corner. "I liked last night, too.

You were all excited, and I can see why. It rubs off."

"Way too many dirty puns in one go." I hugged his neck to me and kissed the side of his head. "I'm glad you enjoyed that, though. It means a lot to me." Maybe he wasn't like Emma. "Okay, so this is a closed set." We approached the apartment where Sophie was pacing and rehearsing lines with herself. "It means fewer people and silence. You can say hey to her later, yeah?"

"Of course." He nodded. "You do your thing. I'm going to, um...yeah." He retrieved a notebook from his messenger bag.

I smiled and inclined my head. My musical genius was ready to work.

"All right, everyone. Focus!" Lucia came up from behind me and got busy.

She must've taken the stairs.

Those who had no business here scattered, leaving only nine or ten people. No one approached Sophie. She knew her mark, and we'd discussed everything before lunch.

She blew out a breath and rolled her shoulders. No longer a movie star, but the young graffiti artist on the run from her family. April was not only bipolar, but she had schizophrenia too, and she refused medication because she thought everyone was conspiring against her.

Her sole focus was to tell her story through art, so her son would know her truth.

Brooklyn's company Shadow Light had been hired for the project, and she'd worked her magic on Sophie. With makeup, she had sunken-in eyes and a more defined bone structure, and a ratty cotton dress and unwashed hair finished her look of poverty and neglect.

Lucia took a step back after everything was done, knowing I wanted to take this one.

"Cameras rolling," I announced. Ignoring the monitor next to me, I stood by Paul instead. "Action."

Sophie continued her pacing, and slowly but surely, her muttering and whispering became louder. She gestured with her hands and shook her head, at war with herself.

"They're wrong," she mumbled over and over. "I'm good for

him." She spoke of her son, whom she was in no condition to take care of. "Nobody else, nobody else…" She stuttered a breath and walked over to her canvases. "My baby will see. You will see, baby—they're wrong!" she screamed.

From there, she lost it. She tore through her apartment and threw breakaways at the walls. Bottles, paint jars, cans, a lamp, and a chair.

I wanted close-ups of glass shattering against the wall, paint thinner splashing, and paint brushes landing on the floor.

"Mommy's gonna make it real nice for you," she cried. Reaching her bed, she yanked off the stained pillowcases and sheets. "They can't find us here, and when you get back, you'll see. It's our home. I'll make it pretty and safe because Mommy loves you, and—" She broke off on a sob and fisted her hair. "They don't know, they don't know…"

The meltdown continued, and I made a rolling motion to keep it going. Eventually, she reached the climax of the scene, and I felt it to the bone when she bent over and let out a blood-curdling scream.

I checked in with each operator, making sure they got that, and they nodded in return, slowly moving back the dollies the cameras were set up on. Only Paul stayed, and he jerked the camera to the side as Sophie ended up on the floor.

She panted.

Everything was quiet, the tension electric.

"Cut!"

She would get some good fucking loving from Tennyson after I sent him the footage.

"You aced it, sweetie." I walked over to her and helped her up off the floor. "You okay?"

"Yeah." She grinned and took a deep breath, her hands shaking. "God, that was draining. Did you get everything? I'm sorry I suck on seconds and thirds."

She sure as fuck didn't suck, but yeah, we got it. "You're a star." I kissed her on the forehead before returning behind the camera. "Moving on, people!"

I glanced over at Julian and grinned. His expression could

only be described as passionate. In the moment, caught up. He scribbled quickly in his notebook while twisting a lock of hair between his fingers.

Whatever he was jotting down, I didn't wanna interrupt, so I got back to work, and fuck it if I didn't enjoy having him here.

CHAPTER 13

Two weeks later

"You're right." I rubbed a hand over my beard and sighed tiredly. "How did I fucking miss that?"

Tennyson shook his head and shut off the flat screen. "Give that question to the script supervisor instead."

Either way, this meant retakes. The scene that followed April's meltdown had a major continuity error, in that Sophie's character was wearing an accessory on the wrong goddamn finger. And I called it major because the ring, with a butterfly on it, would be in focus during the following scene, and it had to be on the right finger.

At least I had an excuse to cancel my last session with Dr. Kendall. This would set us back one day of shooting, so there was no way I'd have time for a shrink appointment. Which I didn't feel like I needed, anyway.

"I'll give Shawn and Lucia a call," I muttered.

"Dinner's ready, guys!" Sophie called from the kitchen. "Kayden! Ivy! Go wash up!"

"I'll go get Julian," I said, pulling out my phone. I could call

Shawn on the way.

Tennyson stood up. "I heard he won his first Five Dollar Friday today."

I chuckled, peering down the hall to see Kayden and Ivy rushing into the bathroom. "He did, yeah." I faced Tennyson again. "It caught him off guard, so he followed Sophie's lead."

It was customary for directors, actors, and others who were above the line, so to speak, to give it to someone else if they won, or buy everyone a beer or whatever.

Sophie had won once, and she'd doubled the pot and drawn another name.

She was popular, and now so was Julian.

Technically, he was on the payroll as my PA now, though he hadn't started working yet and didn't feel comfortable taking winnings when—in his words—he'd cruised right on to a film set without accomplishing anything for it.

Kayden and Ivy yelled that their hands were clean, and I took my leave and headed across the hall. Shawn didn't answer his phone, so I left him a message.

Entering my loft, I was about to call out for Julian, but I closed my mouth before I did. Nicky was evidently here, and I heard them arguing in Julian's room.

This was where I was supposed to give them privacy.

Supposed to.

Instead, I was the nosy motherfucker who moved closer to his door to listen in.

"I'm just sayin', I'm getting sick of waiting," I heard Nicky spit out. "It sucks that you're depressed, but I have a life, too."

I was taken aback by that. Instantly furious with Nicky and beyond worried about Julian. I knew he was on antidepressants, but he went to Kendall. Weren't things going better?

Goddammit, I should've paid more attention.

"I can't exactly control how I feel." Julian's voice was less condescending. "I told you from the start I wasn't ready for much—"

"It's not about that!" Nicky was pissed, and fuck, so was I. If he pushed Julian, I'd have no goddamn issue putting him in his place. "You of all people should know I couldn't care less about a relationship. I wanna have *fun*, and it's been months since you even touched me."

"No one's stopping you from having fun," Julian snapped. "Call one of your four other guys and screw them all you want. I've *fucking* told you, I'm not in that place."

You tell him, kid.

I was proud of him. Hell, I was impressed, too.

"Are you jealous?" Nicky asked.

Julian laughed. "Quite the opposite, Nick. I like spending time with you, *especially* when you've just been with one of your playthings. Less pressure on me."

There shouldn't be *any* pressure on him. Not that kind.

"I feel tossed aside, though," Nicky said. "I mean, I went to all that trouble for tomorrow, and you turn me down like that?"

I tensed up.

Tomorrow was Julian's birthday. If he bailed on us, I'd be bummed, no lie. He didn't know we were throwing him a party; however, I'd told him not to make plans elsewhere.

"I wasn't born yesterday," Julian replied impatiently. "Telling me you have a hotel room booked and a romantic dinner planned only means one thing. You want to score."

Damn straight. Christ, cheap move. Hotel room? This wasn't prom night.

"Besides," Julian went on, "you know Noah's got plans."

Nicky scoffed. "That fuckin' dude… He's no different from the other Hollywood pricks. I can forgive him for putting me out of work for no reason at all, but can't you see he's playing you?"

The fuck?

"Listen to me, babe." He lowered his voice. "He obviously needs you, and whenever he feels you slipping through his fingers, he does something to reel you back in. Now he's got you hooked on his movie. It's all you talk about."

I clenched my jaw, furious, but an insecure part of me wondered if it was true. For about two seconds, and then I shook my head. He was fucking crazy. I wanted nothing but the best for Julian. He was everything to me.

Holy fuck.

That was a cold shower and a slap in the face all at once.

It was true, though, wasn't it? Julian meant the world to me.

I swallowed hard and ran a hand over my head, my heart pounding.

What the fuck did this mean?

"You don't know him like I do," Julian said quietly. "He's a good man. There's no hidden agenda with him. So you can either be happy for me, or you can be bitter. I know I got my job unfairly, but I work hard. I'm writing around the clock, and I'm feeling really good about his film. I think it's magnificent."

Fuck. I wasn't sure I deserved all that praise. It did something to me. My chest felt tight and warm, and not in an uncomfortable way.

"I support you," Nicky was quick to say. "Come here."

I was pretty sure I was figuring Nicky out, and if I was right, I'd punch the daylights outta him. He wouldn't be using Julian—or any of us—as an *in* into the industry. Over my dead body.

Their fight seemed to be over, so I backed off. I had a feeling Julian's head was spinning. He was a smart guy. He'd see Nicky for who he was.

"You should go," Julian said, clearing his throat. "I have dinner at Tennyson and Sophie's."

That was my cue to go. No need for them to find out I was an eavesdropping asshole.

*

I was up with the sun the next morning, first to run and then to get Julian's gift at Brooklyn and Asher's house in Malibu. Next, I drove out to Daniel and Zane's beach house to let in the party planner and the caterers.

Daniel was the man. His idea to throw Julian a party there was brilliant.

"We'll all be here around four," I told the party planner. "Daniel and Zane get in from New York earlier, though, so they'll be here to bug you."

She giggled. "I've worked with Daniel before. I know he's a hard-ass."

All right, then.

I got back on the road. Traffic was a drag, but I got some work calls made along the way, so I wasn't complaining.

At my last stop, I picked up breakfast, and then I returned to the loft. Julian was still sleeping, so I checked in on his gift, making sure it was still...*alive*, which it was, thank you very much. Adjusting the lid, I placed it on the couch for now, and then I set up breakfast at the table.

"Damn." I was spent. I hadn't showered yet, so I got that done too, before throwing on a pair of sweats and a wife-beater.

Time to wake up the birthday kid.

I grabbed the box and knocked on Julian's door.

He mumbled something incoherently, and I took that as an invitation.

"Rise and shine, sleepyhead."

As I sat down on the edge of his bed, he threw the covers over his head and muttered something in German. It held the same tone as *get lost*, but it probably meant he was happy to see me.

"Hey." I put my hand on his hip and shook him a little. "You gonna miss out on your own birthday?"

He grunted into his pillow. "Mom would let me sleep in."

"*Dude*." I didn't fucking think so. "Don't you make up lies about my sister. She did no such thing, the little terror."

That earned me a sleepy chuckle, and he knew I had him. If people thought I got up early, it had nothing on Mia.

"You lazy fuck, get up," I said. "When I was twenty-four, I'd already been up for hours."

He snorted and pushed away the covers, scrubbing his hands down his face. "When you were twenty-four, you probably hadn't gone to bed yet."

That, too.

I averted my eyes from his exposed upper body and placed his gift next to him. "Open your present."

He grinned lazily and sat up. "Aren't you supposed to sing?"

"Not unless you're suicidal." I widened my eyes. "That would be cruel."

"Fair enough," he chuckled. "Okay, so…" He eyed the box and fingered the lid. "I just open it?"

"Try." I smirked.

He rolled his eyes and then removed the lid, and he froze when he saw the cat I'd adopted for him the other day. The chunky fur ball wasn't a kitten, though she wasn't fully grown, either. And like a true Hollywood pet, she would soon be fit for travel so Julian could bring the little shit to Paris.

I rubbed the back of my neck, hoping he'd like it. "I, uh, I bought food and shit for it, too. Her, I mean. A litter box—"

Before I could finish my sentence, Julian threw his arms around my neck and squeezed the fuck out of me.

"Thank you. I—thank you."

I let out a breathy laugh and hugged him back. "You're welcome, sweetheart."

Jesus Christ, it felt good to have him in my arms again. It was the same goddamn sense of relief.

It went beyond comfort, though. I had to suck it up and admit I was inexplicably drawn to him, no matter how fucking difficult it was. Spending my life avoiding complications would get me nowhere.

I wasn't sure I was capable of avoiding this one, anyway.

I pressed a smooch to his shoulder, *wanting.*

Fuck you, Dr. Kendall. Fuck you all the way off.

She'd poked and prodded with her mind-fucking, always curious, always wanting me to talk about Julian. This was why I had refused. I hadn't been ready to admit *shit.* Although…somehow, I was betting on her knowing, either way. She'd dropped it at "attraction," while knowing it was more.

I hadn't been blind. Well, maybe that too, but mostly it had been denial. Part of me still was in denial. But she—that sneaky bitch—wouldn't have ranted about my family wanting us to be happy if she hadn't, on some level, known my fears.

Julian eased out of the hug, and he picked up his new pet.

I watched them, having nothing better to do. It was kinda cute, though. Julian didn't say anything, and I guessed it had something to do with his eyes being glassier than normal.

"You might wanna put the cat on a diet," I said. 'Cause she was sorta fat. All white, or beige-brown—whatever—and fluffy and fat.

"No way. She's perfect." Julian grinned as the cat licked its fur. "Ragdolls get big."

"Ragawhat, now?"

"Ragdoll. It's a breed—the only one I know, really. Our cat in Berlin was one," he murmured. She seemed to like him, if rubbing herself all over him was any indication. "Is she adopted?"

I nodded and scratched my beard.

"Makes sense she's a mixed breed, then. There're some faint stripes here. I love her." He stroked her belly, and she turned and twisted, wrapping her tail around his wrist. "Linda named our old one Fluffy." He grimaced, and I couldn't blame him. "I'll think of something better for my new cuddle girl."

"Great, I'm jealous of a fucking cat." I rolled my eyes and stood up. "Come on. You and your girlfriend are invited to breakfast."

Julian chuckled and pulled on a pair of jeans. "Noah Collins jealous? Maybe hell has frozen over. What do you have to be jealous over?" He picked up the cat again and followed me out to the living room.

"I miss cuddling," I said with a shrug. Everything was set up on the table; I just needed a quick detour to the kitchen to get the coffee. "I'm a proud cuddle slut."

"I thought you had one of your million casual flings to cuddle with. Or that Summer woman." He sat down at the table and let the cat get familiar with the living room. "Damn, Noah. You didn't have to go through all this trouble. Did you buy *everything* I like?"

I ignored that, stuck on the Summer bit. "Summer?"

He nodded with a mouthful of donut. Of course, he'd go for the unhealthy crap first. I should've waited.

"I found her card in your jeans when I did laundry." He took another bite. "I've seen her name pop up on your phone a few times, too." He shot me a grin, though it looked strained. "I didn't mean to pry, but I saw the preview of one message. She is apparently fond of your kissing skills."

That was…strange. I wasn't sure a kiss a few seconds long was enough to show off any skills.

"You'd know better than her." I shrugged and poured my coffee. "Here." I sat down and slid him the pot.

"I would?" Julian did that thing where he pretended to be too busy to look me in the eye. "I thought maybe it was serious."

He was fucking cute. Was he digging?

"Nope." I leaned back and sipped my coffee, and I had to admit I enjoyed this. It was dawning on me that I was fucked where Julian was concerned. I wanted him bad—which was a goddamn kick in the head—and that was my hell to deal with. My complicated mess. But that didn't mean I couldn't draw some pleasure from Julian's old infatuation with me.

I assumed most of it had faded, with maybe enough attachment lingering not to be thrilled to see me with someone else.

That was how crushes worked, in my experience. From the Playboy models I'd gawked at as a teenager to the one-nighters I'd hooked up with all my life. I could be irrationally possessive at the oddest times if I were interested enough, though I let go quickly.

Usually.

Julian was an exception. It'd been a fucking year.

"We went out on one date. That's it." I opened a container with a mixture of pineapple, strawberries, blueberries, and grapes. "She's not my type, I guess."

"Oh." Julian bobbed his head and nibbled on a bagel. "So anyway…" He cleared his throat. "What's the plan for today?"

I smirked at how fast he moved on, and how he'd brightened noticeably.

"Pool party and barbecue with our closest," I revealed. "Danny and Zane are hosting it at their beach house, so don't forget sunscreen."

Julian's eyes lit up. I reckoned he approved.

*

Julian came to life the minute we stepped foot inside the beach house. We'd kept it small, though a couple additions had shown up after Sophie and I had seen Julian get along great with Lucia and Shawn from the set. Along with Tennyson, Sophie, Asher, Brooklyn, Daniel, and Zane, it was shaping up to be one hell of a day.

Tennyson and I were the grill masters while Sophie and Brooklyn flitted back and forth to fill the table on the terrace with condiments, salads, bread, drinks, and God knew what else.

Music poured out from the living room, the sun was dipping low, Julian and Zane were embarrassing Shawn and Asher at volleyball in the pool, and the last time I saw Danny and Lucia, they were discussing politics.

Old Noah would've been appreciating the sight of so many beautiful women in bikinis or other beachwear. Married and obsessed with their husbands or not, it was okay to look. Yet, every fucking five minutes, it was Julian my eyes sought out.

The kid who'd acted like an outta-breath smoker after a ten-minute jog was a lot more athletic these days, and it showed. He didn't run with me in the mornings all that often; instead, he liked going swimming. He certainly had the body for it.

"It's becoming glaringly obvious, my friend." Tennyson flipped a couple steaks and eyed me over the frames of his shades. I frowned at him, to which he chuckled and nodded at Julian. "You stare at him like I stare at Sophie."

I cursed and chugged my beer.

"You still believe it's wrong?" He turned to me, brow furrowed. "Initially, I understood your panic—somewhat, anyway. But you're way past that, Noah. If it had been an unhealthy attachment founded on the grief you share, it would've faded by now."

My jaw ticked, and I wanted to tell him to shut the fuck up. Yet, I couldn't. He was the one person I'd told. He didn't know Julian and I had actually been intimate, but he knew more than Dr. Kendall. He knew my personal thoughts, and it was a heavy-as-fuck issue to carry.

No one was nearby, so against my better judgment, I opened

up a bit.

"It's my sister." I needed something to do, so I took over for Tennyson and started putting the hot dogs and my tofu burgers on the grill. "Imagine if she knew? Hell, all of them. If they were alive and found out… James's folks? It'd kill them."

It made me wanna throw up.

"I won't sugarcoat anything," he replied, lifting a brow. "It probably would have gotten ugly. But your family, Noah—you were so close. Eventually, they would've accepted it. I firmly believe that. Same goes for Julian's grandparents."

I wasn't so sure.

I couldn't shake the feeling of it being like pissing on their graves.

I'm sorry I lost y'all, but don't worry, Julian keeps me warm at night.

"Listen." Tennyson clasped my shoulder. "I'm the last person to push. It took Sophie and me three years to realize our fling was a lot more than that. I know what it's like not to be ready."

True. They'd had an on-set romance years ago, but with their differences—their ages being one—they'd walked away from each other, both depressed as fuck and hiding it poorly. Only, Sophie had ended up pregnant. They'd raised Kayden together from day one, although as single parents. Still…they'd practically been a couple anyway. Nobody could come between them, even when they were too blind to see it themselves.

We'd had a bet going on to see when they'd finally get it.

"Picture yourself in my shoes," I told him.

"I have, actually." He pointed toward where Sophie was giggling about something with Brooklyn and Lucia by the table. "And I wouldn't let anyone come between us. She and our children are everything to me."

Everything.

"Just run me the fuck over already." I needed more beer.

*

I lost count of the times we toasted to Julian. The alcohol made us merrier and forgetful, and after a while, he stopped squirming at the attention. He even butted in with his own digs when Tennyson and I were grilling Asher about the cardio he loved to brag about.

This from the only dude who wore a shirt to hide his love for beer and pizza.

Brooklyn threw her head back and laughed but was quick to kiss her hubby to show solidarity.

"I keep telling you to come with me and Sophie to RJ's, little brother," Tennyson told Asher. "Or go with Noah on his runs. Though, I hear he's a sadistic trainer."

I winked and tipped my beer bottle at Asher.

"What's RJ's?" Julian asked.

"An indoor climbing place," Sophie supplied, giggling. "Funnily enough, it used to be their thing—as brothers. But at some point, Ash stopped going."

"To hell with all of you," Asher said. "I do cardio."

"Once a month," Brooklyn mouthed behind her hand.

"And work is busy," Ash went on. "Hundreds of scripts go through my office every week. It's not easy being a producer."

"Yeah, I bet you cry in your Lexus all the way home to your mansion, beautiful wife, and two daughters every day," Daniel deadpanned.

"Maybe that's it. Do you turn to food for comfort?" Tennyson asked with a smirk. "The pizza cannot hug you back."

That one cracked me up, but the women decided we'd been mean long enough now.

"I could use some cake," Asher grumbled.

I sat back and pinched my lips together, and it looked like Tennyson and Daniel were struggling to hold back their mirth, too. We let it go eventually, and I was the next one to be roasted.

Champagne and cake came out, and Sophie placed the gigantic, chocolaty goodness at the head of the table where Julian sat. I was next to him, and I had to say the cake made my dormant sweet tooth ache. I didn't indulge very often 'cause, frankly, I didn't want to, but damn.

Meanwhile, Sophie, Lucia, and Brooklyn imitated me and how I—apparently—came off as a director. Julian had a fucking *blast* at that. He could barely stop laughing to blow out the candles after Brooklyn delivered her impersonation.

Leaning close, I patted his thigh under the table. "Easy there, kid. Don't forget to breathe."

"I'm trying," he wheezed out.

God, he was fucking beautiful. All carefree and enjoying himself.

His fingers brushed over my hand on his leg, and I had the strongest urge to just hold his hand.

"He's the worst with the lighting," Sophie said. "Admit it, Collins. You're a lighting *snob*." I shrugged and reluctantly gave her my attention, and she cleared her throat and did her best to pull off a gruff, manly voice. "The fuck you doin'? I told you I want floodlight! More floodlight! No, scratch that. Give me a forty-degree Rembrandt and Van fuckin' Gogh and-and-and put a meat ax on that goddamn lens!"

While the ladies guffawed, those of us who actually worked with lighting and directing—and generally knew what we were talking about—shook our heads.

"You just spoke complete gibberish, princess," Tennyson chuckled. "There are no degrees to a Rembrandt."

Sophie waved a hand.

"What's Van Gogh lighting?" I asked.

"Beats me." Shawn grinned and shoveled some cake into his mouth. "Either way, I think Noah's the most easygoing director I've worked with."

"Pardon me?" Tennyson cocked a brow. "You've worked with me, you know."

Most of us laughed, and Shawn smirked and said, "I remember."

Sophie reached over the table and pinched Tennyson's cheek. "God knows I love you, but laid-back you are *not*. On set, anyway."

"Or very humble," Asher huffed.

Tennyson smiled sarcastically. "I see, so it's my turn now?"

"A director shouldn't be humble while the camera's on," I said.

Tennyson and I bumped fists.

The mockery continued, though an unspoken rule prevented us from grilling the ladies. We did that when we were alone, 'cause…we weren't stupid.

Of course, riling each other up brought out our competitive streaks, and once we'd let the food settle a while, some of us headed to the pool. We had a score to settle, so Brooklyn picked a game for us.

She placed a towel on each short-end of the pool and picked up the volleyball. It was me, Tennyson, and Daniel against Julian, Sophie, and Zane.

Or… "The old against the young and gorgeous," Brooklyn said with a wink.

Considering Brooklyn was my age, we men only exchanged a look.

"Shut the fuck up," Brooklyn snapped.

I held up my palms.

"We didn't say anything," Tennyson said.

"You were thinking it," she retorted. She fluffed her hair and continued. "Anyway, pretend the towels are baskets. All you gotta do is touch your team's towel with the ball."

All right.

"Take it easy, love," Zane cautioned Daniel. "I don't want you to pull anything."

"Oooh, shots fired." I dove into the water, the rest following, and it was easy to see which tactics most were going with.

Sophie adjusted her bikini in a way that had Tennyson fucked in the head, so I snapped my fingers in front of his face.

"Seriously?" I shook my head at him.

Zane was doing something similar, showing off his modeling skills, abs, and that ridiculous pose when someone came up from the water and pushed back their hair.

Danny, Danny, Danny.

Turning to Julian, I…fuck. Jesus fuck, game time, no losing focus. I refused to be *that* guy. But yeah, he looked good. He looked ready to fight dirty. There was a gleam in his eyes, which I noticed after averting my gaze from his tight swimmer's body, ink, and piercing.

Head in the game.

I flashed him a cocky grin and folded my arms over my chest, making sure to flex my biceps. "You know you can't win, right?"

He swallowed and faltered for a second, then scowled.

"Pshhh! Don't listen to your uncle," Sophie told him. I made a face that Tennyson found funny. Julian merely chuckled. "I know his weaknesses," she added, and then she whispered something in his ear. Except, we all heard it. Mocking vegetarianism wouldn't work at all. I was far from militant.

I rolled my eyes. "Brook, we gonna play or what?"

It took the youngsters some time to dick around and stall, but eventually Brooklyn threw the ball toward the middle of the pool, and Tennyson caught it.

It was completely dark at this point, and aside from lanterns illuminating the terrace, there wasn't much helping us.

"You can do some cardio while we set the record straight, Asher," Daniel said.

Ash flipped us off from the terrace, and the other spectators made bets.

As Sophie went for Tennyson, Zane tried to cover Daniel, and I dove underwater and swam between Julian and Sophie. I resurfaced behind their pathetic defense line, and Tennyson passed me the ball.

What I hadn't considered were Julian's abilities in the water. He turned out to be fast as fuck, and he reached me just as I slammed the ball onto the towel.

"Goddammit." Sophie glared as she clung on Tennyson's back. "This isn't going to work."

"No shit," I drawled. I eyed Julian. I'd definitely have to watch him.

"Well, fuck the rules, then." Brooklyn removed the flimsy wrap around her hips and pulled back her hair in a high bun. "Come on, Lucia. Shawn, you too. We're with Sophie and the boys."

My mouth twisted into a lazy grin. *Now we're talking.*

"What about me?" Ash frowned.

Brooklyn gave him a loud smooch. "You're our DJ and

referee, of course."

*

"Do I gotta do all the fucking work?" I barked out. Grabbing Sophie by her waist, I pressed her against the wall of the pool as Daniel tried to get in between Shawn and Julian with the ball. "Cover Brook!"

"I'm free!"

Since Sophie was goddamn tiny, it didn't take much effort to keep her in place while reaching out to wrap my fingers around Julian's wrist. I hauled him closer, panting from exertion, and positioned Sophie behind me, still pushed up against the tiles, and Julian in front of me. He was stronger, so I wrapped my arms around him.

"Let me go!" Sophie yelled.

"The fuck would I do that for?" I grunted, desperate for Julian to keep fucking still, so I bent down and bit his neck.

"Jesus!" he hissed.

"Daniel!" Tennyson held up his hand in the air, to which Danny passed the ball.

Lucia and Zane were on him like a leech.

"Motherfuck!" I snapped. Karma was a bitch with teeth, and it was my turn. Sophie's teeth sank into my shoulder blade, and I lurched forward enough so she could escape. "You better run, Sophie!"

"I've got her." Daniel swam toward her.

Julian kept squirming and pushing at my arms, and with only him around, it got…sexier. I couldn't even blame alcohol for clouding my mind. It was all him.

His perfect little ass was distracting.

"Stop moving around," I growled in his ear.

He froze, the air around us becoming charged in an instant. My cock was pressed right fucking *there*. If I didn't let go soon, I'd have to think about baseball stats before I left the pool.

"Damn it," he whispered. "I can play unfair too, you bastard."

It hadn't been my intention to play unfair what-so-fucking-ever, but I couldn't help myself now. It pushed me on to a new path and train of thought, and I wanted to be selfish. And greedy. I wanted a hit from my goddamn drug that was Julian.

I gripped his hips harder as arousal flooded south, and it was probably the worst time to taunt him. "You don't have an ounce of deviance in you. I doubt you could."

"Nailed it!" Daniel boomed out.

It broke the tension, even though my mind was still foggy. Needing some clarity, I let go of him and dunked my head underwater.

Fuck.

When I reached the surface again, Julian was several feet away from me, and the dare was clear in his eyes.

Fuck, fuck.

CHAPTER 14

At around two in the morning, I ordered car service for Julian and me. Neither of us was fit to drive my truck home, and I couldn't be assed to deal with Uber or cabs tonight. Back when Nicky worked for me, he'd hooked us up with drivers contracted to the agency he was at, and it was convenient. Someone would be here soon.

Lucia and Shawn had gone home, and the others were staying at the beach house. We had a fucking cat to go home to. First day in her new home, it was probably not a stellar idea to leave her alone too long.

Julian had named her Blue at some point tonight, for the color of her eyes.

Beats Fluffy.

After hanging up the phone, I returned to the living room. Brooklyn and Asher bid everyone goodnight before heading upstairs, and I sat down next to Julian in the loveseat. On one couch, Tennyson was sprawled out with his head on Sophie's lap, and Danny and Zane were on the other looking all lovey-dovey.

Sickening.

I wanted it.

Paris was the topic, so it was easy to catch up.

"Are we doing a dinner when we get there?" Sophie asked. "I've only shot with Little Paul. Some bonding with my fellow cast wouldn't hurt."

We had two Pauls on the set, so the kid who portrayed April's son had been nicknamed Little Paul. He was a great actor; Tennyson had found him.

"Well, you'll meet them next week," Tennyson said pensively.

I nodded. "We're shooting the scenes where your family packs your belongings."

Sophie pouted. "Is it wrong I'm on April's side?"

That was the whole mindfuck of the movie. It was about April's love for her son, and parallel to that, we had a devastated but determined family searching for her. 'Cause she was, despite all her love for her son, unfit to care for him, and her family was on a quest to take him away from her.

"I'm on April's side, too," Julian said quietly. "I get that she can't be the mother he needs, but damn. She loves him so much. Who wouldn't want that?"

I hummed. "Sometimes it's not about what you want. Needs come first."

I was beginning to worry I was mixing the two up, though. For a year, I'd tried to do what was best. *Tend to needs and not only desires.* What if what I desired was also what I needed?

As the others continued discussing the film, I distracted myself by keeping it about Paris with Julian. He'd only been there once on a school trip.

"I'm guessing you did all the boring museums then," I murmured.

"It wasn't boring." He chuckled quietly and traced patterns on my shorts. "I heard it would take a whole week to see everything at the Louvre."

I almost forgot he'd majored in art. "You wouldn't mind that, would you?"

"No, it would be a dream come true." He grinned tiredly and shifted in his seat. His legs ended up over mine, and he snatched up a blanket before leaning back against the armrest. "When will the car be here?"

"An hour." I fanned out the blanket some more and stroked his calf. I couldn't *not* touch him anymore. "Please your boss in Paris, and he might give you some time off to have fun at the Louvre."

I'd make sure he regretted thinking hiring him was a favor. On set here in LA, he focused on the music. He and Tennyson worked closely together, so I hadn't heard anything. In Paris, Julian would be my bitch. He'd work harder than the other PAs just so he'd learn nepotism wasn't always a perk.

"Should I call you sir, too?" He smirked and found my hand under the blanket. He played with my fingers absently, resting our hands on his stomach. "Or maybe Professor. You did promise to teach me the weird slang you use around sets."

Fucking hell. Images of me giving him assignments and tests flooded my brain. I did remember his fantasies. Professor and student was one of them. So was boss and employee.

"We can start right now if you want." I racked my brain for a common term as I brushed my thumb over his abs. His eyes darkened, and he swallowed hard. "What's an over?"

"Um." He drove me fucking insane with his expressive eyes. "Over easy, how you like your eggs in the morning?"

I chuckled darkly, my mind screaming at me to stop.

"Yeah, Brooklyn told me Peter's springing for a private plane for the cast and the big shots," I heard Zane say. "That's great. Daniel and I will be waiting by the phone for a call from the adoption agency that can come when-damn-ever, and you're all going to Paris in first class. I'm stoked for y'all."

I saw my exit. I didn't wanna take it, but if Julian and I went any further, I'd attack as soon as we were home.

"Hey, guys, I'm trying to teach Julian some on-set slang," I said, clearing my throat. "He doesn't know what an over is. Any guesses? Not you, Tennyson."

He *hmphd.*

"I know," Sophie sang. She faced Julian. "It's an angle. Like, if I have my back to the camera and they film the person I'm talking to—over my shoulder."

I nodded and sat up a bit, 'cause I needed a break from Julian before I mauled him. "That's right. So you get an F on that one, kid." I gave his leg a squeeze and then stood up. "I'll go pack up your gifts."

He'd received a bunch of things for his cat from Brooklyn and Asher, gift cards from Danny and Zane, and studio time with a well-known music producer from Tennyson and Sophie. And I figured carrying out cat furniture to the front of the house would work better than baseball stats.

*

The problem was, when we got in the car to go home, I was back to not being able to stay away. He was so fucking sweet, talking excitedly—albeit sleepily—about Paris, working on a film set, seeing the sights, and being back in Europe, that I couldn't manage any distance between us anymore.

A touch here and there, a shift, a scoot. We moved closer to where I wanted him, and he dove into a story about French food while I put my arm around him and kissed the side of his head.

Was he even aware?

It was pretty fucking clear he was still attracted to me. I wasn't that blind. But like I'd told Dr. Kendall, which was actually true, attraction wasn't everything.

"Hey, you're that director, aren't you? You used to work a lot with Tennyson Wright?" The driver eyed me in the rearview. "And you lost your family in a plane crash."

I threw him an irritated look. "I haven't forgotten."

Julian had grown quiet and uncomfortable.

Not that the driver noticed. "Yeah, I'm a screenwriter." Of course he was. We lived in a town where drivers were screenwriters, waitresses were actresses, and bartenders were stuntmen. "Do you take scripts? I heard you're filming with Sophie Pierce now."

Julian spoke for only me to hear. "Is he serious?" He scowled and grabbed my hand.

"Unfortunately, this isn't very rare." I chuckled quietly and threaded our fingers together. Then I addressed the driver. "I assume you've heard of Asher Wright?"

"Of course," he replied.

I inclined my head. "Send your script with a pizza to his office. He'll read it."

While Julian turned his head to stifle his laughter against my neck, the driver eagerly agreed and said he'd send it first thing on Monday. After that, it was quiet again, and I returned my attention to Julian.

"Did you have a good time today?" I pressed my nose to his hair, smelling chlorine and shampoo.

"Understatement. I can't thank you enough." He was killing me. His hand slid up my thigh, and he squeezed it gently. "The only thing missing is-is, um, birthday sex."

That sent a rush of heat through me. "Are you drunk?"

"No… Just tipsy enough to have the balls to ask that of you."

I groaned under my breath as the tip of his tongue licked my neck.

"I wanna be weak tonight, Noah," he murmured. "Please?"

No fucking clue what he meant by weak, but it fit well, I supposed. 'Cause I was too weak to resist.

"Okay." I cupped the back of his head and tilted it back so I could cover his mouth with mine. At the same time, his hand landed on my crotch, and I grunted into the kiss.

I stroked his tongue with mine, sucked on his bottom lip, and struggled to hold back so I didn't end up taking him in the back of the car.

"I've been thinking about this all day," he admitted. "When're we home?"

I broke away from his mouth. He kissed down my jaw and neck, and I looked out the window long enough to see where we were. Then I took his mouth again and kissed him deeply, managing to let him know we'd be home in ten.

He moaned. "Why do you have to be so fucking sexy?"

Why can't I get you outta my fuckin' head?

I hummed, out of breath, and nipped at his jaw as I applied pressure to his hand on my cock. "Jesus fuck, you make me hard."

His breath hitched, and I pulled him in for a brutal kiss so he couldn't reply. I didn't need his questions on my sexuality. It was as if he couldn't understand that I found him sexy, too.

We spent the rest of the ride kissing and teasing each other senseless, not giving a shit about the driver. He certainly didn't have any more requests about scripts.

*

"My bed," I managed as he pressed me up against the wall in the hallway between our rooms. "I won't fuck you in the bed you share with your boyfriend."

"Dick. It's not like that." He scratched up my back, our teeth clashing as we kissed. "What about you, you manwhore? Don't make me feel bad when you've screwed half of LA."

The jealousy was seeping out. For both of us, it seemed.

"You're exaggerating." I pulled off his shirt and threw it on the floor. "And I sure as shit didn't bring any women to our fucking home."

I was pathetic. I'd had to get wasted before going home with those broads, and I'd still ended up nauseated the day after, despite bad recollections of what had happened. I'd accomplished absolutely nothing by trying to move on.

"It's not really—I mean, Nick—"

"Don't speak his fucking name." I hauled him up against the other wall and slid my hand down his shorts. "I'm still clean. Are you?" I grasped his cock and stroked it teasingly.

"Yes," he gasped. "I wouldn't let him—I swear I've been safe. About everything."

Good.

I dragged him into my room and pushed him down on the bed. As he yanked off my tee, I got rid of his shorts, and then I kissed my way down his body.

"Oh, *God.* Noah, I…*fuck*!"

I licked the underside of his cock, then closed my mouth over the head and took as much of him as I could. Last time I gave a blow job was in college, so I had to rely on instinct and how I liked getting them. Julian didn't seem to have any complaints. He moaned and whimpered and cursed, and I got a steady little flow of pre-come in return.

Around the same time my jaw started aching, he cried out for me to stop and squirmed away, panting and shaking.

"Too close." He collapsed again and threw an arm over his face.

I crawled over him and kissed his chest. "Get lube, Julian. I'm taking your ass."

He nodded quickly and practically flew out of the room. In the meantime, I kneeled on the bed and stroked myself, spreading the fluids that seeped out of my cock. Then he was back, and I told him to lie down on his stomach.

His ass was fucking perfection. Tight, smooth, and soft enough to drive me wild. I spent ages tongue-fucking him, squeezing and rubbing his cheeks, and fingering him.

By the time I slicked up my cock, he was a pleading mess. He gasped for air and pushed out his ass for me, and I fisted my cock and pressed teasingly against his opening.

"Fuck, please," he groaned. "I need your cock, Noah."

I leaned over him to kiss his neck, and then I slowly pushed in. Caught between me and the mattress, he was completely at my mercy. That urge to consume him was back, and this time, I knew it wasn't going anywhere.

I screwed my eyes shut and bit into his shoulder. Forcing my way deep inside him, *feeling* him…it was out of this world.

"*Christ*." I hissed and stilled when my cock was buried. "So fucking good."

His breathing stuttered, his hands trying to grab at my legs. "I need—oh hell, *yesss*… More—I want to feel you."

"In a minute." Lifting my upper body, I palmed both his ass cheeks and watched my cock work his tight hole. "What a sight." I slowly fucked him into the mattress, mesmerized. My cock came out slick with lube, blood pulsing fast and making me more sensitive.

I needed to see him, though. Pulling out, I told him to turn over, and he was more than willing. He spread his legs for me and yanked me down on him. His kiss was hungry, deep, and filled me with both relief and pleasure. And the need for more. I pushed in once more, and I set a steady pace. I fucked him in long strokes and grabbed the headboard to fuck him harder.

"That's it." I shuddered and dipped my head to capture his mouth with mine. "You're gonna turn me into an addict, baby."

"Good." He wrapped his legs around me and dug his fingers into my back, rocking to meet my every thrust. "I like it when you call me that."

I smiled then rolled my hips to get deeper. It made him cry out, and I felt the sticky mess he was making on his stomach. I stroked him as my orgasm approached, wanting us to get off at the same time.

"It's what you are, isn't it?" I groaned as he licked a bead of sweat from my neck. "My musical genius and my baby."

"Fuck," he whimpered. "Yeah." He nodded and kissed me even more hungrily than before, and I could tell he was getting close. His breathing was choppy and shallow. He tensed up, and he shook.

Pleasure pooled in my gut, like a ball waiting to explode. It kept building up, and I went harder and deeper. My sac felt tight, and it slapped against his skin every time I rammed into him.

"Look at me." I grabbed his jaw. My breathing was growing out of control, and it wouldn't be too long until I couldn't hold back anymore. I didn't say anything else to him, but I stared. I saw his desire, his vulnerability, and I knew I'd never seen anything sexier. Or more beautiful. *God, I've missed him.*

Moments later, he lost it. His eyes fell closed, he sucked in a breath, he gripped my arms, and he started coming.

The sight of rope after rope of come hitting his chest did me in. I groaned and slammed my cock deep inside his ass, and then I lost it, too. I breathed through clenched teeth as I filled him. Every inhale made me salivate at the scent of sex that lingered heavily in the air.

Afterward, I collapsed next to him and waited for my heart rate to go back to normal. I was spent and deliriously sated, and I'd hit a new low of stupidity if I even attempted to say this was an itch I could scratch. Unless the scratching was forever. There was no goddamn way I'd get over Julian.

I couldn't lie; I was slightly panicked about it, but what good would it do to fight it? I'd tried and failed for a year.

Acceptance. I needed to accept it. It would probably take a while, but I was done denying it.

"I'm going to be so sore tomorrow," he whispered.

I grinned and blew out a heavy breath, my heart still beating fast. "I'll take that as a compliment."

"You should. Damn." He chuckled sleepily and winced a little. "I need a smoke."

"The hell you do." Sitting up, I planted my feet on the floor and held out my hand. "Take a shower with me."

That seemed to surprise him, though I had no clue why. His smile was hesitant. Almost shy.

"Yeah?" He sat up too, and slipped his hand in mine. "Okay."

I pulled him to me and walked him into my bathroom while sniffing and kissing his neck. He smelled deliciously sexy and *him* there.

"This is different," he said with a small laugh.

I knew it was, and I needed this. He wasn't a quick fuck, and I wasn't running away from what I wanted anymore. I fucking couldn't.

Turning on the water, I walked over to the toilet and took a leak. Julian stepped into the shower, and I joined him shortly after. I had questions I wanted to ask, though I wasn't sure it was the right time.

His argument with Nicky was still fresh in my mind. Everything about the extent of their relationship and how Nicky treated Julian, to his antidepressants and why he took them.

Exclusive or not, he and Nicky were evidently close enough for Julian to tell him more than me. There was so much I didn't know.

It'd been a long day, though. A good one. I didn't wanna ruin it.

I poured some shower gel in my hand and began soaping up Julian, all while he looked up at me with a funny expression.

I smirked lazily as I rubbed my thumbs over his nipples. The one that was pierced was clearly more sensitive. "You got a problem with me doting on ya?"

He shook his head slowly, still studying me.

Farther down, I swiped a sudsy hand over his ink. I'd never really paid attention to the details before. Everything was in black, shadowed perfectly. A piano was in focus, and along waves of sheet music, I could see family. *Mom, Dad, Linda, JJ.* There was a mountain and a Bavarian castle in the background. Lyrics, his birth date, a chain with a broken link.

A tattooed semicolon caught my attention. I knew it was a symbol for depression awareness.

Yeah, 'cause me and my big mouth could shut up now…

I started innocent enough. "Tell me about the castle?"

He looked down, shrugged, and peered up again. "Favorite childhood memory. We went to Neuschwanstein castle. Mom was pregnant with Linda, and it was just a perfect family day." He closed his eyes as I moved up to rub his shoulders. "The good times before I knew I was gay."

That shit again.

I decided to save the semicolon for another day. Instead, I continued with the topic we were already on.

"James and Mia never knew, did they?"

He shook his head and opened his eyes again, then went for the shower gel. "My turn." Well, that was abrupt. He cleared his throat. "I shouldn't have brought that up." I turned around when he gave me a nudge, and then I felt his hands on my back. "I'm—I'm ashamed of some decisions I made in the past. I don't like talking about it."

I mulled that over, trying not to get too into the spectacular massage he was giving me. "We've all done things we're ashamed of, haven't we?"

"Sure, but it affects us differently," he mumbled. "My decisions ruined the latter part of my childhood." He paused as he reached my lower back, and he was quiet while he rubbed a knot I didn't even know I had. "Mom and Dad would be disappointed if they'd known."

I knew a thing or two about that, considering who I was in the shower with.

"My birthday isn't over until we go to bed," he said. "I want more birthday sex."

I snorted a chuckle and hung my head, enjoying his hands on me. It didn't hurt that he'd gotten to my ass. The hot water combined with his magic touch was outta this fucking world.

"How long are you gonna dodge this conversation?" I asked.

"Forever."

"I can't allow that," I murmured. "I wanna know. You're on medication, Julian. That's serious to me, and I can't help if you won't let me in."

He hummed and sank to his knees behind me. "Speaking of letting someone in…"

Worst goddamn pun ever, but I lost my focus, anyway. Holy fuck. He stroked a finger along the crease of my ass, and his tongue followed.

"Jesus," I muttered. I placed a hand on the wall for support and groaned when he started rimming me softly. "Fuck, it's been years, baby… Don't stop."

"Oh, I won't."

CHAPTER 15

Two weeks later

"Someone at security is asking for you, Noah," Lucia said as she passed us.

"I think it's pretty fucking clear I don't have time." I went over the scene again with Shawn, who made adjustments because I'd changed my mind about the lighting. I wanted a sunbeam, a distinct one, a real-looking one.

Lucia came over to the monitor again. "His name is Nicky?"

I grunted, irritated. "Tell him to go fuck himself."

Of course, it was the jealousy speaking. Mostly. And god-fucking-shit-dammit, I didn't have the time. My personal life had no business at work.

We'd wrapped everything with April's brother, her ex slash father of her son, and two parents. All we had left before Paris was Sophie's post-meltdown scene, and it had to be perfect.

"Someone's mad today. Again." Sophie came up behind me with Brooklyn in tow. "I'm actually glad we're doing this retake." She closed her eyes while Brooklyn did the final touches. "I don't think I nailed it last time."

"You can't say that in front of the director." One of the operators seemed genuinely appalled, though he didn't know our dynamic very well.

Sophie scoffed. "I can say whatever I damn well like."

"Diva," I coughed.

I was full of shit, and I didn't care. I didn't need her to point out that I'd been pissy these past two weeks.

"I'll wrap this up," Shawn said. "Shouldn't take more than ten."

I checked my watch, bugged about whatever the fuck Nicky was doing here. But if he had info on Julian, I had to know. "You have until I get back," I told him, and then I made my way to the elevator.

My PA was just exiting with a to-go cup from Starbucks. "Oh. For you, man."

"Thanks, kid." I accepted it and stepped in, at which he walked over to the panel and pushed the bottom button. "I kinda hate to lose you, you know."

Nothing bad about Julian, obviously, but Michael was like a twenty-five-year-old version of me. He worked hard, spoke my language, and didn't panic or run in circles to get shit done.

"I appreciate that." He nodded. It looked like he was gonna leave it there; instead, he smirked slyly. "You have my number if you ever need a PA on another set. Or anything else."

I chuckled and inclined my head. "Noted." A local set, though. His being a single dad made it impossible for him to travel. I'd definitely remember it for local gigs. "Before I forget." I patted my pockets and took a sip from my coffee, handing him a piece of paper. "You said you're going back to school, so recommendations won't get you anywhere right now, but this can come in handy. You wanted to be a sound mixer, right?"

"Yeah." He took the paper eagerly and scanned the list of independent studios I'd worked with. Email addresses that went further than some receptionist's desk. "Wow, this is… Thanks, Noah."

"Any time. If you have a spare minute, stop by at the party tonight." The elevator door was pushed open, so I clapped him on the shoulder and got out, aiming straight for security.

"I'll try," Michael called.

Tennyson was over by the trailers, busy signing documents all while having the monkey that was Ivy clinging to him.

I was about to break his budget, so I left him alone for now, and I doubted he'd be at the bar tonight. Hell, I didn't wanna go. We had a flight tomorrow, but it'd be rude not to show up. The LA crew was done, so they wouldn't be around for the wrap party in August.

As I got to the exit, I nodded at one of the security guys to let Nicky through.

"Make it fast. What's up?" I took a sip of my coffee, eyeing him.

"Is Julian here?" he asked impatiently. He adjusted his tie and glanced around the set. "He's not returning my calls."

"I thought he was staying with you." That one stung to bite out.

I hadn't seen Julian in a fucking week. He sent me texts to say he was all right and needed some downtime, but he wouldn't pick up the phone when I called. Which hurt.

I'd been…a bit different the day after Julian's birthday. Maybe to test the waters, both his and mine.

I'd developed goddamn feelings that ran *deep*, so I'd been sweeter. I'd pulled him close and kissed him, and it had evidently not been welcome. In the days that followed, he'd grown distant—until he left a note one day saying he needed some space to think.

"No." Nicky scowled. "Last time I spoke to him was the day before his birthday."

Well, hell. Now I was worried.

Julian's last text came this morning though, so knowing he was okay enough to keep in touch prevented me from panicking. I made a mental note to call Dr. Kendall. The anniversary of the plane crash was the day after tomorrow; who knew where his head was at?

"I don't have time for his drama," Nicky said, "but this is on the way to my new job, so I thought I'd find him here. He needs to make up his damn mind—"

"*You* need to fucking watch it," I told him. That wiped off the arrogance from his face. "I heard you guys arguing before his birthday, and if you for one goddamn second think you can use him to get ahead in the industry, you've got another thing comin'."

He stared at me hard, his front wafer-thin. He wanted to be the big, macho motherfucker, and maybe he could pull that shit with Julian to a certain degree, but sure as hell not with me. And he knew it.

"Let's be realistic, Noah." He went for reasoning, though it came off patronizing. I wasn't amused for shit. "This is how LA works, and Julian knew very well what he got himself into. No feelings involved. A good time that also took us places—"

My glare shut him up.

"Where the *fuck* does a good time with you take him?" I stepped close, throwing the coffee in a nearby trash can. "Let me make this clear so you understand." I dusted some lint off his shoulder. "Stay away from Julian. He's got too much on his plate to deal with your God complex. And if you don't? If I hear about you bitching at him like some little cunt again, I'll make it significantly more difficult for you to get a job in this town under your name. You follow me?"

He gritted his teeth, and I didn't think he'd say anything, so I turned around and started walking back to the building.

I should've known better.

"I know about you two," he called.

I stopped and clenched my fists. Then I headed back to him, not stopping until I was in his space, towering over him.

"A friend of mine drives around rich fuckers like you for a living." He tried to come off assertive and threatening. "Guess who he drove home after a birthday party a while ago?"

I said nothing, seething. It was strange that I didn't care he knew. There was even some pleasure in knowing he did. What did piss me off royally, however, was Nicky's agenda.

"I also know you and Julian had a relationship last year," he went on. He swallowed and straightened, as if he could grow in height to look less pathetic. "He told me. I get it. You forgot you were straight, and he got to warm your bed until you'd had enough.

You ruined him. And I bet you don't want that to get out." He smirked. "Noah Collins banging his nephew? Fucking disgusting, man."

The only thing that packed a punch was the possibility of me ruining Julian. I didn't know what he'd told Nicky, though I'd find out. In the meantime, I could take my miserable state out on the fuckwit in front of me. Who the hell did he think he was?

I smiled faintly and took a step back. "You just killed your future in this industry. Well done." Next, I jerked my chin at one of the security guards. "Get this motherfucker off my set."

Back to work.

*

"Action!" I checked the monitor, where the main operator let me see April's world and how it was tilted off its axis.

The meltdown was over, and Sophie lay on the wooden floor. We filmed her from a low angle, and she slowly lifted her hand to the sunbeam flowing through the window. Dust particles were going to swirl in the wake of her destruction.

She let out a sigh. Peace surrounded her. She was off in her own fantasy world. The ring she wore glinted in the light, and I nudged Lucia and my script supervisor to make a note. I wanted extra coverage there.

Zooming in on the butterfly ring April's brother had once given her, I waited patiently for Sophie to bring it home. She hummed lightly as her fingers danced slowly with the dust.

"Don't worry, dear boy," she sang softly, "Mommy can shelter you well. Don't worry, dear boy, Mommy can catch you stars." It was perfect. Her voice was angelic but held a note of scratchiness, the only reminder of her previous meltdown where she'd screamed and trashed the place. "Don't worry, dear boy, Mommy can keep you safe. Don't worry, dear boy, Mommy can catch you stars."

The song morphed into a quiet humming again, and I paused for a beat before I called cut. Everyone waited for orders while I spoke with the script supervisor, and when I saw Tennyson watching in the background, I went over to him.

"The lullaby," I said, looking around to see where Julian was. "What do you say about Sophie recording an extended version?" It hit me that Julian wasn't here. I was an idiot. This was what work did to me. I forgot everything around me, and now that the memories flooded back, so did the unease in my gut.

"Recording it for the score?" Tennyson inquired.

I nodded and pushed aside my personal life again. "The next scene is April's family closing in on her in Paris. So in this scene, the song is a lullaby. But it could grow from there as the next one begins."

Tennyson evidently approved. "It would be more of a warning of what's to come. I like it. I'll speak to Julian. I've come to value his opinion, and I think he could make this powerful."

Well, now it was fucking impossible to keep my personal life off the set. "When was the last time you talked to him?"

He shrugged and scratched his jaw, pensive. "Last night, I believe. He was in the studio all day, so I stopped by to hear what he had so far."

Ah. I rubbed the back of my neck and frowned at the floor, honestly feeling cast aside. I had no doubt that if I texted him about work, he'd reply. He was professional and took shit seriously, but I didn't know why he was avoiding me. Hell, I didn't even know where he lived.

"Are you two okay?" Tennyson asked.

I forced a smile and lifted my gaze from the ground. "I'm not really sure. He's keeping to himself." Glancing over to the set, I saw everyone was still waiting for me, so it was time to finish this. "Maybe I'll see him tonight at the party, or it'll be tomorrow at the airport. See you later, man."

"Noah?" He stopped me, and I looked back at him. "You know where he's staying, yes?"

I suppressed a sigh. 'Cause it sucked that others knew more about him than I did. It wasn't some goddamn competition, but Christ. "No," I admitted.

"Daniel and Zane's beach house."

Fucking great.

"We thought you knew." He frowned. "We don't pry, but I have noticed he's looking more tired lately."

I nodded with a dip of my chin and offered another tight smile, and then I got back to work again.

*

"Can you at least pretend to be happy?" Sophie asked. "Or tell me why you're PMSing." That part was grumbled as a doorman let us in to the bar Tennyson had rented for the evening.

"I'll be happier after a few drinks." I scowled and adjusted my crotch. The only downside to our being neighbors was that she sometimes played dress-up with me if we had an event that required more than jeans and button-downs.

These gray dress pants from some uppity designer could certainly get me laid, 'cause fucking hell, my ass looked *good*, but I had to be in the mood for it. Years ago, I wouldn't have complained. *Years* ago.

Back when I didn't have Julian to obsess over.

The trendy bar was packed with crewmembers and their spouses, and after greeting only a few, I was feeling suffocated. I unbuttoned the top two buttons of my shirt and aimed for the bar. I'd already lost Sophie to Brooklyn, both of whom were enjoying a night away from mommy duties. Tennyson and Asher were catching a game—lucky bastards—and they had the kids with them.

While I waited for my beer, I checked my phone. There was nothing new. Last text from Julian came a couple hours ago, and he'd said he'd be here.

Away from the set, everyone was more chill, and crewmembers who wouldn't normally approach a director for fear of interrupting his work were now coming forward in droves. I was flattered as fuck, though.

This attention was new, and I was beginning to see why Tennyson had adapted to a hermitlike lifestyle. Sophie had brought him outta his shell a bit, though he preferred peace and quiet. I got it. It was a bit overwhelming.

"Noah! Over here!"

I'd drained my third beer when I looked out over the crowd and saw my escape. Michael had made it, so I excused myself from two wardrobe girls and made my way over to him.

"Hey, kid. Glad you made it." Checking my watch, I wondered where the hell Julian was.

"Yeah, me too. My sister's watching my daughter, so that's gonna cost me, but…" He shrugged and grinned. "You stoked about Paris?"

Couldn't he tell? Fuck, I didn't know what was wrong with me.

"It'll be fun." I nodded and tried to muster some enthusiasm. "You haven't seen Julian by any chance, have you?"

There was no big plan. I didn't know what I'd say to Julian when I saw him, but I was done with his hiding. And he didn't need to worry about me crossing any more lines. Someway, somehow, I'd get over him. I hoped.

"Uh, yeah, sure." Michael craned his neck to look past me. "I think I saw him in the back. Come on. I'll take you there."

I was fully capable of finding the seating area in the back myself, but I followed anyway. With Michael, I looked busy. Fewer people stopped me, so that was good.

Someone called out for me way back from where we came, and I pretended not to hear it. The music was loud, making it a plausible excuse.

Rather than continuing to the back, Michael turned toward the bathrooms in a corridor behind the main bar, which confused me. Though, before I could ask what was up, he faced me with an odd expression. Seriousness mixed with nerves, and he ran a hand through his light hair.

I folded my arms over my chest and leaned a shoulder against the wall. "If you saw Julian here, it's called cruising."

"Heh. Cruising." He pulled a strained laugh and took a step closer as two ladies passed to get in line. "Funny you should mention that."

Oh, really.

I narrowed my eyes, wondering if I'd become so whipped and

focused on Julian that I'd missed something obvious.

His gaze strayed before he faced me again. "You're kinda difficult to get alone, you know."

Yup, I'd missed something.

I let out a chuckle and scrubbed a hand over my face. "You flirtin' with me, kid?"

This attention, I was used to. Flattering for sure, except I had no interest. Nor would I have taken the bait back in the day. If there'd been a beautiful woman on his arm, fuck yeah. But only one guy had captured my attention—and pretty much everything else—and he wasn't here.

"I don't work for you anymore," he said, "and I owed it to myself to try." With that, he stepped close enough so our chests were touching. His flirting was bold already, so I hadn't expected another move from him. But before I could decline, the fucker planted one on me.

What the hell?

It was surreal, and I just fucking stood there. Did I make dudes' gaydar go off all of a sudden? I cursed internally and broke away.

He looked confused. "You're not gay?"

"Uh…" I chuckled, 'cause it was all I could do. "It's not—" *that easy*. Fuck. "I'm not into—" I sounded like a stuttering moron. Then I didn't give two shits 'cause that was when I saw Julian at the opening of the hallway. "Goddammit, I'm too old for cliché bullshit." He was quick to bail, and it made me groan. As I grew anxious, I gave Michael a tight smile and squeezed his shoulder. "It's been nice working with you, Michael. Not interested, though." I left it there and took off after Julian.

I'd only gotten a glimpse of him, but it had been enough. He was drunk, and he'd looked shocked and wounded to see me with another guy. Fuck it, I couldn't blame him; however, if he'd been sober, he would have seen it for what it was.

"Julian!" I pushed past the chatty ladies who worked for Brooklyn in makeup and finally caught up to him when he reached the exit. "Not so fast, kid."

"Let go of me." He flinched away and headed outside, and I

followed with a fucking sigh. "It was a mistake to come."

The last couple of weeks came rushing back, and he was pissing me off. I didn't do drama. I didn't *chase.*

"Hey!" I stopped on the sidewalk and glared at his back.

The anger in my tone made him stop, and he turned to me.

Deep breath. We needed to talk, not yell. He was in a bad way, shadows back under his eyes, hair messier than usual. The kid knew how to worry me. With a jerk of my chin, I told him to follow me, and I walked between the two buildings so we could get some privacy.

It wasn't a deep alley, and I came to a stop some fifteen feet away from the sidewalk.

"What the *fuck* is going on with you, Julian?" I asked, frustrated. "Did you know I had to hear from Tennyson that you're staying at Danny and Zane's place? I'm fucking worried here, but you won't talk to me."

He laughed darkly and kicked at a bottle on the ground. "You didn't seem very worried in there."

"Fuck you," I told him. "Fuck you all the way off for that. Maybe it looked bad, but I didn't instigate *shit.* Nor did I kiss him back. But even if I had?" I widened my arms. "So what? I'm a free man, aren't I?"

As soon as those words left me, I regretted them. They were true, except I had to fucking cool it. He frustrated me so damn much because I could *see* the state he was in. He'd never been able to hide his moods or how he felt; he only refused to talk.

"You gotta level with me, kid." I took a gentler approach and placed my hands on his shoulders. "You look like shit."

"Thanks."

I rolled my eyes and hauled him in for a hug. "You know that's not what I meant." I sniffed his hair, smelling cigarette smoke and… Well, he probably hadn't showered in a few days. "Why did you leave the loft?"

"I needed space." He wouldn't hug me back yet, though I could be a relentless motherfucker. "I told you."

"You never tell me why." That was the problem. "Why did you call Danny instead of Nicky?"

He tensed up. "I don't feel like being anybody's fuck toy."

Fuck. His tone… Was that what he thought I wanted? Just sex? Nicky, sure. He was a cunt stain. I wasn't Nicky.

Of course, I hadn't been very verbal with my own intentions. I barely knew them. Or, maybe I did, but sweet mother of mercy, I had a heart to protect. Emma had managed to put a dent in it, yet it was nothing in comparison to what Julian could do.

That said, his happiness came before mine.

That much was clear to me now.

Unfortunately, I'd been crap at showing Julian I gave a fuck. I hadn't even called around and asked my friends if they knew where he was. Mostly because I'd assumed he'd go to Nicky, but also 'cause I didn't want them to know I didn't have it all together.

"Are we done hugging?" he muttered.

"No." I hugged him harder because of that. "Not until you tell me how you're doing. Give me *something*, Julian."

He shuddered a breath, and I could tell from his posture that he didn't have much fight left.

"I don't know what to say." His hands came to rest carefully along my sides, just above my belt. "I don't feel very good—"

"Try again, baby," I murmured. I hadn't meant to cut him off, but I wanted honesty.

He paused, struggling, then admitted defeat. "Everything sucks. Okay?"

It wasn't okay, although now I had something to go on. "Is it the anniversary?"

Painful reminder, though I had expected it to affect me more than it did. There was going to be a moment of silence at the airports in both Philly and Orlando for the lives that had been lost, and I had asked Julian weeks ago if he wanted to go. Luckily, we were on the same page. We were moving on, and we were remembering our family our way—privately.

Regardless, I had other worries that weighed heavier. Namely, the one I couldn't let go of. Literally.

"Some, yes." Slowly, his arms circled me until he clasped his hands at my lower back. "I want to tell you the rest, Noah, but it scares the crap out of me. I don't want you to hate me."

"Hey." I moved my hands to cup his cheeks so he'd look up at me. The sight of his eyes brimming with unshed tears fucking tore at me. "I could never hate you."

He swallowed hard and averted his gaze. "I'm tired. I'm so damn tired."

"Let's get you some rest, then." I pressed my lips to his forehead, fucking relieved to have him near. Felt like that was a goddamn running theme. The relief. "What does Kendall say?"

"That I should talk to you."

Good. That was good. "We'll get there." I brushed my thumbs over the shadows under his eyes. "No more running away, though."

He cringed. "That makes me sound childish. I'm sorry."

I shrugged and draped an arm around his shoulders. "We all cope differently, yeah? It ain't exactly mature to drown your miseries in a bottle of whiskey either, but I'm a champ at it." I grinned faintly and started ushering him out of the alley. "There's one thing you and I have in common when we're immature dicks, though."

"What's that?"

"We evidently stop showering," I replied wryly.

"Shit, I'm a mess." He made a face, visibly embarrassed. "I can't say I feel like going back into the bar."

I laughed quietly. "Don't worry, I'm taking you home."

That gave him a pause. "Blue is at the beach house. And my luggage."

"We'll get her and your stuff before we go to the airport. Deal?"

"I suppose she can survive one night without me."

CHAPTER 16

The plane was fucking huge, and there was even a part in the back where kids could nap. Which the castmembers who traveled with their children appreciated.

So did I. Saved me from hearing their sleepy whines. God knew I loved Kayden and Ivy, but I also loved handing the runts over when they got fussy.

I stayed in the front with Tennyson, Lucia, Julian, and a few others who were focusing on work during the flight. Sophie and Brooklyn were mingling with the cast and being all mommylike, and for a moment, I envied the actors. They only worked when the camera was on, aside from learning lines and characters.

Then I remembered how much I loved this, and it was all good again. But fuck if I'd ever pull a Tennyson and try my hand at being a creative producer. The man was drowning in paperwork. Legal shit, permits, deadlines, conference calls, and puzzling everything together.

"Refill my coffee, will ya?" I extended my cup to Julian, who sat next to me with his laptop.

"But I'm—" He stopped there. I knew he was busy with the music software he had up, but we were on our way to Paris now. He was my PA. He sighed and got up. "Yes, *sir.*"

I stifled a grin and got back to transferring notes from my pad to my own laptop.

"You're having way too much fun with that, Noah." Tennyson occupied one of the four seats across the aisle, documents spread out on the remaining seats as well as on the table in the middle. "He's on the payroll as a songwriter now, not a PA."

"He didn't think I could make him suffer." I stretched out my legs and rolled my shoulders. "He asked for it, Wright."

"He's certainly stubborn." He inclined his head and side-eyed me. "I wonder where he got that from."

"Fuck off," I chuckled. "You're hardly one to talk, buddy."

"We're not discussing me now." He smirked.

"How convenient," I deadpanned.

"What's convenient?" Sophie joined us and shut the curtains that separated us from the next section. "Ivy and Kayden are finally asleep."

Tennyson smiled as she plopped down on his lap, and what followed wasn't meant for an audience. Jesus Christ, where they trying for another kid?

"Get a fucking room," I said, turning back to my work.

Sophie beamed and flushed while her hubby whispered shit in her ear. "I didn't think you were against a little PDA, Collins," she told me. "You didn't seem to mind it yesterday."

"The fuck?" I frowned at her.

Julian returned at that point, so she merely shrugged and grinned impishly.

What the hell had she seen? I guessed it was Michael, when he'd kissed me. In which case it had nothing on Tennyson and Sophie molesting each other.

Either way, it was nothing I wanted to discuss.

"Your coffee, almighty one." Julian sat down and slid the coffee my way on our table. "Let me know if there's anything else I can do for your holiness."

"You can treat me with the same respect you would a boss you don't call family."

That gave him something to think about.

*

After dinner was over, I called it a day where work was concerned. It was getting dark, and the cabin crew dimmed the lights, anyway. It got quieter.

Julian had Blue in his lap as he scribbled on his iPad, Tennyson and Sophie were dozing off, as were the others.

Pulling off my hoodie, I got comfortable and adjusted my seat so I could lean back and check out Netflix on my tablet.

"Are you going to watch a movie?" Julian asked.

"Or a TV show, haven't decided yet." I grabbed a blanket, glad I'd gone with sweats today. Sleeping in jeans was complete shit. "You wanna watch something with me?"

"Okay." He was quick to stow away his iPad and put Blue back in her travel carrier, which wasn't as easy as it should've been. She was a fucking brat. "When you fly commercial and they show movies you've worked on, is that weird?"

I smirked lazily. "Nah, it's fun. I usually end up watching them."

"But you see everything behind too, right? You see more than what the average public sees." He pulled a blanket over him as well and pushed up the armrests between us so he could take up more space, the little fucker.

"Sure, it's like a scrapbook. Every scene comes with a memory or a dozen." I focused on the app as he placed his head on my shoulder. It wasn't distracting at *all*. "What're you in the mood for?"

"I'm not choosy. You pick."

He looked good, all snuggled up next to me, and it was a struggle not to go further. A blind person could see there was something between us, but it wasn't enough. Otherwise, Julian wouldn't have avoided me or turned me down when I was affectionate the day after his birthday.

That better stop stinging soon.

"Hey, can we talk instead?" Julian asked.

"Yeah?" That surprised me. "Of course." I set aside my tablet and leaned back again, wondering if he had a topic in mind. I hadn't pushed him about anything after last night, and it seemed a little soon for him to open up already. One could hope, though.

"We're spending almost two months in *Paris*," he murmured. "It didn't hit me until this morning."

I smiled and looked down as he tilted his head up.

"Will you have any free time so we can sightsee?" he wondered.

The trip was work. I wouldn't be there to sightsee, but taking *some* time off was doable. I'd always loved Paris, and of course, I had my favorites. If he hadn't already been there, I wanted to show him Parc des Buttes Chaumont, catch a show in Pigalle, have lunch by the river…

I could picture it, and in not a single one of the scenarios did I view him as a family member. I wanted *dates*. Hand-holding, sappy photos, kisses on bridges, dinners, and all the goddamn time in the world to explore him. No more "just this once" or "to get him outta my system."

A fucking relationship.

"I'll make time." I pressed a kiss to his forehead instead. It was what I seemed to be able to get away with before he pulled away, and I couldn't take that anymore. "We arrive in the morning local time, so technically we start with two days off."

"We should distract ourselves tomorrow," he said quietly. "I don't think I can sleep the entire day, as much as I would've wanted it."

I agreed. The anniversary wouldn't be a walk in the park. Mentally and emotionally, I had moved on fairly well, I thought. But on days like birthdays, anniversaries, and holidays, I was a masochist. That was when I pulled out photo albums and reminisced.

There would be no photo albums for tomorrow, though that didn't mean much. My head was packed with memories, and I was sure I'd assault myself with them.

"You know what?" A memory came to me then, as did a plan. "My folks honeymooned in Paris, and Ma always said she loved the view from that cathedral—" I snapped my fingers, trying to remember the name of it. "Sacré something. Sacré Coeur?"

Julian nodded. "Yes. It'd be a sweet tribute to Nana and Pops if we went."

"All right, it's a plan." I'd even light a candle for them. Ma would've liked that. "I think the view is supposed to be better than from the Eiffel Tower."

"It is." The art major in Julian appeared. I reckoned history mattered to him, too. "Three hundred steps to the top, Mr. Athlete."

I was game.

For the next couple of hours, we talked more about Paris. He spoke animatedly of art and history, and it was impossible not to smile at him. I knew that passion. I felt the same about filmmaking, and he was fortunate to have two subjects that got him going, the other being music. He was gifted and proved it on a daily basis.

Here and there, my thoughts wandered. Perhaps 'cause we'd be balls deep in the city of love. Nevertheless, I couldn't get that out of my head. What I wanted. What I should've wanted *more* when I was with Emma. I had loved her deeply. I had given her everything. Or everything I'd had at the time, maybe. 'Cause it felt more now. I couldn't fucking explain it.

Hard to think it'd been exactly one year since I ended things with her. It wasn't really on my mind, but God knew it would be if it'd been Julian and not her.

And he didn't have a single goddamn clue how I felt, which... Christ, it was fucked up. If I wanted him to be open with me, I had to return the favor. He wasn't stupid. He *had* to know I was attracted. But beyond that? How would he know? I'd told him he was sexy, beautiful...whatever. Actions spoke louder than words, and I'd been shit at showing him.

I winced internally, remembering the times I'd come home in the morning, wearing the same clothes as the night before when I'd told him I was going to a bar.

I couldn't really say I regretted it. I guessed it was one of those mistakes—or several—I had to go through before accepting what I wanted. And it wasn't any of the women I'd fucked after my first night with Julian.

Even so, he saw it. He knew what I was doing. He saw me as

more straight than…anything else. Goddamn labels. I didn't blame him. I just had to change it. I had to show him what *had* changed, rather.

Then, it would be up to him.

*

"Noah, it's time to wake up."

Fuck no. "Another hour." I rolled over and buried my head in the überfluffy hotel pillow. "How'dju even get into my room?"

"You mean suite." He snorted, and I felt the bed dip as he sat down. "As your devoted PA, I have a spare key. I guess you already forgot."

Guess so.

"What time is it?" I grumbled sleepily.

"Three. I ordered car service, hope you don't mind."

"Sounds good." I let out a yawn and stretched a bit. "As my slave, could you be a good boy and gimme a back rub?"

"Would you say that to a regular PA?" he retorted.

Touché. I wouldn't have.

"It would explain why Michael shoved his tongue down your throat," he muttered.

That made me laugh. "There was no tongue action, kid." He was cute when he was jealous. Unlike me. I was just a dick. "All right, give me ten minutes, then I'll meet you downstairs. I need to shower off the jet lag."

*

We arrived in Montmartre an hour later, and we were dropped off at the bottom of the hill with Sacré Coeur in front of us. The large church was located at the highest point in Paris, and I didn't doubt Julian when he told me it was four hundred steps from here. Ninety to get to the top of the hill, then three hundred inside the church to reach the lookout in the main dome.

"I wonder how many stories it would be," I mused as we started heading up. There were tourists and vendors everywhere, and for every landing we reached, there was someone trying to sell us crappy plastic souvenirs.

"Well..." Julian squinted toward the top. "If my math is correct, it should be around...twenty-eight stories? From here to the top, I mean."

"This should be fun, then." I turned my ball cap backward and pushed up the sleeves of my Henley. "Let's work up a sweat, yeah?"

He didn't seem amused, though he followed me when I picked up the pace to a jog. There was no way he could be surprised. I'd gotten dressed in sweats and running shoes, and he'd lived with me long enough to know better.

We reached the church in a few minutes, and as I caught my breath, I pictured my parents strolling around here decades ago. I could imagine what she'd point to and tell Pop to take a photo of. The trees, the stunning view, the church itself, the expansive staircase, and all the countless angles.

"It's official," Julian panted. "I hate cobblestones."

I chuckled and looked down where he stood, bent over. "That was just the first ninety steps, kid. You spent already?"

He ignored that. "I really need to give up smoking."

"Best thing you've said all day." I clapped him on the back and peered up at the church. "Come on. Let's climb that dome thing before we go inside the church." I had a feeling I wouldn't be interested in any workout once I'd seen the interior and assaulted myself with more memories of my folks.

To the left of Sacré Coeur was the entrance for those who wanted to go all the way to the top. I made sure I had cash to pay the fee, and then we ended up standing in line for a solid half hour.

"I'm glad we came." I draped an arm around his shoulders and leaned on him a bit. "Maybe next anniversary, we can go to where Mia and James went on their honeymoon."

Julian scrunched his nose and looked up at me. "You want to revisit the place where my mom and dad got it on like rabbits?"

Okay, I hadn't thought that through. I'd just thought it was sweet, the whole tribute thing. And it beat talking to some random fucking gravesite in Pittsburgh. They weren't even buried there. Or anywhere.

If I remembered correctly, Mia and James had gone on some romantic cruise, anyway. It would be different than sightseeing in Paris.

"Never mind." I scratched my nose. We were almost there, thank fuck.

"I like the idea, though." He nudged me with his shoulder. "I'd like to go somewhere that meant something to them next year."

I smiled and nodded with a dip of my chin. "Me, too."

It was finally our turn, and I paid for us before we were let in some narrow-as-hell spiral staircase. Jesus fuck, I could barely fit. A few inches narrower and it would be the same width as my shoulders. Everything was made of stone, and running was out of the question.

"You go first." I pressed myself against the wall so he could pass, which he did with a quizzical look. I smirked and shrugged. "I wanna enjoy the view." There weren't many windows, after all.

A claustrophobic person would freak.

"Casanova," he muttered.

I laughed, and it echoed. "Only for you, baby."

There. I had officially started giving him truths.

He didn't reply, but every now and then, he glanced back at me. I could see his mind was spinning.

As it turned out, climbing up to the dome of Sacré Coeur was a slow fucking process. The people in front of us evidently didn't exercise very often, and there was no place to stop. In fact, it got narrower and narrower the higher we got.

The last leg of the race, even I was getting winded, and it was nearly impossible to fit. Low ceiling, bad air, uneven steps, and everyone was exhausted. But we made it, and when we stepped outside and got the first glimpse of the view, I understood why tourists flooded the church.

I grinned, strangely happy despite the date.

The sun peered through the clouds as we entered the lookout area that surrounded the dome. An all-stone balcony embedded in the building gave us a 360-degree view of the city, and Julian's eyes lit up.

It was breathtaking, no lie. Both him and Paris.

As he snapped off a few photos with his phone, I walked up behind him and wrapped my arms around his middle. He only froze for a second, maybe getting used to my wanting to be close. Fuck, always close. I craved it.

We could see for miles, yet it was him I had my eyes on.

I recalled the day of the memorial service. He'd stepped out of the car a hot mess. Stricken by grief and despair. He'd been my nephew then, sort of. And if someone had told me I'd one day look at him and believe he had the most beautiful soul and was the sexiest person I'd ever seen…? I would have thought that person was high or off his goddamn rocker.

I pressed a kiss to his shoulder. "You make me happy, Julian."

"Um." He chuckled awkwardly. "I can feel that."

I smirked. Maybe I was sporting a semi. Not my fault.

"Not the happy I was talking about." I trailed more kisses along his neck and hairline.

He blew out a breath and turned around in my arms. Uncertainty was written all over him.

"Why are you telling me this, Noah?"

I brushed a lock of hair away from his forehead. "'Cause I want you to know." It angered me now, that I hadn't been more open to him before. He deserved it.

"I, uh…" He stumbled over his words, heat rising to his cheeks. "I think we're supposed to be able to see the Eiffel Tower from the other side."

I quirked half a smile and took a step back. The last thing I wanted was to freak him out, and he was clearly not ready to talk. I'd give it some time. An hour was good, right?

I was ready for any outcome, be it rejection or reciprocation. I could admit I felt it was leaning toward rejection from him. I needed to know, regardless. Otherwise, there'd be no moving forward.

We did get to see the Eiffel Tower on the other side of the dome, and I even got a tourist to take a photo of Julian and me together. I grinned and kissed his temple, and he was smiling and blushing and trying to look composed all at once. With the stunning view of Paris in the background, it became my new screensaver on my phone.

Julian gave me another quizzical look for that.

Eventually, we began the trek down again. Knowing we were about to go inside the church turned me into that masochist, and a blanket of melancholy covered me. In moments like these, I would've given anything to have my sister back. She'd been good at helping me decipher the shit tumbling around in my head.

There wasn't all that much left to decipher, though. It was just…messy.

The staircase that led down was as narrow and stifling as the one that we'd climbed, but going down was easier than up, and it didn't take nearly as long to reach the bottom again. Once there, we didn't say much. Julian lit up a cigarette, and I didn't comment.

It wasn't the time.

"I'll head in, okay?" I put my hands down in my pockets, and after his nod, I went inside the church. Despite the crowds of tourists, and despite having no real attachment to religion, it moved you. It was quiet and peaceful, candles lit everywhere, and worshipers filling the pews with their heads bowed.

No shit, my ma had shed a tear or two in here. She'd always been emotional.

My chest felt heavier.

I lit one of those damn candles, dropped a few Euros in a box, and then found an empty pew near the back.

Thoughts and emotions swam inside me, and I didn't know where to start. It was stupid. Did I speak to my folks? They couldn't fucking hear me.

Julian passed me, picking a pew closer to the altar.

I sighed and scrubbed a hand over my face, having no goddamn clue what to do here. I guessed I'd thought it would come naturally. I'd think back on some shit, tell my folks I missed them, and then be done.

An old lady behind me said something in Italian. I got the feeling she was talking to me, so I looked over my shoulder and told her I didn't understand. One of the two phrases I knew in

Italian, the other being a request for more beer.

She laughed softly, her eyes showing a youth her body didn't anymore. "Ah...*come se dice*...you, ah, tense?"

"Yeah, I guess you could say that," I admitted with a wry smirk. It fell pretty fast. "I don't know what I'm doing. I don't really pray."

No need to tell her I didn't believe in God.

"You let..." At a loss for words, she patted her chest—or heart. "It speaks. Someone will listen." She nodded firmly. "You...too young and handsome to be troubled. *Sí?*"

I chuckled quietly. "Maybe. *Sí, grazie.*" Someone would listen, eh?

She gave me another nod before she clasped her rosary beads and bowed her head to pray.

Rather than mirroring her move, I faced forward again and gazed up at the mural in the apse above the altar.

Someone will listen.

My gaze fell to my lap, and I frowned. Maybe the listener was me. Maybe apologizing to my family would help *me.* I'd never get answers from them, and I had to move on somehow. I couldn't carry the guilt anymore.

If my sister and the rest of my family *were* here, I would say I'd done everything in my power to...well, not to cross any lines with Julian. I had failed over and over but kept trying. Nothing worked, and it had gotten to the stage where he was worth everything.

He was more important than the risk of rejection, than the disappointment of my family.

I'm fucking sorry, guys.

I missed them. My vision became blurry, and I leaned forward and pressed the palms of my hands to my eyes.

I'm fucking sorry, but he comes first for me now.

I blew out a breath and rubbed my jaw, glancing over to where Julian was sitting. He was on the other side of the aisle, and I could only see a little bit of his face. I didn't know if he was upset or what he was thinking about.

That worried me more than whether or not my sister would've approved—eventually—of me being with Julian.

I had to believe she would, though. Like Tennyson said, it wouldn't have been easy. We probably would've argued a lot first, and maybe even had a falling out. But in the end…

It didn't really matter anymore.

I'd always miss our family, but it was time to take the next step. It'd been a long year. Grief, conflict, confusion, internal battles. I was tired of it.

Standing up, I quietly made my way out of the church. There was a sense of letting go; it was cathartic.

It was bizarre how different the atmosphere was right outside the doors. Upbeat tourists taking photos of everything, some having picnics on the steps.

I waited for Julian, and he didn't take very long. He was introspective, so I held back some. We began walking down the hill, not saying anything, and I took the opportunity to look around, imagining more spots my parents probably took photos of. When we got home, I'd have to check the memory chest. Their album would be there.

"Are you okay?" Julian asked, sending me a careful glance.

I said *fuck it* to myself and grabbed his hand, kissing the top of it before I threaded our fingers together. "Yeah. You?"

He nodded and looked down at our hands. "It was somewhat liberating. I got some thinking done."

"That's good. So did I." I descended another step and turned to him. It made him as tall as me, and I wanted him at eye level for this. "Have dinner with me tonight."

His brow knitted together, and he cocked his head. "Um, well, sure—"

"A date." I stepped closer and cupped his jaw. "I wanna take you out on a date, Julian. You and me."

His mouth formed an "o." He'd really had no idea. It made me feel worse than before.

Considering how little I had actually paid attention to his past, unless it revolved around his education and our family, I didn't know what he'd told himself about how I felt. That he'd only been a good fuck to me?

"What do you say?" I pressed my forehead to his. "Give me a

shot?"

He swallowed audibly and closed his eyes, but he wasn't shutting me out. His hands ghosted carefully along my sides. "Are you serious?" he asked quietly. "A date, even if I were to say I didn't want sex at the end of the night?"

Jesus fuck, I was no better than Nicky. Maybe I should blacklist myself from the industry as a punishment, too.

"Yeah. In fact, I'm ruling it out right now," I told him. Not able to help myself, I kissed his nose, then his eyelids. "I want a chance. I've been a dick. I should've been more open to you, too."

He frowned, though his eyes remained closed. "No… You haven't done anything wrong, but I had no idea—"

"Which is kinda fucked," I chuckled, my gut twisting. Shit, I was nervous. That was a first in…ages. "I've been fighting my feelings for you for months." That made his eyes fly open, but I wasn't done yet. "In retrospect, I should've given you more. It's all obvious in my head, yeah? Even Tennyson's noticed I can't keep my eyes off you. But I haven't told you shit, and I don't know how you've perceived things."

Julian cleared his throat and glanced to the side as a group of tourists passed us on the steps. It wasn't the best place to have this conversation, but whatever.

"I knew the terms," he murmured. "I'm an adult, Noah. You didn't owe me anything. You still don't."

Well, what-the-fuck-ever. We could debate this endlessly.

"Agree to disagree," I said. "But I *want*." I gripped his chin and kissed the corner of his mouth. "Fuck what's owed and not. I wanna do couple shit with you. You have no idea how much."

He let out a soft laugh and covered his face, and I knew incredulousness when I saw it. "God…" He shook his head and let his hands fall again, a wobbly smile in place. "*You* have no idea how much I've fantasized about you wanting more. This is nuts." He grinned crookedly, and I smiled back. "Especially recently—you've been so affectionate with me. That was very rough."

"It's outta my hands." I kissed him quickly to prove it. "I'm a strong motherfucker, but you've got me on my knees, kid. Figuratively speaking." For now, anyway. I wouldn't mind dropping in a literal way soon. "So is this a yes on the date?"

"I think quoting Ivy when she says *duh* is fair." He smiled softly, eyes closed once more, and slid his hands up my biceps. "This means I won't have to avoid you tomorrow to get another clean break, yes?"

"No more breaks." I slipped my hands down the back pockets of his jeans and gave his ass a squeeze. "No more one-time-only." This time, I kissed him for real. I went deep 'cause I needed it. I tasted him, teased his tongue with my own, and fucking basked in the moment.

Surely, nothing could come between us now. I was done denying, and Julian would open up to me in time, as he grew to trust me and so on. Telling his grandparents wouldn't be easy, but I hoped for the best.

"I've missed this," he sighed into the kiss.

"Me too, baby." I trailed kisses down his jaw, remembering that we were in an extremely public place. "Fuck, me too."

He cursed under his breath. "You know, room service for dinner doesn't sound bad. Then we wouldn't have to leave the bed."

I groaned a laugh and stole one more kiss. "Don't fucking tempt me. But no. Indulge me. I want—"

"The couple shit?" he quipped.

I inclined my head and smirked. "That's right. Besides, I thought we said no sex."

"*You* said that. I was being hypothetical."

Good to know. I gathered his hand in mine and pulled out my phone. "Dinner out. Then…yeah, like I could keep my mitts to myself at this point." Ridiculous. I found the number to our driver and pressed the phone to my ear. "I'll have you chained to my bed if it's up to me."

"Oh, kinky." He smiled. "Will I ever get to feel your fine butt, too? I prefer it when you top, but…you know…"

Fuck. For a beat, that had me anxious. I'd never fucking bottomed. But with patience and preparation—and maybe a shot of whiskey—of course I wanted that with Julian.

"I'm sorry," he said quickly, "I'm getting ahead of—"

"I'm all for equality." I winked. "Just be gentle with me."

His jaw dropped. "You're…you're…"

"Yeah, an ass virgin. I can be wild in the sack, but I'm not *that* experienced." That was when the driver answered, so I tuned out the sex talk and focused on getting us out of here.

Holy shit, I was stoked. If being with Julian before had offered an immense relief, besides the obvious one, it had nothing on this.

*

That night, I got exactly what I wanted. We found a bistro by the river and dined outside while the sun set. For the first time, everything was completely at ease and relaxed between us. I'd lowered my defenses and could tell him more about what this year had looked like in my noggin'.

We sat next to each other as I shared the conflict, the guilt, the mourning, how I'd fought my feelings and why. In return, Julian rolled his eyes and told me again he was an adult. I had no responsibility toward him, but I couldn't help that part. If we didn't protect family, what did we do? It was how I functioned, and thankfully he understood. Even so, he called me stubborn several times.

"I can relate on some level," he conceded as a waiter brought us new drinks. "I've dealt with the sense of…*wrongness*, I suppose, since I was sixteen and saw you in a very new light." He paused and dipped a piece of bread into his ratatouille. "But with everything else, I guess wanting more with you wasn't that much of an issue anymore."

It was the "everything else" I wanted to know. It was more than losing our family.

"I get it." I scooped up the last of my salmon and salad on my fork and crammed it into my mouth. "So the Nicky shit was an attempt to move on, right?"

"Well, yes." He shifted in his seat. That topic made him uncomfortable. "I made a mistake there." He cocked a brow and sent me a little smirk. "Not unlike you and all your one-night stands, I'm sure."

"Ouch," I coughed on a chuckle. "Touché." I shook my head and wiped my mouth. "I don't really remember it. Just going out to get wasted, and then… I drank even more when I couldn't get you out of my head."

"I'll take some weird pleasure in that," he told me with a grin. "I was so jealous."

I felt bad, 'cause I knew the feeling. "Ditto. Seeing you with that motherfucker… Christ, it made me boil." I took a sip of my beer. "While we're on that subject, I should probably tell you what happened the last day on the set in LA."

He rolled his eyes and sat back, full. "You mean when you threatened to blacklist him in the industry? He told me."

Ah, all right. "I followed through, too."

"You mean…"

I nodded. "Before our flight, I made some calls. It's not impossible for him to get work, but he can kiss the major studios goodbye." I wasn't even sorry. "He threatened me, Julian. I don't respond well to that. I want us to go out in public; case in point—" I waved a hand at where we were. "But it will always be on my terms—or ours, obviously. That cocky little prick needed to be taken down." Seeing he had food left, I pointed to his plate next to mine. "You gonna eat that?"

He shook his head in amusement. "Go ahead."

I fished out what was left of the lamb chop and dug in on the ratatouille and bread.

"I ended things with him, you know." He gave my thigh a squeeze. "That was why I showed up intoxicated at the LA wrap party. I called him to say I didn't want him in my life anymore, and he felt the need to tell me I was pathetic for pining after you. I suppose it struck a chord. Or eleven. So I had a few drinks."

Perhaps I'd call a couple more people to ensure Nicky would have the mother of struggles to get anywhere.

"For his sake, he better not show his mug around me again." I scooted my chair closer to his so I could kiss his cheek. I didn't know if all restaurant tables were tiny in Paris, or if it was just here outside, but it worked for me. I could stuff my face and be handsy at the same time. "Topic change? I wanna focus on us."

"I'm okay with that." He seemed to think it was funny how much I ate, though he couldn't be surprised. "This is certainly about us: do you think we can keep things professional around work and colleagues?" He bit his lip, appearing nervous. "You know I feel guilty about being your PA without even having applied for it, and adding romance to it…"

I understood that completely. Work was for work. It was how I wanted it, anyway. I couldn't afford distractions on set.

"Besides, I've been thinking," he went on. "At some point soon, I need to tell my grandparents I'm gay. I don't have to tell them we're doing *couple shit* if you're not comfortable; this is very new. But I have to be honest about who I am. I've hidden that for too long."

I took that as progress. "I'm with you every step, baby." Perhaps it meant he was ready to say why he'd felt the need to hide his sexuality. Aside from some slight apprehension around Tennyson and Sophie when they'd learned he was dating Nicky, Julian had acted pretty natural. As if he'd been out for a longer time. "You're prepared for them not approving of us, right?"

He nodded and looked down. "Yeah." When he faced me again, he wore half a smile. "It won't stop me, though."

Damn, that tugged at the heartstrings.

I swallowed and gripped his chin, quick to kiss him. "It wouldn't have stopped me, either." He needed to know this was big for me, as well. "I want this—you and me."

He nodded quickly and kissed me harder, and we spent the rest of the dinner being sickeningly lovey-dovey and talking about more sights we could see when we were off work.

It almost felt too good to be true.

CHAPTER 17

Two weeks later

"From the second mark!" Lucia hollered before turning to me. "We have approximately forty minutes before we lose too much light."

I nodded and turned, and Julian extended my little notebook and my coffee to me. "Okay, let's get crackin', then. Cheers, kid." I took a sip of my coffee, waiting for the actors to get back to their marks.

Sophie crossed the cobblestone street to the door that was supposed to lead to her apartment, and the two men playing her brother and ex—also the father of her son—took their marks on the curb.

Going through my notes, I frowned and wondered why I wasn't satisfied with the scene. Something was missing, and I didn't know what. I squinted over at Sophie. Brooklyn was doing a quick touch-up, and it hit me. Sophie wasn't looking unkempt enough.

We hadn't shot the scene that followed this one yet, so I could add changes. Walking over, I told them about my idea, and Brooklyn got started. Sophie suggested a tear in her dress, and I ran with that. Indecency wasn't the picture of good parenting, so a three-inch rip exposing more of her chest would sure as fuck work.

"Should I worry about the fact that you're undressing my wife, Noah?" Tennyson called from behind us.

"Yeah, I finally convinced her to run away with me," I said.

Lucia joined us, and I told her to tell the script supervisor about the change. While we spoke of continuity and additions, I overheard Sophie giggling about her not being my type. And it wasn't the first time I'd heard something similar and laden with innuendo since we'd arrived in Paris.

"You got somethin' to tell me, Sophie?"

"Hmm?" She grinned and exchanged one of those girly giggle expressions with Brooklyn. "I'm not sure what you're referring to."

"Cut the shit." I waited until Lucia had left, and then I sent Sophie a look to show I meant business.

She sighed. "Fine." She looked to be struggling pretty fucking hard to withhold her smile. "Rumor has it you're dating your former PA now."

"Rumor?" I rolled my eyes.

"One of my girls saw you." Brooklyn rushed out the words as if she couldn't bear keeping them in any longer. "You and Mike were kissing by the bathrooms at the bar."

Ri-fucking-diculous. "Well, gossip broads, do I got news for you." I draped my arms around their shoulders and huddled us closer. "Am I batting for the other team now? It would appear so. But the batting doesn't involve Michael, whatsoever. The kid kissed me, and then I went home with someone else."

Brooklyn furrowed her brow as she tried to figure it out, and Sophie looked to me expectantly.

Fuck that.

"Now, *back to work*," I said firmly. Turning around, I let out a sharp whistle that got every crewmember to pick up the fucking pace. This was a movie set, not a goddamn gossip factory.

Thankfully, even Sophie and Brooklyn took me seriously, and I returned to my monitor and put on my headphones.

"Any problems?" Tennyson asked.

I shook my head. "Not for me, anyway. You might wanna

prepare yourself for a shrieked 'you knew this all along and didn't tell me?' from that little ball of energy you married."

"Oh, joy." Tennyson chuckled. "So this means…?" He lifted a brow.

I glanced over at an oblivious Julian and stifled a grin. "Yeah. It's not official yet, though."

Tennyson smiled and nodded but didn't say anything, fully aware we were in the middle of work.

"Camera rolling!" Lucia called out.

I faced the monitor again, my gaze flicking between the screen and the actors. Then I called for action and concentrated on Joel, who played April's ex.

His despair was written all over him, and he visibly struggled to keep it together as he approached April by her door.

"Is—Is he up there?" he asked tightly. "I deserve to know, April. I'm his dad—" He swallowed hard, both angry and sad it had come to this. He was worried as fuck, having not seen his son in months. "We're here to help."

"You're lying," Sophie said flatly. "You want to take him away from me."

April's brother stepped closer. "You're not well, butterfly. Please let us take care of you. We love you so much."

"Cut!" I yelled. Goddammit, when Joel finally nailed his part, the other fucked up and acted with less emotion than a robot.

"I'll go talk to him," Lucia said.

Looking over my shoulder, I saw Tennyson walking toward my trailer. "You not sticking around, Wright?"

"Nope," he said with ease. "This was why I wanted you to direct, Noah. You know what you're doing, and we share the same vision."

I grinned to myself and returned to work.

*

I had a late dinner with Tennyson, Lucia, and Shawn that day, so it was nearing midnight when I finally dragged my tired ass back to the hotel. I expected to find Julian passed out in bed with Blue;

instead he was sitting by the desk, flipping through a notepad.

Damn, he was a sight for sore eyes. Seeing him brightened my mood regardless of how I was feeling.

"Hey, baby." I rolled my neck and removed my belt, looking forward to a shower. "I thought you'd be asleep."

He looked up from the desk and bit on a pen. "You gave me homework, Mr. Collins. Don't you remember?"

Well, fuck me.

I unbuttoned my jeans, looking him over. It wasn't until then I noticed he was dressed like a fucking schoolboy. Button-down, uniform jacket. A pair of glasses sat on the desk. I couldn't see what pants he wore, but I was itching to find out.

"Close your eyes and hold that thought," I told him. Suddenly I wasn't tired anymore, and I wanted to do this right. While his eyes were closed, I got a pair of dress pants and a nice shirt and tie from the closet. "I need a quick shower, all right? You can open your eyes when I've left the room." I grabbed shoes, too. It was all or nothing.

"Yes, sir," he said with a smile in his voice. "I'll finish my homework."

It was the fastest shower in history, and I fought a hard-on the entire time. I was getting used to that. We'd lived together for a year now, though it didn't hold a candle to sharing a suite with him when there was nothing to hold us back.

We hadn't had many opportunities to go out and see more of Paris together, but we'd sure as fuck taken advantage of our bed. Tonight, it looked like we'd get use of the desk.

After drying off, I put on the pants Sophie had bought me for the party in LA. I zipped up carefully and then buttoned my shirt. I tucked it in, went on with the tie, then put on my shoes. That'd do.

Time to see what homework I supposedly gave Julian.

I strode out of the bathroom with purpose, wanting him to get the full experience. No pussy-ass teacher here. I could be a strict motherfucker when the situation called for it.

Julian lost composure for a beat as he spotted me. Parted lips, eyes widening, and then a whispered curse as he dropped his gaze and became the student he wanted to be for tonight.

"All right, let's see what you've got, Mr. Hartley." I rolled up the sleeves of my shirt and came to his side of the desk. "You realize you have to impress me if you want me to change your grade, yes?"

"I, uh…yes. Um." He side-eyed me as I leaned back against the desk right next to him.

There was no way I'd let him get off with a cliché "I'll do whatever you want if you give me an A" fantasy. The power should be in the teacher's hands, yeah? Not the fucking student.

"They're, um, terms I heard at work." He tapped a finger on the piece of paper. "Instead of asking you what they mean, I researched and looked them up myself. But I didn't finish all of them."

I withheld a smile. It did things to me, that he was serious about learning the language we spoke on set. He could've gone with anything for this. Even though we'd joked about it, me giving him homework, it didn't really matter until now when I saw he actually meant it.

"I thought maybe you could test me?" he asked.

"Fair enough." I pushed off the desk and leaned over him a bit to see what he'd scribbled down. His breathing quickened, and I took longer than necessary to read his list. It was only the terms, not the meanings, so this should be fun. "Okay, start with the first one. Explain who the gaffer is."

*

"Excellent." I massaged his shoulders slowly, keeping him flustered. He was good, though. He'd done a great job at memorizing a shitload of terms, and we were already halfway down the list. "And the next one. If a director says broom it, what does he mean?"

Julian stuttered on a breath as I subtly pressed my erection against his back.

"It-It means he wants it—something removed from the set."

He was catching on. He'd noticed I rewarded correct answers with not-so-accidental touches. As for incorrect answers… I got stricter. I was catching on too, and it was clear he enjoyed a firm fucking hand.

"Very good." I stifled a groan as I eased away to give my cock a solid squeeze. If I didn't get out of these pants soon, I'd go postal. "If you know the next one, I'll be impressed."

"*Gone with the Wind* in the morning, *Dukes of Hazzard* after lunch" was the saying. Tennyson had quietly used the phrase on me last week as a reminder, and Julian must've overheard it.

"I know it, I know it," he promised. "Um. Fuck—"

"Watch your mouth." I grabbed a fistful of his hair and yanked his head back. He gasped, eyes growing large. "You do not curse in my office."

"Yes, sir."

I nodded and let go, and he struggled to remember the task at hand.

"The answer, Mr. Hartley. Don't waste my time."

"I'm sorry, I don't remember," he said quickly, a blush spreading across his cheeks. "Only that it was something about not spending too much time on…something…"

"I need more than that." I walked over to the seating area and grabbed the leather belt I'd worn all day. "If you know *anything* about film, it's self-explanatory."

The patronizing tone was evidently effective. It turned me on beyond belief to see him so worked up. It was as if he got really lost in the moment, and I liked it more than I could say. Fuck, imagine all the kinky fun we could have.

I returned to the desk, the belt in a firm grip, and I told him to stand up and put his hands on the tabletop.

"I don't have all day, little boy," I growled.

"Oh, fuck." He sucked in a breath and scrambled to obey me.

When I had him where I wanted him, I took a step back to watch him from behind. I stroked my cock through my pants, all the possibilities of where to take it from here rushing through my head.

"Push down your pants," I ordered.

"Um, but, sir—"

"Do it," I snapped. "I thought you came prepared, but you

don't seem to know very much."

"I'm sorry." He fidgeted with his zipper and trembled as he yanked his black pants past his delectable ass. "Is there anything I can do for you to forgive me?"

There it was. That line.

It wouldn't work with me.

How strict would I be if he could win me over with a blow job?

I don't think so, kid.

Leaning over him, I brushed a hand over his crack and spoke quietly in his ear. "You can give me the right fucking answer, Mr. Hartley." I rubbed and squeezed his ass cheeks, warming them up for his punishment. "You won't tell anyone about my…*unconventional* methods, will you? Hmm?"

"No, Mr. Collins," he breathed out. "I promise."

"Good boy." I backed off a bit and gave his ass a smack. He yelped then moaned, and I did it again. "Now, think back. What was going on when you heard that phrase? What were we doing, and so on."

He went on to ramble nervously about the filming, what scene we'd been shooting, and I took the opportunity to get the lube from the nightstand. Blue blinked sleepily, licked her paw, and then she was out again. Lazy little shit.

"Can I please have a hint, sir?"

I hummed. "It's going to cost you."

"Anything."

I stroked his ass and set down the lube in front of him. That had his attention…until I raised the belt and let it make a resounding impact on his left ass cheek.

"Oh my fuck, Noah!"

I nearly lost it right there. "What did you call me?" Needing to touch him, I let go of the belt and grabbed his hips, pulling him back to me. A few inches south, I found his cock smooth, hard, and leaking. "Jesus Christ, you're making a mess."

"I…I…God, I'm trying to remember…" He moaned as I scraped my teeth along his neck. "I want to be good, I promise."

He'd get his hint.

After I learned how fast I could turn his ass red.

I used both the belt and my hand, and every now and then, I reached around him to rub his cock and spread the pre-come up and down his shaft and balls. At one point, I almost stopped. His eyes were welling up, yet before I could worry myself to death, he choked out that he was close.

Holy fuck.

"I spent hours nitpicking over details in that first scene," I told him, kneeling behind him. I had maybe a couple minutes' worth of restraint left. Maybe. "Fuck…" I leaned in and licked him from his balls to his perfect little asshole. At the same time, a clear string of come landed on the floor. My mouth watered, and I was thankful when he remembered the answer.

"T-Tennyson warned you be-because—oh, shit—because if you kept fretting about minor details, you'd have to, um…" He hauled in a breath as I began tongue-fucking him slowly. "Oh… Um, you'd have less time with the following shot, and it would turn out, uh, not great."

Finally.

I stood up and uncapped the lube. "On your knees."

"Thank fuck, at last." He turned in a flash and sank to his knees, his fingers working my zipper until he could push down my pants. The second my cock was in his hand, he sucked me into his mouth, and we gave up on the charade.

"Perfect, baby," I groaned. "Hold out your hand."

He hummed around me as I poured some lube in his hand. Then I swiveled the chair around and sat down, perched on the edge so he had better access. He followed automatically, kneeling between my legs. His mouth went back to my cock, and he sucked me long and hard, as if he'd been deprived.

I wasn't near ready for his cock in my ass, but I'd grown addicted to his fingers. He stroked and rubbed and teased, and then slowly pushed one digit inside. It caused pulses of fluid to seep out of my dick, to which he moaned and swallowed around my head.

"Goddamn, I missed you today." I wove my fingers through his hair and fucked his mouth gently, keeping the same pace as him. "I almost bent you over the couch in my trailer at lunch." It stung in the best ways, and when he added the second finger, I gritted out a curse and shoved my cock down his throat. "F-Fuck!"

He choked and then breathed through his nose. Slowly pulling out, I felt his tongue swirl along the underside, tracing the vein.

"I wish you would have." He licked his way down and spent some time sucking and tonguing my sac. I was in fucking heaven. Two fingers inside me, one hand stroking me off, a perfect mouth on my balls. "You're so sexy when you're in the moment. I love watching you work, Noah."

I groaned, the heat rising, my chest expanding with every breath I managed to suck in. "I need your ass, Julian. Now."

Considering how fast he pulled out and bent over the desk, I figured he was more than ready for the same. I reached for the lube and slicked up my cock, and then I positioned myself behind him and, inch-by-inch, pushed my way in.

It wasn't until I was balls deep the frenzy settled slightly. My need to come was over-fucking-whelming, but simply being with him satisfied me for the moment.

I kissed his neck and stroked every inch of his body I could reach. Buttons were unbuttoned, and clothes fell to the floor. But even with his naked body pressed against mine, close wasn't close enough. I'd never fucking felt that way before.

"Gimme your mouth." I drew a shallow breath and cupped his cheek, and he turned his head to meet me in a kiss. "I'll never get enough of you."

He whimpered into the kiss, and his hand slid down my side, back to my ass. "Me neither—fuck, I…" He shivered. "Never."

With a firm hand on his hip, I drove in deeper and stroked his cock with my right. The kiss didn't break. It was sloppy, messy, needy as fuck—until it was just mouth on mouth and heavy breaths. The occasional nip, the occasional taste.

My body strained and burned.

"I'm so close," he groaned.

"Yeah." I gritted my teeth and sped up, chasing my orgasm.

He tried to say something, but no sound came out. Instead, he fell forward, his hands thudding against the desk, and a violent shudder made him quiver. Warm come filled my hand as he started coming, and I lost it right away, thankfully before he became too sensitive.

Sweet mother of...

I was exhausted.

A shiver traveled down my spine as my cock pulsed with the last drops. I felt feverish and sticky, but even as a blanket of perfect satisfaction covered me, the smell of us made me want more. The relief I'd initially felt with Julian was kinda constant now, but that heavy rush had been replaced with something much more intense.

Actually, it had been there a while. Now, it was only becoming a struggle to contain it.

"Shower and bed?" he croaked sleepily.

"Bath," I murmured. "I wanna feel you up and make sure I wasn't too rough earlier with the belt."

He laughed softly then winced when I drew out of him. "Noah, you made one of my biggest fantasies come true with that spanking. Hot damn."

I chuckled and pulled him close for a hug. "I'm thrilled to hear it."

He kissed my sternum and then smiled up at me, all sated and lazy. "You're the first I want to explore with. For real. I mean...some fantasies, you kind of need to trust the person."

He was the sweetest fucking man. He humbled me, too. And the thought of him with someone else now...?

I kissed his fingertips, then his forehead. "Thank fuck you're mine now. You've turned me into a possessive bastard."

"I sort of like that, though." He grabbed my hand and began walking us to the bathroom. "I suppose you'd be pleased to know your cock is still the only one I've sucked off."

I groaned and hugged him from behind. "Ridiculously pleased. I'm screwed in the head, but I don't give a shit."

He laughed and reached around me to pinch my ass. "It's all good. It's relaxing, in fact. Now I know I'm not the only one feeling irrational at times."

Yeah, this honesty was good for us. We should've done it sooner.

CHAPTER 18

We finished earlier on set the next day, so after dinner at the hotel with Julian and the crew I worked closest with, I grabbed some essentials I'd ordered. Then he and I got in a taxi to the Trocadéro, which was, in my opinion, the best place to see the Eiffel Tower.

The gardens spanned out over a hill that sat right in front of the tower, lawns on both sides of a spectacular and, of fucking course, phallic-shaped fountain. It was Europe.

"Are you going to tell me what's in the backpack?" Julian asked.

"Romantic shit." I smirked down at him and gave his hand a squeeze.

He chuckled and kissed my shoulder.

The steps were packed with tourists at the top of the hill, though the crowds thinned out a bit as we descended. Checking my watch, I saw we had just missed the hourly spectacle where the tower sparkled like the rock on some Hollywood diva's finger. We had time, however.

"Tired?" I murmured, catching him yawning.

I was running him ragged on set, but he took it like a champ, and he was good at what he did. When I didn't need him, he continued working closely with Tennyson, writing and composing, so Julian didn't get much more sleep than I did.

He smiled crookedly. "A little, but it's mostly a food coma."

Well, I had dessert covered when he was ready.

"That looks like a good spot." I jerked my chin toward an empty spot on the lawn.

It was Paris, so obviously we weren't the only couple around. Illegal street vendors sold roses and fake champagne, which said a lot about the tourists around us.

I sat down in the grass, and I made room for him to sit between my legs. He plopped down with a satisfied sigh, and maybe he'd spent too much time with Blue. He purred like a fucking cat as he leaned back against my chest.

"This is perfect." He took out his phone and snapped off a few photos of the massive tower, a couple of the fountain to our right, as if he wanted to get that over with.

I did the same so I could focus on him. Then I dug out a blanket from the bag and wrapped it around us. It kinda cocooned Julian, and he hummed in approval and cuddled closer.

"Have you always been a romantic?" he asked quietly.

"Hmm." I'd done plenty of romantic stuff for Emma. The few times I'd found myself in a relationship, no matter how brief, I did enjoy taking care of the other person. Even spoiling them to a degree. But I guessed with Julian, it was different. It was less for him and more for the both of us. "Yes and no, I suppose. You matter more." I pressed a kiss to the side of his head.

Julian shivered and tilted his head back to look up at me. It'd been a while since I saw so much uncertainty in his eyes, so that put a rock of unease in my gut.

"You okay?"

He bit his lip and sat up. "I feel like a damn fraud. I want to go all out with you, like you do with me, and not worry about anything…" He turned sideways so he could face me without it being uncomfortable on the slope of the hill. "I have this crap holding me back, so…perhaps it's time to rip off the Band-Aid. Because this is sort of killing me."

I held on to what he'd said about wanting to go all out with me. That kept me sane while he mulled over what he needed to say.

I assumed it was about his past.

"Whatever it is, it can't be that bad, baby."

The irony wasn't lost on me. I'd wanted him to open up for a long time, yet a selfish part of me now hoped we could've forgotten all about it and moved on.

"Some of it is. To me, anyway." He tugged on a lock of hair that had fallen down at eye level. "But you're actually right. I made things much worse than what they were—or are. I did this to myself, and I've paid for it."

I waited him out and placed two sodas next to us while he warred with himself. And that worked. The selfish side of me shut up. Once he'd gotten it all out, I could finally help him move past this. It was what it boiled down to. I didn't want him carrying that shit.

"I was bullied in school," he admitted. "Even before we moved to Germany. Classmates called me girly, and I didn't play sports like the other boys. And it continued when we moved, so in a way I believed there was something wrong with me."

That angered me. Bullying always had.

Knowing Julian, who never wanted to be in the way, he'd hid it from James and Mia.

"I was somewhat of a late bloomer," he went on, absently picking at the grass. "By the time I suspected I was gay, JJ was five or six. He ran to the TV when Dad watched soccer, he had the same hobbies the boys who used to bully me had, and Dad lit up every time JJ was in the same room."

That packed a punch. I remembered talking to James back in the day. He always worried about Julian fitting in.

Julian offered a weak smirk. "JJ was the junior. Dad's pride and joy. I was the older emo kid who only wanted to play piano."

I gave his hand a squeeze. "Please tell me you know James was proud of you, too."

He nodded and looked down. "Like I said, I did this to myself. I've spoken to Dr. Kendall about it, and she helped me understand. Dad didn't prefer JJ because he started playing soccer. He just related to it more than me and my music."

That made sense, though it didn't erase the hurt Julian had carried.

"I didn't give them enough credit." He swallowed and withdrew his hand from mine. "Mom and Dad showed up at every recital and every coffee shop I played in, but I already had that mind-set. I couldn't stop thinking there was something wrong with me, so I did my best to be as happy as JJ was. And Linda, eventually. I kept it to myself."

He reached for one of the sodas but didn't open it. Instead, he traced the bottle cap and looked way too uncomfortable for my liking.

"I had a boyfriend at uni, and we sort of lived together." He cleared his throat. "It wasn't my first, but it was the first who wanted us to be out. He was going through similar issues, but he'd been to a therapist and was ready to come clean to his folks. I wasn't. I kind of froze, and understandably, he broke up with me when I refused."

If my math was right, he'd been around eighteen or nineteen then. Another couple years to go before he went on antidepressants.

"I became a douche after that." He made a face. "I closed myself in even more, I got stoned a lot, I got a tattoo and expanded it pretty quickly, I got the piercing. I took up smoking, I was out every weekend, and I only did casual hookups." He winced. "I took a sabbatical, which worried Mom like crazy. Dad and I were arguing because…you know, he didn't like my double major. Studying music, he understood. Art, not so much. And he was pissed when I took a year off."

James would've understood today. In our industry, it blended together—art, music, film. He'd been a fretting parent. I'd already told Julian how my pop had reacted when I'd gone to study film. The old man had nearly shit a brick.

"Have you talked to Kendall about this, too?" I murmured.

"Yes." He nodded. "Dad was only worried. Of course, back then, it translated to he wasn't pleased with me and who I was. I was such a fuck-up."

"Hey." I tilted up his chin so he'd face me. "None of that.

You were a kid, Julian. Should you have opened up to your parents? Hell yeah. But you didn't keep anything to yourself out of spite or for shits and giggles. And parents fuck up all the time. Everyone makes mistakes. I bet there was some other approach they could've tried with you, but you all did that you could. Yeah?"

He blew out a heavy breath and looked down at the grass again. "I see that *now.* I only wish I could've seen it sooner."

Looking at him, I could tell he wasn't done. There was something else weighing down on him.

"Tell me?"

He nodded jerkily. "Yeah. Um. So I stopped living destructively in my last year. I was depressed, and I saw a therapist. It helped somewhat. I focused on school and gave everything to get good grades. I also started working up the courage to come out to Mom and Dad. I worried myself sick a few times and clammed up when I tried to tell them. So I promised myself, after graduation."

He never got the chance. He'd graduated in May, and our family had died in June.

Fuck.

"I was staying at Mom and Dad's when I heard about the crash." He paused, clearly in pain. He clutched his stomach, and his eyes brimmed with tears. It was fucking killing me. How bad could it be? "God, I hate myself." He covered his face with his hands, and I tensed up. "I swear I didn't mean it, Noah."

"Mean what? You gotta tell me, baby." I tried to draw him closer, but he wouldn't have that.

"I was relieved." He whimpered into his hands. "My first thought when I found out about the crash was that I didn't have to tell them anymore. I was relieved."

Jesus fucking Christ.

I couldn't explain the reaction I had to that. There was a shitstorm of emotions rushing through me. I was shocked, but then it made sense. I was sad for him. I understood him. I was relieved to have it all out there. I felt horrible he'd carried this for over a year, and I'd been bitching about my attraction to him.

"Come here." This time, I didn't take no for an answer. I

pulled him close to me and wrapped my arms around him.

"I didn't mean it," he croaked. "It was only a second. I'm so fucking sorry, Noah—"

"Shhh." I pressed my lips to the top of his head and gave him a tight squeeze. "I know, Julian. Trust me, I know."

I released a heavy breath, slowly swaying him. It was soothing, and I needed a minute to get my act together. We could go on forever and carry guilt we shouldn't. Hell, I was feeling guilty as fuck for not making him tell me sooner. But that implied he wasn't an adult who could make his own decisions.

It was what it was. All we could do was take it from here.

"I saw it on the news," I murmured into his hair. "I was in the private lounge at the airport in Santa Monica. I'd just landed, and Tennyson and Daniel were trying to get to me before I learned about the crash from somewhere else." The memories of that day were fuzzy at best, but I couldn't forget my initial reaction. "I laughed, Julian."

He sniffled and stilled. "Wh-what?"

"It was too much to process," I answered. "I sat at some bar and saw the footage from Florida on the news. And I laughed."

Julian didn't say anything for a while, and that was okay with me. As long as he didn't pull away, he could be quiet all damn night if he wanted.

A low murmur traveled through the gardens as the Eiffel Tower began sparkling with millions of flashing lights. The blanket had fallen off my shoulders at some point, so I grabbed it and fanned it out over Julian's and my legs.

"You're not upset with me?" There was nervousness in his tone, his voice soft but scratchy from crying. "I would understand if you are."

"I have no reason to be upset with you." I leaned back, my hands supporting my weight on the lawn. "Are you pissed 'cause I laughed?"

"Of course not. It's actually quite common to laugh instead of cry when you've lost someone."

"I know." I smiled and kissed the top of his head again. "And considering you spent years hiding a part of you, it's no surprise your mind went there first."

He turned his head and buried his face against my chest. "You sound like Dr. Kendall."

I chuckled quietly. "Don't tell her that. She'd be offended."

"No way." He tilted his head and sent me a brief smile.

Seeing his face, I stroked his cheek and brushed away the last remnants of tears. "Beautiful." I dipped down and kissed his forehead. "I'm glad you told me everything, Julian."

He sighed and closed his eyes. "I feel weird about it. I still beat myself up over it, but I've been told it can take a while to condition a new behavior." He extended a hand over my leg and uncapped his soda. "I honestly thought you were going to be angry with me. And this last month…you've been so fucking nice and affectionate…"

I could fill in the blanks. I'd tried to get closer to him, and he'd been thinking, *"If only you knew the truth."* No wonder he'd been a skittish animal. But I did know the truth. I knew a shitload about Julian, and this didn't change anything. Not negatively, anyway.

"Noah?" He raised himself up a bit and faced me.

I leaned forward and playfully nipped at his nose. "What's up?"

He smiled and shook his head. "I love you. That's what's up."

"*Jesus.*" I choked. I hadn't expected that right at this moment. I'd kinda known it was around the corner… But fuck me sideways, he was hitting the feels with that one. "Come here, baby." I yanked him closer and kissed him hard. Knowing he felt the same was in-fucking-describable. A rush more intense than I'd experienced before. "I love you, too. Like you wouldn't fucking believe."

Julian moaned something unintelligible into the kiss and locked his arms behind my neck.

CHAPTER 19

Two weeks later

"Cut!" I barked out. Turning to my script supervisor, I removed my headphones and asked what'd gotten her fucking panties in a twist.

"I went through the footage of the scene this leads up to, and we need to change the order of the canvases," she replied in a rush.

I glanced across the street where Sophie and the man playing April's brother were holding three large canvases, which April had painted for her son. Each one had a theme. In toned-down graffiti, using muted colors instead of flashy neons, April told her stories topic by topic. Love. Betrayal. The future. Dreams. Lies. Conspiracies…

Her misguided legacy.

"What're you waiting for?" I asked. The clock was ticking.

While the script supervisor scurried off to correct the error, I spoke to Lucia about her taking a second unit to do flyover coverage next week. I'd work almost exclusively with April's brother and ex, so it should be a quiet one, and I could manage without Lucia.

"Noah!" I heard Tennyson call.

"Yeah?" I turned around and saw him by the trailers. "What's up?"

"I need a minute of your time."

Had to be serious for him to interrupt shooting, so I made my way over, and he opened the door to the trailer Sophie used.

"I got off the phone with Asher a little while ago." He headed to the seating nook and adjusted a laptop so I could see the screen. "The West Coast is up, and this is spreading like wildfire."

I scanned the headline of a gossip site, my chest tightening with anger.

"Director of Sophie Pierce's new movie finds love with his nephew!"

"Oh, fuck." I drew a hand over my hair and pulled out my phone. "I can't believe this. We gotta call it a day to do damage control." As my blood started to boil, I texted Julian to get his ass in here. "Mother*fucking…*" My jaw tensed, and I nearly hurled the phone at the nearest wall.

This could set Julian off. He hadn't told his grandparents. He and I weren't even official yet, having decided to tell our closest once filming was over.

"It'll be okay, Noah." Tennyson gave my shoulder a squeeze. "We'll take a couple days off to get to the bottom of this. It reeks of insider gig."

"What do you mean?" I muttered, my jaw clenching at the thought of a particular motherfucker who could've given out information to the press.

"We haven't created any buzz for this project." He bent over the laptop and more articles about Julian and me popped up. "I want to sell the film at Sundance or in Cannes, so location sites and dates haven't leaked out. Finding Sophie isn't very difficult; there're vultures everywhere. But…" He glanced over with a cocked brow.

I nodded. Our sets had been clear of press, which limited the options of knowing who the fucking director of her new movie was. Industry folk always knew more. Between studios and various companies involved in filmmaking, the chatter was constant, though it tended to stay internal. Unless it was intentional to leak the information or if it was a huge scandal involving a star.

Then there were supposed friends. Or ex-boyfriends…

Even so… "I'm not famous enough for this," I told him. "I'm of no public interest whatsoever."

That was why Julian and I hadn't hesitated to roam freely in Paris. Nobody gave a fuck.

"You are now." He flipped to a page where a series of photos of Julian and me were revealed. "First of all, congratulations." He smiled wryly, with a spark of genuine amusement in his eyes. "You two are clearly in love."

I cocked my head, studying the photos. Somewhat grainy but clear enough. They were all taken a few days ago. Julian and I had had dinner at another bistro, and we'd sat outside. The photos showed laughs, us sitting close, hand-holding, a few kisses… The last one was of me ushering him into a taxi.

If not so much was at stake, I could've laughed it off or said I didn't care. And we did look all cheesy and lovey-dovey together. But I didn't know how Julian would react, and this wasn't good publicity for the film.

In print, my relationship with Julian looked bad. Ignorant fuckers would see incest or an older man taking advantage of a much younger one. I wasn't even fucking old, but forty-one against twenty-four could be portrayed as a fuckload.

"This can ruin things, Tennyson." I had to put that out there, 'cause he was too chill about it. Maybe it hadn't occurred to him, though that didn't make any sense. "There are scandals and there are scandals. This ain't the kind that will drive more people to see the film."

"Oh, screw that." He slid into the booth and took a sip of his coffee. "Worst-case scenario, we keep a low profile and wait for the next season. Either way, I don't believe this will affect the film much at all. Perhaps in the next few weeks or so, but Hollywood forgets quickly."

There was a knock on the door, and I let Julian in as a wave of nausea came over me.

"I'll give you some privacy, and then we'll talk back at the hotel," Tennyson said.

*

It was getting ridiculous.

Julian had been staring at the laptop for half an eternity.

Or ten minutes.

He went from article to article and read the gossip about us. I hadn't even read the bullshit. It was probably lies, anyway.

"It says you seduced your nephew," he mumbled. "You took advantage of my grief after our family died to get me into bed."

I sighed heavily and sat down across from him. "I don't care about any of that. I'm only concerned about how you feel."

He made a face and went to another gossip site. "Basically, I am a weak child who can't stand up for myself, and you're a perverted uncle preying on me. Wonderful." He shook his head, finally facing me. "You're waiting for me to freak out."

"Your grandparents…"

"I know." He swallowed and averted his eyes to the screen. "This isn't how I would've wanted them to find out, and it's not like I can jump on the next flight to go see them. We have another month here."

"You can do whatever you want," I told him gently. "Family comes first—"

"You come first for me." His tone was soft, but he held my stare firmly and didn't break away. "I'm not sure you've realized that yet."

Maybe I hadn't. It was difficult to embrace, difficult to understand I was so important to someone else.

For this conversation, I felt it was best to start over. I got up and joined him on his side of the booth instead, and I cupped his cheeks and rested my forehead to his.

"Tell me what you want."

He scowled, though he didn't withdraw. "No… It's what *we* want."

He had a point. It was about us. But even so, they weren't my grandparents. They were his.

"I get that, baby. I do. And maybe I even needed the reminder." I brushed some hair away from his forehead. "It's not my grandmother and grandfather, though. So what I'm saying is, I'll be with you every step of the way, but you gotta tell me how you wanna play this."

His brows knitted together, and he looked down as he thought about it. "Like I said, I—*we*...can't be on the next flight to Pittsburgh. So I don't know. As long as we deal with things together, we'll work it out."

I nodded. "Together."

He quirked a grin and kissed me quickly. "Admit you thought I was going to have a meltdown."

"Perhaps..." I let out a small laugh, more relieved than I could say. "I've never had so much to lose as I do now."

This time, he kissed me deeper and lingered. I cupped his cheek and stroked the tip of his tongue with mine, knowing this could get outta hand too fast. I'd been fucking worried, and now when I could relax, I wanted to maul him.

"You know who did this, right?" He climbed onto my lap and straddled me, his piano fingers scratching my scalp as he kissed me harder. "Or maybe I'm assuming too much."

"No, I have a pretty good idea. I'm sure you do, too." Fuck holding back, fuck timing. I pushed him down on my cock and didn't protest what-so-fucking-ever when he began undoing my belt. He made me lose my head every goddamn time. "We gotta tell our closest today. Tennyson wants to talk when we get back to the hotel."

"Okay." He swallowed nervously, and I was quick to derail his thoughts. "Um..." He grunted as I released his cock from his pants and stroked him firmly. "What—what should we do about Nicky if it is him?"

That one was easy.

"I'll fucking bury him."

*

That night, Julian and I made our way to Tennyson and Sophie's suite. It was on the same floor, and we passed Sophie's PA along the way, who was taking the kids for ice cream.

I'd barely knocked when Tennyson opened the door, looking tired but wearing the same wry smile that was practically his trademark expression.

"Come on in, you two." He opened it wider and stepped aside. "Apologies in advance for my feisty little wife. She's just learned I've known about you a while."

I smirked and squeezed his shoulder. "I bet the sex will be fucking spectacular, though."

He winked.

Passing him, I grabbed Julian's hand and aimed for the seating area in the living room. Sophie was on one of the couches with a tablet, looking freshly showered in a robe and damp hair. Tennyson said she was catching up on the recent gossip about us.

She didn't even look up until we'd sat down on the couch across from her and Tennyson's. She eyed our clasped hands and huffed.

"I still can't believe you didn't tell me," she muttered to Tennyson.

He smiled and placed an arm around her. "You would've done the same thing, princess. Don't even try to deny it."

She scowled but didn't say anything.

"I put him in that spot, hon," I told her patiently. "If you wanna be mad at someone, aim it at me. Not at him." I glanced at Tennyson. "If it weren't for that bastard, I would've lost my marbles once or twice too many."

Julian gave my hand a gentle squeeze.

Tennyson inclined his head at me, a mere acknowledgment. For being assertive and quite fucking arrogant about his profession—as he should be—he was ridiculously humble off the set. He didn't take praise very well.

"I mean it, man."

He furrowed his brow. "I didn't do that much."

I sighed and slid my gaze to Sophie. "Peg him or something."

Tennyson laughed, and it became impossible for Sophie to stay *huffy*. She hid a grin behind the lapel of her robe and rolled her eyes. I could tell she had a lot more to say, but hopefully, she knew this wasn't the time.

"So…we gonna talk about this media shitshow now?" I placed my arms along the back of the couch. I needed physical contact though, so it didn't take too long before one of my hands found Julian's neck. "Based on how tired you look, Wright—no offense—I'm guessing you've been on the phone nonstop since we left the set." I absently rubbed the back of Julian's neck and played with the soft curls of his hair. "Who's in the loop?"

"The world?" Sophie quirked a brow.

I chuckled. *Touché*. Bad wording.

"I've made a…*few* calls today, I suppose." Tennyson sat forward and rested his elbows on his knees. "The good news is that this will die down fast. Asher's people have dug around a bit, and it appears we're looking at a single source who won't say anything else."

Julian and I exchanged a quick glance before he cleared his throat and faced Tennyson.

"We believe it's Nicky who's behind this," he said quietly.

"Your ex?" Sophie tilted her head.

I gnashed my teeth together.

Julian nodded. "Yes. Noah and I talked earlier, and it's the only possibility, we think. He knew the location, when we'd be here, who we are, and so on. He's also bitter about losing a chance at getting further in the industry."

I took it from there and explained to Tennyson and Sophie about some of the things that had gone down with Nicky. The motive was sure as fuck there, and they could see that, even before I'd finished telling them how Nicky had threatened to expose us.

Tennyson cleared his throat when I'd finished. "So, legal actions—"

"Fuck that," I said. There wasn't a whole lot we could do, anyway. "I've already had his name blacklisted at major studios. By the time I'm through, he'll be lucky to get hired as a fluffer."

"Déjà vu." Sophie grinned and nudged Tennyson.

I remembered. One of my old roommates had been hooked on Sophie before she and Tennyson got together. Then things had blown up a bit, and Tennyson had threatened to destroy the guy's career in physical therapy so he would end up giving massages to porn stars in the Valley or some such shit.

I'd been wasted that night, but witnessing Tennyson Wright go from stoic and chill to seething and feral was an unforgettable sight.

"That little fucker had it coming," he muttered. "Though, I never had to make good on my threats. This Nicky appears to be a whole other matter." He slid his gaze our way. "Leave it to Asher, and consider Nicky finished in this industry."

I inclined my head, thankful. "We'll do some digging first, in case, but we're pretty sure already."

Who else could it be? We couldn't completely rule out random strangers; weird crap made people bitter and jealous. Then, they'd have to have had access to information in order to reveal so much. Julian had shown me some of it since I hadn't bothered to read the specifics earlier, and not many "sources" could say he and I had been seen kissing after a birthday party in LA.

What we did know was that Nicky knew the driver who'd taken us home that night we'd been so careless.

"By the way, if Asher gets a script delivered with a pizza, tell him the script's a waste of time," I said. That oughta teach the driver to keep his mouth shut and respect others' privacy.

Tennyson frowned. "Okay…?"

"Long story." I waved it off. "Work-wise, how will we deal with publicity for the film?"

He was quick to move on. "I've spoken to a few publicists, Sophie's included, and they're all in agreement on ignoring this. It'll blow over, and I'm not submitting the film to Cannes until the deadline in March next year." That was good to hear. A fuckload of gossip would circulate in Hollywood in the next eight months. "Now, if we get selected by the committee," he went on, "Sage suggests doing a subtle interview." He spoke of Sophie's publicist, one of the fiercest and most experienced in the industry. "She said it was a non-issue and prattled on about a piece on unconventional love in Hollywood."

"A highlight to remind people it should be celebrated," Sophie chimed in. "That way, it could silence the most critical bastards before they've even opened their mouths."

"And we'd be able to enjoy Cannes without anything hanging over our heads," Tennyson finished.

I nodded slowly, internally adding it'd be easier to sell the film to a major studio if Hollywood didn't see me as a fucking pervert.

Defending myself for who I was with didn't sit right with me, but I'd get over it. That was how things worked in the industry. If you were famous enough, privacy wasn't cheap.

Maybe Sophie took my silence for something negative, 'cause she spoke again. "Don't worry, Sage's discreet. You know that. Tennyson had her on speaker before, so I heard her saying she could add lots of couples. The focus wouldn't be only on you. She's creative as hell."

"Nah, it's fine," I assured her. "Small price to pay. I appreciate you both for this." I pressed a kiss to Julian's temple. "What do you think?"

"No objection here." He shifted in his seat and squeezed my leg. "I'm not familiar with how Hollywood works yet, but one interview doesn't sound too terrifying."

I slanted a grin, knowing he was probably a little overwhelmed. We'd work it all out, though. Besides, he was undoubtedly more worried about his grandparents than the rest of the world.

Frankly, so was I.

We'd already decided it was best to contact James's parents over the phone—soon. We didn't have any other option, really. We couldn't leave the set.

"Are we done talking about this now?" Sophie looked to all of us. "I've barely been able to process this. Seriously, Noah…you're in *love*. I've never, ever seen you this way. I should've known sooner. I mean, come on! I called it from the first time we had dinner when Julian had moved out to LA. Remember I texted you?" I laughed, remembering very well. She'd said we'd been very aware of each other. "This needs to be celebrated—as soon as you're both off my shit list, of course."

"Don't ask." Tennyson smirked.

I stupidly ignored that and lifted a brow at Sophie.

She huffed, since she was good at that. "Well, for one, I'm

selfishly annoyed because you didn't tell me sooner—Shut up, honey." She threw Tennyson a *look*. "I know, I know. It's big, they had to work things out, blah-blah, I *get* it. Hence, selfishly. *Jeesh*." She blew out a breath and Tennyson and Julian chuckled. "And, secondly, Noah and Julian are on my shit list because I'm not the reason my trailer smelled like sex earlier."

"Oh my God." Julian buried his face in his hands.

Tennyson grinned, and I winced before amusement took over.

CHAPTER 20

When Julian and I returned to our suite, I could tell he was anxious.

"It's late…" He scratched his head and walked toward the bedroom.

Checking my watch, I saw it was past midnight. I followed him and silently helped him remove the bedspread. I didn't wanna push him; however, if he wanted his grandparents to learn about us from him, he couldn't wait forever. James's folks were hardly gossip readers, though that wouldn't stop younger generations in their lives from finding out and telling them.

I gave Julian some time while we changed into sweats and brushed our teeth, but it was becoming clear he wanted to avoid the phone call today.

"I'm so tired." He left the bathroom, and so did I after turning off the light. "We should get some sleep."

"Julian."

He didn't face me. Instead, he adjusted his pillow and pretended to be busy with setting his alarm. As if we didn't have the day off tomorrow.

"You should call them, baby," I reminded gently.

"Like I said, it's late—"

"Not back home."

This time, he turned to me. Had this not been so serious, I would've cracked a grin at his look of frustration and annoyance. It was cute.

"Come here." I walked over to him and cupped his face. "I know it's hard, and there's a chance they won't approve. Unfortunately, our hands are tied. It's either finding out from you, or from the press."

He swallowed hard and looked down, and I kissed him on the forehead.

"I have a feeling I know the answer to this, but do you want me to call 'em?" I'd be happy to; I'd rather take the brunt of any amount of anger. But to confirm my thoughts, he shook his head. "I figured." I kissed him again. "I'll be here, though. You can put them on speaker. I'll do my best to shut up."

A promise I could keep unless things got ugly.

"You're right," he sighed. "I've postponed enough in my life. I have to stop being a chickenshit."

I didn't like how far he went with that, but his determined expression made it clear he wouldn't listen. The guy was on a mission now, and he gave me a quick kiss before he retrieved his phone and started pacing by the foot of the bed.

A moment later, he put the call on speaker, and I heard the dial tone.

It put a rock in my gut.

"Hartley residence, to whom am I speaking?" It was Trudy who answered.

"Hi, Grandma. It's me—Julian."

I sat down on the edge of the bed, near where he stood. His voice had faltered a bit, and I realized it was easier said than done to be a bystander. I wanted to protect him from everything, even though that would do him no good.

There was a pause before Trudy spoke in a careful tone. "Oh…hello, dear."

Fuck, they knew.

I scrubbed a hand over my beard and made sure I looked confident when Julian threw me a nervous glance. I gave him a nod; he could do this.

"I, uh—" He cleared his throat. "I-I take it good news travel fast?"

Reaching over, I tugged him closer to me. The distance was fucking unbearable.

"So, it's true? It can't be." Trudy almost sounded like she was pleading. That couldn't be good. "He's your *uncle*, Julian. I can't believe he'd take advantage of you in such a way—" She cut off as she got emotional, and I clenched my jaw, steeling myself. "When the girls at the club told me at lunch, I refused to believe it. I thought he was a good man."

Julian looked panicked. "Grandma, that's not—"

"I don't want to hear you defending him," she said abruptly. "I know how these things work. Predators play mind games." Holy fuck, that was a punch in the gut. *Predator?* "You came to him for support and understanding because your grandfather and I clearly failed you after James died. That's on us." She sniffled. "We are so very sorry, darling. And I want you to listen to me now. Come home. We will get this sorted. We'll get you help—"

"That's enough!" Julian had evidently built up some anger. Meanwhile, I felt sick. "I don't need *help*. I love Noah. Stop thinking I'm some gullible prey, for the love of God. I'm a grown man!"

There was silence on the other end, and Julian stepped between my legs and placed a hand on my cheek.

"This is serious," he told her, holding my stare firmly. "I apologize for the way you found out, but I wasn't hiding this because I was ashamed. It's just new. We weren't ready to go public." When I tried to avert my gaze, he didn't let me. The little fucker. He knew I'd taken a hit, I guessed. "You should look up the photos of us that've been published. Only an idiot would say it's anything but real."

"You don't understand, Julian," Trudy exclaimed. "He can make you believe it's genuine!"

"That's fucking insulting," he snapped. The fire in his eyes even took me off guard. "What's next? Are you going to say he tricked me into thinking I'm gay, too?"

"Hardly," she replied stiffly. "This may come as a surprise to you, but we know you. We've suspected that for years."

That made Julian pause. He opened and closed his mouth a few times before asking, "Who's we?"

"Your family, of course." Trudy sniffed. "Your parents, me, your grandfather. Do you remember us, the ones who actually want what's best for you?"

I managed to push aside my own crap, and I tilted my head to kiss Julian's palm. This was a good thing. His eyes brimmed with tears, 'cause he was fucking relieved. James and Mia had known—or suspected—and the world hadn't come to an end. They hadn't stopped loving him. They'd accepted him.

It was something I'd known all along—that they wouldn't have loved him any less for being gay—but I understood the desire to have it confirmed.

"Noah's who's best for me," Julian whispered. He leaned down and pressed his forehead to mine. His eyes fell closed, and he grinned to himself. It made it all worth it. "I'm sorry you feel this way, Grandma. I'm sorry you think poorly of a man who's basically saved me." When he opened his eyes, I mouthed an *I love you* to him. His smile grew. "Should I assume Grandpa feels the way you do?"

"He's furious with both of you," Trudy answered irritably. "I'm afraid I must be strict here. We love you with all our hearts, Julian. We'll forgive you if you choose to come home. But you're not welcome as long as you let that man manipulate you—"

Julian hung up the phone and threw it somewhere behind me. Before I could open my mouth to speak, he dipped down and kissed me hard.

"I don't care," he muttered. "I don't care."

He did. So did I, but if he needed…this, whatever it was he wanted right now, I'd give it.

"She's wrong." He pushed me back and climbed on top. My mind was fucked, and I couldn't really keep up. I let him lead. I'd get there eventually. I hoped.

We lost our clothes and ended up in the middle of the bed. While he mumbled about not giving a fuck, I struggled to process the phone call.

"She hurt you." He left a trail of kisses along my chest as he tried to get me hard. I was a red-blooded male with a hot-as-fuck man on top of me; it wouldn't take forever. But my priority was his well-being.

"I'll get over it," I said, pushing myself up on my elbows as he went south. "I didn't expect her to call me a manipulative predator—that's all." I grunted the second he sucked me into his mouth. "*Jesus*. Shouldn't we talk about this, baby?"

He shook his head, his warm, wet tongue swirling around me.

I gave him an exasperated look. Fuck if what he was doing to me wasn't making my mind fuzzy. *Focus*. "This is a big deal. You gotta be upset."

He released me and used his hand instead, my cock thickening and growing harder against my will. "Not at the moment. I will probably fret like I usually do tomorrow, but not right now. I will not let her venom ruin my night. She's so wrong about you—about *us*."

That much was true. I knew that. I wasn't a fucking predator. I'd fought my feelings too goddamn long. James's mother wasn't gonna cheapen anything about our relationship.

"Momentary lapse," I said. Then I cursed. He'd gotten me hard enough to deep throat me. "I'm already feeling better. Much…much better…*fuck*."

My turn to make *him* feel better.

*

I was alone in bed the morning after, not counting Blue. I could hear Julian in the other room. It sounded like he was on the phone, and he was laughing. I got up, took a piss, and pulled on my sweats, then joined him in the living room.

"That's what I was thinking," he told whomever he was on the phone with. His smile was weird. Almost sinister lookin'. "No, you were right. I should have listened to you. I was nothing to him."

I frowned.

His words confused me, and so did seeing him holding my phone close to the one he was speaking into.

As he spotted me, he winked. Which I'd never seen him do before.

"I don't care about the money," he replied. "I want him to suffer for hurting me."

My brows rose, and to me, he mouthed, "Nicky."

Jesus fuckin' Christ.

My legs carried me over to him without me really noticing until I was inches away. Julian tilted my phone so I could see the display, and I saw he was recording. Holy fuck, he was playing Nicky to get a confession. At least that's what I presumed.

"Actually, we don't have to meet up when I get back to LA," Julian told Nicky. "The real reason I called was to get you to tell me you were the one who told the media about us."

I automatically leaned closer to hear Nicky's response.

It was quiet a beat, aside from his breathing, and then I heard him bite out, "You're *kidding*, right?"

I grinned. Fuck if I wasn't proud as hell of Julian. And maybe a little turned on. My boy was devious.

"Afraid not, and now we know the truth," Julian said.

"Don't tell him about any plans," I whispered.

We didn't wanna risk anything. Nicky would always know who buried him, but there'd be no proof. Though, judging by Julian's expression, he was well aware and didn't need my reminder.

"This isn't over," Nicky gritted out.

"That's where you're wrong." Julian toyed with the drawstrings of my sweats. "It's very over. Anyway, I have to go. Noah sends his absolute best. Take care, Nick." With that, he hung up the phone and ended the recording.

"Have I told you lately that I love you?" I put my hands on his hips and captured his mouth in a kiss.

He laughed softly and tossed our phones on one of the couches. "Not today."

"Well… I love you." I teased his bottom lip with a playful bite. "How did you think of this?"

"It was bugging me most of the night," he admitted.

"Eventually, I gave up on sleep, and I plotted and fretted a few hours." He slid his hands up my biceps. "I figured it was safest to paint myself as some victim. Everyone else seems to think that's my thing." He was clearly not too thrilled about that. "So I called him and thanked him for leaking things to the press. Because it showed me your true colors, and you'd decided I wasn't worth the hassle."

"Liking this less and less," I muttered.

He chuckled and rolled his eyes. "I know that's not the case, doofus. But it worked on him. At first, he didn't want to admit anything, but when I mentioned making you suffer, he confessed pretty quickly and even told me some bullshit story about it being for my benefit."

I sighed and yanked him in for a tight hug. At least we had that outta the way now. Tennyson could give Asher the green light to ruin any opportunities Nicky could have in the industry.

"How're you feeling about last night?" I murmured.

Blue chose that moment to circle our legs, which we knew meant she wanted food.

"I'm not sure yet." Julian kissed my neck and pulled away a bit. "It stings—a lot—but I won't let anything stand in our way now. I want us to be open. No more worrying about what others think."

I touched his cheek. "Sounds perfect to me. Bet you're relieved to hear about Mia and James, though."

He smiled and ducked his head. "Yeah. God, I was such a moron."

"Hey." I lifted his chin. "Everyone's got insecurities and fears."

Losing him had turned into my biggest fear. Having him was terrifying and elating and powerful all at once, something I'd probably never get used to.

"I love you." He nipped at my finger.

"Ditto." I took a step back while he picked up Blue. "Wanna go out and get some breakfast? I'm starving."

"Yes, definitely." He smiled and nuzzled Blue's fur. "Oh, can we go to that place with the awesome hot chocolate?"

"Of course." As long as I could get coffee, I was game.

*

Regardless of how focused we were at work, film sets were a place one always made new buddies. Julian had made a few, and I'd gotten even closer with my AD and DP. People were curious and had texted us a fair bit since the gossip broke, and we used the breakfast to send brief confirmations saying yeah, we were a couple.

We'd remain discreet on set, obviously, just no more hiding.

"Brook's filled in the girls in wardrobe and makeup," I said, pocketing my phone. "That's a relief. Those broads can talk." And it was better if they had the correct information.

I sat back and crammed the last of my croissant into my mouth. Julian, who claimed I was a messy eater, smirked and dusted some flakes off my shirt.

"I half expected reporters to come at us," he confessed.

"Nah. Had we been at home, then yeah." Traveling to Paris didn't come that cheap, though. I wasn't even on the radar in French media, and they'd only send paparazzi overseas or from the UK if I'd been more famous. "Like Tennyson said, it'll blow over fast—"

"Uh-oh." Julian was staring at his phone. "Sophie's PA texted me this." He showed me the display, and at first, I didn't know what I was looking at. It'd been ages since I was on Twitter. "Your ex made a comment on Twitter, and Sophie responded."

"That fuckin' cunt." Emma's involvement was the last goddamn thing I needed. I should've seen this coming. "Can I see what Emma wrote? Sophie had to have been enraged if she got in the middle of it."

Because of Sophie's past as a teenage diva, she'd learned her lesson and kept a low profile these days. She didn't even use her official Twitter much. Her PA and publicist handled that.

Julian handed me his phone, and there was Emma's message with a link to one of the countless articles about him and me.

This explains so much. No wonder I couldn't save our

relationship.

I rolled my eyes.

Was she fucking serious?

She didn't have any particular status in Hollywood, but thanks to Sophie's response, each comment was going viral. There were a few, evidently.

"Where's Sophie's reply?" I asked. As soon as the words left me, I found the link, and I laughed.

Followed the link, surprised to see it wasn't a story about you cheating your ass off on the guy you wanted a ring from.

"There's more." Julian updated Emma's page.

One other person doesn't equal 'cheating my ass off.' I guess he lied to you too! #notevenagoodactress

"Mother of Christ, she just admitted the infidelity to hundreds of thousands of people." I shook my head. "I swear she wasn't always so fucking stupid."

Sophie's only response to that was *"Good grief."* Now everything was getting screencapped and retweeted by her fanbase.

"I have a feeling Emma will regret this later." Julian made a face. "It's probably wrong that I enjoyed this. It angers me that she hurt you, though. Plus—jealousy is a nasty bitch."

I chuckled and turned my baseball cap around so the brim wouldn't be in the way when I kissed him. "What do you have to be jealous for, huh?"

"It's irrational, I know." He twisted my nipple and leaned closer, resting his head on my shoulder. "You settled down with her. We'll have that too, right?"

That right there went straight to the heart. "Un-fucking-doubtedly." I gripped his chin and kissed him. "You wanna get a house together?"

I'd come a long way, hadn't I? It was amusing now. When I left Mendocino, I'd sworn, never again. Now, here I was. Everything was different with Julian.

"I love the loft."

I hummed, leaving a slow trail of kisses along his jaw. "We're not getting rid of it. We could always get a second place, though. Maybe a beach house?"

Having access to a pool where I could stare at Julian doing laps was appealing as fuck.

It kinda spiraled from there. Barbecues, runs along the beach, sunsets, poker nights—a new place to fill with memories that were only ours.

Fuckin' hell, I had it bad.

"I really like the sound of that," he murmured.

"Me too." What I didn't like was the sound of my phone going off. "What now?"

Julian's vibrated at the same time, so we checked our messages.

I had one from Sophie, a miles-long apology about not thinking before speaking. Or Tweeting, rather. She was apologizing for revealing Emma's infidelity on Twitter without permission, and now she was feeling awful. Truth be told, I hadn't given it a single thought.

"I got a text from Lucy." Julian snickered, referring to Sophie's PA. "Emma deleted her comments about you. But you know, once it's on the internet…"

I grinned faintly and replied to Sophie.

Don't worry about it, hon. I appreciate it, but I really don't care anymore. Emma's in the past. You did good. ;)

This time, I turned the phone off. "How about we take a lazy day at the hotel?" I suggested. "We could burn some calories in bed, order room service, and forget phones exist."

Julian practically purred with approval. "I only need to meet up with Tennyson first. We have some lyrics to discuss."

I huffed. "And I take it the fucking director's still not important enough to be there for those meetings?"

I was only half teasing. I *was* curious as fuck about what they were working on together, and the score would play a big part once we reached post-production. But I supposed I could wait, and I knew it mattered a lot to Julian to do this independently. He wanted to prove himself.

"Pretty much." He smirked and tucked thirty Euros under the basket where the croissants had been. "Race ya back to the hotel?"

I barked out a laugh. "Oh, you're on, kid."

CHAPTER 21

Two weeks later

"What time is it?" I asked.

The script supervisor was closest, and she told me we were breaking for dinner soon. A very, very late one. Apparently it was already nine PM. We'd been at it all day, same two scenes, and this would hopefully be the last angle I needed.

"Thanks." Heading up the stairs in the narrow apartment building where Sophie's character lived, I joined her and Brooklyn on the landing. "Why you lookin' mopey, Brook?"

She shrugged, finishing the final touch-up on Sophie. "Miss my girls. I can't wait for them to visit this weekend." She side-eyed me. "Why you lookin' frazzled, Collins?"

I checked my watch. "Because…Julian's grandparents should have received the tickets now."

I'd sent them with a simple note. *"Please give us a chance. It's family. Nothing to lose, everything to gain."* Other than that, the address to our hotel, and I'd let them know I'd make reservations for them, too. If they agreed to come next week.

"Have you told Julian yet?" Sophie asked quietly, knowing

Julian was downstairs with the rest of the crew. I merely shook my head no. "*Noah.*"

"You two weren't supposed to know, either." It was most likely my weakest defense ever. Christ, it was bad. I didn't wanna get Julian's hopes up in case the Hartleys didn't show, which was a big possibility.

The only reason Sophie and Brooklyn knew was 'cause they'd walked in on me in my trailer when I'd ordered the tickets.

My initial thought had been that it could be some big, romantic gesture, but I'd gotten over that. I should've told him before I even went online to find flights.

"Anyway, we ready?" I asked.

Brooklyn nodded and stepped back with her makeup case. At the same time, an assistant arrived with Little Paul, who played April's son, and his adult stand-in was done for the day. The rest of the actors got into position halfway up the stairs, too.

"You ready, little man?" I squeezed Paul's shoulder gently.

He grinned and nodded. "Aye, aye, captain."

Lucia hollered for everyone who had no business on set to get the fuck out, leaving only the actors, me, herself, and Paul. He was operating one camera, and I was doing the other.

"Want me to take it from here, boss?" Lucia asked. I nodded as I adjusted the dolly on which the camera stood. "Roll cameras!"

Through the lens, I had Sophie huddling in the corner with Little Paul. Both looked frightened, and they clung to each other as April's family climbed the stairs.

"Action!"

"Get away from us!" Sophie shrieked.

Little Paul buried his face against Sophie's neck and started crying. In the previous scenes, the future star had managed to produce real tears, but I knew he was drained.

April's brother reached them first, quickly followed by Joel, the kid's dad. I zoomed out to make room in the frame, and I was impressed by the intensity in Joel's eyes. Relieved to see his boy, livid at April, torn because he knew she was ill, and beyond exhausted.

"This ends now," he choked out as he made a grab for Little

Paul. "We don't want to take him away from you, but you leave us no damn choice, April!"

"Dad, no!" Paul screamed. "Mommy says you're bad!"

April's ex, as well as her parents who stood farther down, broke at that.

It was April's brother who took charge and managed to wrench the boy away from a sobbing Sophie. Mayhem followed where she tried to get her son back, and Joel got in her face, yelling about how much she'd hurt the family. She was unfit to see it, though. She saw only her own world.

I couldn't help but grin. All these visions flooded my mind. I pictured how it would look on the screen later, the scene slowing down and music taking over. I zoomed in on Joel's hands as he grabbed her by her waist, holding her back. She thrashed and screamed, all while April's parents pleaded for her to see reason.

"Cut!" I yelled.

In the next scene, a doctor would arrive, and they'd have to sedate April. It was a rush. We had plenty of scenes to go, but this was one of the last ones that would be shown in the film, and I was definitely satisfied.

*

"What do you think?" Tennyson asked.

I groaned and scrubbed a hand over my face. "Why now, Wright? Jesus Christ." It looked good. The printouts on the table in my trailer looked *good*. But we already had a location here in Paris where we were supposed to shoot the epilogue.

"Tiff stumbled across it." He spoke of our location scout. "You know why I'm showing them to you."

Of course I did. It was only an adjustment I had to do up in the noggin'. We had three days booked in a psych ward, and so I had the images of that room, that atmosphere, etched in my head. But yeah, the facility Tiff had found in Nice fit my previous mental image. We wouldn't even have to do much with the room.

"They have an art studio, too."

"I give." I threw up my hands. "Have Tiff send a video or

some panoramas."

"I already did." He smirked. "Should be done tomorrow or the day after. You go back to the hotel and get some rest. It's…" He checked his watch. "Almost four in the morning."

"What about you?" Part of me was worried about facing Julian, so maybe I was stalling. "If you need any help, I'll be happy to—"

"Brooklyn ratted you out earlier," he said wryly. "Go talk to Julian."

"Goddammit," I muttered. Well, if he was asleep, I'd wait, anyway. "All right, see ya tomorrow."

I made my way out of the trailer, nodded at security and the lingering crewmembers, and strolled toward the nearest main street where I could catch a cab. My phone burned in my pocket, having been too silent all fucking day.

So far, no response from the Hartleys.

I couldn't say I regretted sending them the tickets, but what the fuck had I been thinking? I should've cleared it with Julian.

Once in a cab toward the hotel, I cringed at the memory of us saying we were finally being open and honest—no more hiding whatsoever. Granted, we'd been talking about the outside world. Being out and open around others. Then, starting that chapter by keeping this from him…?

I hoped he'd see my intentions. Actually, I knew he would—eventually. Despite that, he had every right to be pissed.

Twenty minutes later, I entered the fancy lobby and took the elevator to my floor. I was surrounded by mirrors, and I removed my cap and ran a hand through my hair. I needed to trim my beard. I looked ragged as fuck, but my eyes… I chuckled and shook my head.

Since beginning my relationship with Julian, I was undoubtedly more alive. I guessed it was happiness I saw staring back at me. And some chickenshit nerves for fessing up.

Keycard ready, I exited the elevator and headed toward my suite. Julian was guaranteed to be asleep, so I was looking forward to a quick shower before crashing next to him.

I'd fess up tomorrow.

*

I woke up slowly, vaguely aware of Julian's hands rubbing my back. I groaned sleepily. It felt so fucking good, though I wasn't ready to leave sleep behind.

"Turn around," he told me quietly.

"Mmmmph..." It was like I'd gained a ton overnight. Rolling over took way too much energy. "It can't be time for work already, can it?"

"No." He kissed my chest lazily. I kept my eyes closed, my mind foggy with sleep, though my hands trailed up his naked body. "You rest."

I hummed, relaxing. His slow kisses and touches lulled me back to sleep, and I only roused here and there when he stroked my cock. It was the perfect morning. Perfect way to wake up.

At some point, I felt his fingers wrap around my wrists. I frowned as a dream had a decent grasp on me. Sophie and Joel were practicing lines—I knew it was a dream—and why couldn't I move my hands?

Then my cock was engulfed in warm and wet, and Sophie and Joel were gone. The dream faded, and with it, the cobwebs of sleep. A husky moan slipped through my lips. Julian was everywhere. I didn't have to tell him to get lube; he nudged my legs farther apart and began teasing me with a coated finger.

In a reflex move, I shifted to scrub my hands down my face, and I found myself stuck. It caused me to open my eyes pretty damn quick, and I furrowed my brow and blinked drowsily.

"The fuck?" I was tied. Literally. He'd used two of my ties to restrain my hands to the bed frame. "I usually prefer coffee before I get kinky. Wha's goin' on, baby?"

"You can be quiet now." Julian seemed driven by something. Whatever it was, it made him steelier, more determined, and...feral? It was too early to read into things.

"All right." I gave the restraints a few tugs. He'd done a good job. I wasn't going anywhere. "I'm your willing captive."

He snorted and smirked darkly, though he didn't answer. There was tension. It confused me a bit, but then his magic fucking fingers made me incoherent. Bending down between my parted thighs, he swallowed me down and pushed two digits into my ass.

I groaned, my head falling back on the pillow again. Fuck, it burned good. The third finger even more so, and I let everything go. He was clearly in charge this morning. No complaints from me.

My abs tensed as he twisted his fingers to reach my prostate. I bucked my hips involuntarily. When I asked for more, he *shushed* me. Which was… Sexy. As. Fuck.

I flushed with heat. My head swam, images swirling, thoughts giving me questions. Would he make me beg? I could probably be down with that. It would be new.

"*Fuck.*" I shuddered, clenching around his fingers. Arousal seeped out of my cock, and excitement tore through me in quick bursts of fire.

He got into a rhythm that had me fucking spellbound. I started panting. Gripping my restraints, I used them as leverage as I met Julian's thrusts. My balls ached, my muscles strained, and whenever I got close, he stopped.

Like now.

"Julian!" I growled.

He wore that dark smile as he withdrew and reached for the lube. "I made a decision earlier." Seeing him slicking up his cock was both confusing and making my mouth water. It was unbelievably hot, but why would he…? "Don't worry," he said and leveled me with a stare, "I'll consult with you afterward."

"Wh…" *Oh, fuck.* The memories came rushing back.

Julian inched closer and rubbed the head of his dick against my ass.

"You know."

He nodded. "I received a text when I woke up: 'Be sure to tell your uncle we are certainly not accepting his tickets or his invitation to visit you in France.'"

Fuck, fuck, fuck.

Despite the fact that my hands were tied, I could stop him. His gaze was almost more difficult to break, and I broke neither. I stared back, strangely turned on by the fire in his eyes that was no doubt sparked by anger.

"I'm sorr—"

"Shut up, Noah." Leaning over me, he positioned himself and gave a small thrust.

My jaw tensed. His face was close to mine, and I could tell he was searching for my reactions. I sucked in a breath through clenched teeth as he slowly pushed in.

Holy fuck, this would take some getting used to. I did my best to push back and relax, and he decided to rip off the Band-Aid and bury himself completely.

"Oh, damn," he moaned. As his forehead hit my shoulder, I closed my eyes and breathed through the burn. "Fucking *hell*, love."

Hearing his voice dripping with pleasure and hunger ignited a different kind of fire. His hot breath hit my neck in quick puffs, and it sent shudders through me. I needed to be able to touch him.

"Untie me," I gritted out.

He was quick to lift his head, eyes widened with worry. "A-Are you okay?"

"I'm fine." I kissed him chastely. "But I want my hands free."

His anger was gone for the moment. He reached for my left wrist and untied it swiftly, then went for the right.

Once I was free, I slid my hands down his back until I could grab his ass. Hard. And pull him deeper inside me. His eyes grew large once again, and it was easier to swallow the pain this time. Julian shuddered, his cheeks flushing with desire.

Good fucking God, he was stunning. I brushed away a lock of his hair. The anger remained distant, so maybe he was saving it for later. Maybe he'd momentarily forgotten it. Either way, he had run out of his will to be in charge, too. So it was up to me.

"Fuck me." I tilted my head and kissed him deeply. "Go ahead, baby. I want it." And I did. The burn was fading, leaving more room for pleasure. It felt better taking the lead, too.

Topping and bottoming had shit-all to do with who fucked whom. It was about this. Me taking decision-making away from him in moments that were only ours. Him giving it away, trusting me enough to let me decide for him.

Keeping one hand firmly on his ass, I used the other to stroke his cheek. He searched my eyes for a brief moment, and at my nod, he began moving once more. He inched out slowly, then pushed in. I groaned as the pain mingled with the intense bliss, and then I sighed into a kiss as he wrapped his fingers around my cock.

It didn't take him long to get me hard again.

Given that he was already losing himself in me, I put all my focus on him. I tasted him on my tongue, grabbed at him, stroked every inch I could reach, met his thrusts, and didn't give a flying fuck about chasing my own orgasm. It was secondary.

He gasped and started fucking me harder. "I want to make you—"

"No." I grunted and took away his hand from my cock. "You can give me your sweet mouth later." *After I'm off your shit list.* "Let me watch you."

He let out a moan, pressing his forehead gently to mine. And I watched. My hands wandered his lithe body, feeling his tight muscles flexing beneath his smooth skin. I memorized his reactions. Almost as if he were in pain, every time he slammed into me, his face contorted with restraint and concentration.

The lust and love swam in his eyes. It was fucking electric.

"You're there, baby," I murmured. "Give me everything."

He hissed a curse, rammed in a last time, and scrunched his face as he came.

"I love you." I kissed his cheeks, his nose, and his eyelids. He shuddered, riding out his orgasm. "Sometimes I can't fucking believe how beautiful you are."

"Oh God, Noah…" He collapsed on top of me, panting and shivering.

I hummed and pressed my lips to his damp skin. Wherever I drew my fingers, goose bumps rose. His weight on me always felt good. A perfect fit. And I was fucked for life. Getting this sappy was another new experience, though it only made me grin now.

Eventually, Julian regained his breath and pulled out of me, only to roll over next to me instead. I winced at the soreness, but it felt oddly hot, too. Add an orgasm and I'd grow to want him to fuck me plenty.

"Are you all right?" he asked softly.

I nodded and turned my head to him. "More than." I gazed at

him, wondering if we were both waiting for the moment to pass so we could discuss the point he sure as hell made. "For the record, I'm on board with you taking my ass." I cracked half a smirk to test his mood.

He narrowed his eyes, irritated but not doing very well to hide his amusement, small as it may be.

I sobered. "I'm really sorry, Julian. I wanted to help." He hadn't been totally emo or anything since his grandparents spoke their piece, but there had definitely been moments of sadness. "I hated seeing you upset, so I reached out in an attempt to fix things."

"I know." He was clearly still bugged, but I took comfort in him shifting closer and using my shoulder as a pillow. "I know *you.* But you should have told me."

"I won't make this mistake again, I promise." I was such a shit. I couldn't contain my smile.

He saw it and scowled. "Do you think this is funny?"

"No!" Except, that made me grin wider. "Fuck, I'm sorry. I'm so goddamn sorry, but I love this. Our first fight?" I shrugged, feeling like an idiot. "Maybe it's stupid, but it means something to me."

He stared at me for the longest time, and then he sighed and scooted even closer, close enough to kiss me. "You jerk," he murmured. "You romantic, goddamn jerk." The corner of his eyes crinkled, and there was tenderness in his gaze. "As long as you will do your best not to pull a stunt like this again… It hurt getting that text this morning."

"You have my word." I held him to me and drew the duvet over us. "I'm sorry, sweetheart."

"Water under the bridge," he replied. "You had my happiness in mind. That matters."

I breathed a sigh of relief and shifted a bit, though that made me wince again. He'd really gone to town on my ass. "Next time you fuck me, I need wining and dining first."

Of course, Julian being Julian, he didn't see the humor and went straight to worry. "Are you hurt?"

"*No.*" I chuckled and gave him a hard smooch. "You and I

both know I could've stopped you. I wanted this, and I'll want it again. With a side of whiskey and a blow job."

That finally earned me a smile. "I can help you with one of those right now."

CHAPTER 22

A few days later, I got a weird phone call right before my lunch break was over, and I was having one of those days. My second unit was off shooting, a few crewmembers were down with food poisoning, I had to have another budget meeting with Tennyson later, and adding another distraction was too much.

I told Lucia to take over until I returned, and then I jogged over to Sophie's trailer. She didn't have a scene today; we were shooting with Joel and the others, but she liked being on set. Said it helped her stay focused.

She opened the door after I'd knocked twice, and I wasn't surprised to find her with a script in hand.

"Hey, you. What's up?" She smiled, and Kayden popped his head in the doorway and waved.

"Hey, kid." I smirked and jerked my chin at him, then faced Sophie again. "I just got a call from your publicist."

"Oh?" Sophie frowned.

"Yeah, she said the interviewer was on her way with a photographer." I cocked a brow. "From back home, Wright. They're flying them out."

That only happened to the A-listers, and that was aside from the whole question of…what the fuck was a reporter coming for?

Obviously to interview me and Julian, but we weren't supposed to do that until later—*if* the film was accepted at Cannes.

"That's so strange," Sophie said and gestured for me to come in. "Maybe there was a misunderstanding? I'll give her a call."

"Okay, thanks." I climbed the two steps and entered her trailer, only to have a little hurricane called Ivy crash into me. "Hey there, sunshine."

"Hi, Uncle Director!"

I laughed and picked her up. "Uncle Director, huh? I kinda dig that."

She shrugged, her grin not totally unlike Tennyson's wry one. "Daddy says you're a—um, he used a bad word and great director and Julian is Uncle Piano Man 'cuz Daddy says he is great at that and—"

"And you need to *breathe*, Ivy," I chuckled.

"Oh." She giggled.

Sophie's assistant came over to us at that point and lured Ivy and Kayden away for snacks and a movie back at the hotel.

It wasn't long after that Sophie reemerged from her bedroom with her phone in hand and an apologetic look on her face.

I folded my arms over my chest. "Mix-up?"

"Yeah…" She smiled sheepishly. "Sage's going all out. National magazine, huge spread, seven couples. You and Julian are one of them. The good news is it's for the December issue, so there's time if you want to back out." She paused. "If not, a journalist and a crew will be here the day after tomorrow."

It didn't seem like a smart idea to back out if we'd eventually need some kind of publicity anyway; I just had to talk shit over with Julian first.

"It's a casual interview, Noah." She appeared to believe I was worried about being interviewed. Or maybe exposing Julian…? "This is a highlight, with a focus on your relationship. There won't be any interest in digging for sensitive information, and if there's any question you're not comfortable answering, you simply decline."

She was cute when she was being all reassuring and motherly. I grinned and kissed the top of her head. "I've been interviewed before, babe. Lemme talk to Julian and then I'll get back to you." I took a step back, and she nodded. "You know anything about the other couples?"

"Some from the music business, some from our industry." She shrugged. "I think one couple is polyamorous. One producer is into BDSM, and she's being interviewed with her submissive husband or something."

Unconventional love, eh?

"All right." I ran a hand over my head and scratched my neck. "For now, I gotta get back to work."

*

Julian was nervous, though he agreed to the interview without much hesitation, so two days after my talk to Sophie, he and I found ourselves at another hotel in Paris. The hotel's own bar, to be exact, and it had been cleared out for the interview.

The stylist wanted me in a suit, which wasn't me. I compromised and agreed to some designer slacks and a fitted pullover. Julian, on the other hand, looked like sex in dress pants, a snug shirt, and a skinny tie. The photographer tested the lighting as I stuck my feet into polished shoes and a makeup artist finished with the powder.

"I'd expected an interview over email or Skype," Julian admitted.

I smirked, and the stylist returned to me with a fancy watch. There was nothing wrong with my own, but product placement was a thing.

"If there hadn't been a photo shoot, it probably would've been," I said.

We were shown to the booth where we were supposed to sit, and the rustic feel of the place was hardly a coincidence. It looked almost like a British pub, and I supposed it set a more masculine tone.

I sat down, placing an arm along the back of the booth, and Julian got comfortable next to me. We'd talked about this all morning. I was somewhat familiar with this part of the job. It had taken some coaching from Sophie—who was a pro—for Julian to know a bit more of what to expect.

Felicity, the journalist, knew what she was doing. As she took her seat across from us, an assistant brought us beers and snacks, and Felicity eased into a casual chat about Paris and the filming. It was evident her goal was to relax Julian, and it was working.

She hit the jackpot by mentioning museums. It got Julian going, and the interview as well the photo shoot began without him even knowing it. If the recorder on the table hadn't been on, I barely would've known, either.

"You're in the city of love," Felicity said with a smile. "Have you had any spare time in between filming for romance?"

I smiled and took a sip of my beer while Julian launched into the story of when we visited Sacré Coeur.

*

Our time together in Paris was easy to cover without many questions. It was memory after memory. Once we were past that, though, Julian took the back seat when Felicity asked about our family.

She cleared her throat and glanced briefly at her little notepad. "Noah, what was your first impression of Julian? He and his father came into your sister's life, and they quickly became a family. Were you ever the overprotective brother?" She winked.

Subtle way to put it out there that Julian and I weren't related. It made me grin.

"Mia would've checked my privilege pretty fucking fast if I'd tried," I chuckled. "Besides, she was always a responsible girl. The few guys she brought home before she met James and Julian were good to her." I sent Julian a sideways grin. "First time I met Julian, he didn't say much. Shy and sweet, I'd say."

Julian's mouth quirked up a little. "You were loud and way too cheerful."

That made me laugh, a bit wistful. They were hardly days I missed, yet…being surrounded by family and Ma's cooking… "I was a starving bastard who didn't know how to cook. Not that I could afford much more than ramen at that time. Visiting home meant a mountain of food."

"Did you get to see each other often back then?" Felicity asked next.

I shook my head. "Unlike piano wonderboy here, I didn't have any superior talent to show off when I moved to LA. I studied and worked my ass off, and I was lucky if I saw my family once or twice a year." I smiled faintly at one memory in particular. "Right before my sister moved to Germany, I had to skip a reunion because I'd just gotten the job on my first film set. I was stoked. Then it turned out my only job was to clean up after the crew had lunch."

I remembered being bitter about that one for a while. Not anymore, though. A bunch of those shitty gigs had contributed to the man I was today.

*

Felicity derailed us with more casual conversation while the photographer got his moment to take shots when we were relaxed and just chatting. I had to admit I preferred this to posing.

"How long until you return home?" she asked.

"Ten days or so?" Julian looked to me for confirmation.

I nodded and threw back a handful of peanuts. "Yeah, then we're wrapping up the last scenes in LA."

Julian's eyes lit up. "After that, we finally get to post-production."

I knew he was itching to show me what he'd written, as well as the few songs they'd recorded already. I smiled and pressed a kiss to his temple, enjoying his excitement. The photographer enjoyed it for other reasons.

"You look happy, Noah," Felicity noted with a soft grin.

"Hell yeah." I leaned back again, comfortable. Maybe this interview wasn't that bad. "My work's always been my passion, and I've never been able to really share it with someone."

My not-so-subtle *fuck off* to Emma. She hadn't been on my radar in ages; then the social-media war with Sophie had irritated me.

"It's equally refreshing and amazing to see someone so dedicated," I went on. "I learned that fast about Julian. I admire hard work, and he gives everything. I've lost count of the nights he stayed up to tinker with the piano in the living room."

"That's right, you've lived together a while…?" Felicity looked to both of us, and I let Julian take that one.

"Yes." He nodded. "After we lost our family, I didn't know where to go. Germany wasn't home anymore, and staying in Pittsburgh held no appeal. So I bought a plane ticket and flew out to Noah."

"He dragged me out of purgatory." I stroked his neck absently, thinking back on those awful fucking days. "I wasn't dealing with the grief very well. Having him around made me wanna move forward again."

Julian sent me a shy smirk. "That was mutual."

Felicity evidently found that sweet, and her eyes shone as she drained the last of her wine. "Well. You guys are clearly on a mission to give me cavities." She shook her head and released a breath, then glanced at her notepad. "Never mind, my question isn't on there." She grinned and faced us again. "You obviously found support in each other. You knew what the other was going through." We agreed with that. "That must've had an impact on how you felt, right? I can't even imagine the loss, and to have one person who knew exactly what it was like…"

"It definitely made things easier," I replied. Then I went on to explain the bond we kinda created and how it confused me for a long goddamn time. Attraction came later. It was that connection to Julian I'd never been able to shake. The one I fought for so long because of our…*other* ties.

Julian spoke of my struggles, too. The withdrawing, the avoiding, the denial. I could tell he wanted to clear my name, so I took over after a while. Aside from the grief and worrying we'd been relying on each other for the wrong reasons, today I mostly chalked it up to social norms. Our relationship wasn't *normal* in that sense, and despite how open-minded I considered myself, I supposed it was impossible to remain completely unaffected by what society dictated.

Being accepted mattered.

Felicity's personal opinions shone through here and there. She shook her head at people who couldn't mind their own business and felt the need to spread hate. From a young age, we were encouraged to follow our own paths and be ourselves. Which was pretty fucking difficult when one kept being knocked down for doing just that.

"I'm not sure most people see it," Julian said pensively. "We aren't mindful enough."

"Agreed." I inclined my head and reached for my beer. "We forget how powerful words are and how long they'll follow us."

Childhood bullying was a great example. In Julian's case, it had made him feel like there was something wrong with him. That shit was hard to shake.

"Exactly," Felicity agreed. "Plus, we tend to dismiss or even fear the unknown."

I smirked and tipped my glass at her. "The unconventional."

"There it is," she chuckled. "And here you two are now. You both gave in at some point. That must've been a relief."

"Indescribable." Julian squeezed my leg under the table.

Perhaps Sage or Sophie had given Felicity a heads-up about not asking further, ignoring the topic of what our remaining family felt toward us, because she left the present and the future alone.

"Last question." Felicity smiled. "Does love conquer all?"

I laughed under my breath and exchanged a sideways glance with Julian. I nodded to him, 'cause he may call me romantic, but he was better with words than I was.

"No," he answered, facing Felicity, "but I believe it gives us what we need in order to fight."

Perfect.

*

A lot of things were perfect lately. With the publicity and gossip out of sight and out of mind, we dove back into work. We wrapped Little Paul's last scene, and a few days after, it was time for Sophie's character's family to finish. It was hectic, and Julian and I had little time together. At the same time, having him on set made all the difference.

I craved those brief moments. Whether I turned to see him waiting with my coffee or he was sitting on a crate nibbling on a pen and working on his songs, it reenergized me to see him. We were on the same page; I wasn't losing myself in work while he was merely waiting for me to get off. He was just as devoted.

I may have asked the guy who was documenting the project to take shots of Julian so I could have them developed.

Same went for everyone else I cared for. They weren't merely friends to us. We were surrounded by family, and I wanted moments captured. Brooklyn, always attached to her sponges and brushes. Tennyson, bothering with a shitload of paperwork to pull through something he believed in. Sophie, who'd earned her stardom in front of the camera. Asher, when he visited with his and Brooklyn's daughters.

Daniel and Zane were supposed to visit too, but one day they got the call they'd been waiting for. Then they packed their bags and flew off to adopt a boy and his baby sister.

On the flight to southern France, we celebrated them as best as we could. Sophie, Brooklyn, and I got some online shopping done. They covered the baby shit, and I focused on the daddies-to-be.

"I think they need a flat screen in the bathroom," I said, scratching my nose. "That way, they won't miss out on games during bath time."

Brilliant, I reckoned.

In the meantime, Julian put his headphones on and tinkered with an app where he could compose. He mentioned a lullaby, which I thought was sweet as fuck. Lastly, Tennyson made some calls to hire a party planner for a welcome-to-parenthood shindig when we all got home. Sophie had wanted to do it, but she'd go overboard.

"You know what this means, right?" Sophie, seated behind me, tapped a pen on my head. "You and Julian are next."

I laughed, side-eyeing Julian to make sure he hadn't heard.

Except, he had. He gave me a look of amusement in return and rolled his eyes.

What the hell did *that* mean?

I wouldn't rule it out simply 'cause I couldn't predict the future, but I couldn't say I was interested in changing diapers and giving up, you know, sleep. The uncle gig suited me far better. I did love children, and I also liked the opportunity of handing them back to their parents. Always had.

Julian removed his headphones and kissed my shoulder. "Don't overthink it, love. I'm too selfish to share you."

I let out a sigh of relief and stole a smooch. "Good. There's plenty of other shit I see in our future."

"Oh, yeah?" He quirked a brow and smiled lazily. "What kind of shit?"

I shrugged. Maybe I'd opened my mouth too fast. I didn't wanna scare the kid.

"Well, we're buying a house together when we get home." I rubbed the back of my neck, and it was probably best I left it at that.

"Very true. I can't wait." He threaded our fingers together and gave my hand a squeeze.

"Me either."

*

Our first evening in Nice, I went to dinner with Sophie and the young guy who'd be playing April's son as an eighteen-year-old. Brad was a sweet kid, and Sophie had already taken him out for dinner back home, when he landed the part. But getting relaxed in each other's presence before a scene was always a good idea.

We went over the scenes and my plans for them while we feasted on seafood platters, plenty of beer, and salad the way you could only get it around the Mediterranean. By halfway through dinner, Brad had visibly relaxed, and he was looking forward to shooting. He said he loved acting but was also interested in directing, so when he asked if he could come with us when we returned to wrap up the last scenes in Paris, I agreed right away.

"You can shadow my PA," I said, licking butter off my thumb. "Julian is always nearby."

"PA in this case is short for man of Noah's dreams." Sophie smiled widely. She was a bit lit. It was cute.

"No argument from me, but I'm trying to keep it professional here," I laughed. "Julian almost had my head when I referred to him as my boyfriend on set the other week."

Brad chuckled and Sophie aww'd for some reason.

"He wants to impress you and show his worth," she said with a firm nod. "Speaking of. If I want to show my worth tomorrow, I should get some sleep. *Someone* has to be up at four to sit through a hard-core makeup session."

True, Brooklyn was gonna add ten years to Sophie. And both Tennyson and I were demanding fuckers. We wanted it subtle and real for when I shot close-ups.

*

Sophie wasn't the only one who was up early the next morning, though. So was I. I showed up at the hospital around five, and the parking lot looked like a war zone. The only reason we'd been allowed to shoot here was because the east wing was under construction.

I passed our trailers and the trailers that belonged to the construction site and followed Lucia inside. We'd only flown down with the first unit, so we didn't have too much crew milling about.

She brought me up to speed, and time flew between having the lighting adjusted, covering anything that looked too out of place for an American hospital room, and going over continuity issues with the script supervisor.

"I want a complete run-through of everything before lunch," I said. "See it as a rehearsal." We'd spend the rest of the day as well as tomorrow reshooting and getting more angles, but I wanted to run it all through once before. It would also help my script supervisor keep track of everything on screen.

Another perk of shooting digitally was you could include rehearsals without worrying about wasting expensive film. So regardless of the first results today, there was no waste.

"Understood." She nodded.

Julian showed up little past seven with coffee, breakfast, and a hard kiss.

"We're at work, baby." I smirked and took a sip of my coffee. "I thought kissing was a no-no."

He shrugged and started walking backward toward Lucia and Shawn. "Sometimes I can't help myself." He winked and then turned around.

I chuckled to myself, feeling ridiculous for how happy that guy made me.

Soon, everything was set up, and I slipped into director-mode. Sophie was beautiful, which might've been an odd way to describe her. Beautiful for her role. She looked thin, her hair lacked luster, and her aging had been created realistically.

Brad came down the hall as well, dressed like a shy high school kid with glasses, a flannel over a T-shirt, a backpack, and khakis.

Lucia and I worked together like a well-oiled machine, and as soon as Shawn declared he was ready, Lucia called for cameras to roll.

I didn't use my monitor this time. Brad stood outside the observation window of Sophie's room, and she was inside. The pale walls were empty, and she paced aimlessly, sometimes pausing to draw invisible patterns with her finger.

I called for action, and Shawn filmed Sophie from the outside of the room—Brad's point of view. Then slowly, Shawn included Brad in the frame, revealing that years had passed. We saw Brad hesitating and, in the end, not entering the room.

"Cut!"

We did the scene once more, and then Lucia announced the second set was finished in the art studio.

In there, April's paintings were stacked, canvas by canvas, and some hung on the walls. With the cameras rolling, Sophie mixed some paint and straightened in front of a blank canvas. Head tilted, Shawn catching her expression from the side.

She hummed. Brad watched in the background while she

remained oblivious to his presence.

The humming morphed into the lullaby April used to sing to her son.

I made a motion to keep filming. It wasn't the main angle I wanted, but Sophie was acing it, so I needed to see what she'd bring. It wouldn't be the first time something from a rehearsal shot made the final cut.

"Don't worry, dear boy," she sang softly, "Mommy can shelter you well. Don't worry, dear boy, Mommy can catch you stars." The canvas wasn't in the shot when she started painting. And even though it would be replaced with another canvas to show April's art, Sophie drew the brush gracefully and with purpose. "Don't worry, dear boy, Mommy can keep you safe. Don't worry, dear boy, Mommy can catch you stars."

Shawn moved the dolly backward, a living god with his camera, and I called cut.

It was…somber, the mood on the set. We had some scenes left to shoot in Paris, and the second unit was working around the clock with inserts and coverage, but this still felt like the end. It *would* be the end once the film was finished.

"Last scene!" I announced.

"Ugh, don't say that." Lucia pouted. "I'm not ready for this to end."

I frowned and looked behind me, seeking out Julian. And there he was. It wiped the frown from my face, and his smile made me smile, too. Nah, this wasn't the end at all.

We were only getting started.

EPILOGUE

The following year

We'd found our beach house not too far away from Daniel and Zane's around the same time I turned forty-two in February. But since we'd been buried in post-production work, we'd only managed to make the downstairs feel like home.

This time, I gave a fuck. No matter how much I loved our loft, this house was ours from the beginning, and copying a couple pages from a Pottery Barn catalogue wasn't enough.

Julian took care of most of the furniture. I wasn't picky, though I liked what he did with Sophie's help, mixing old with new, sorta like in our loft. I focused on keepsakes and pictures. I had Julian's script from *Catching Stars* framed, 'cause it had his sheet music doodled across the pages. He'd bought some souvenirs in Paris too that I found spots for in our living room. Combined with photos from our sightseeing and from work, it was beginning to feel a lot like we'd stay here more than at the loft.

I was sure as fuck okay with that.

Now, with *Catching Stars* finished, we had time to tend to the upstairs of our house, too. Asher, Daniel, and Zane were on their way over to help us put together some shit we'd had delivered.

Breakfast was served on the deck outside, and I watched in amusement as Julian laid out a rubber mat in the living room. He was protective of our hardwood floors and said the smallest scratch would shine like a beacon since the wood was dark. It was cute as fuck, seeing him fretting.

One day he'd almost panicked because we didn't have a cover for the pool yet, and he worried Blue was gonna jump in. Snowball's chance in hell; she hated water.

"Isn't it easier if we assemble the furniture upstairs?" I asked.

He replied as the doorbell rang. "Not the desks for our study."

He had a point. We had a study and our bedroom down here; guest rooms and ultimate man cave would be upstairs.

Heading to the hallway, I let the guys in and assured them we'd stocked up plenty on beer and that breakfast was ready.

"Cheers for helping out, guys," I said.

"No problem." Daniel slapped my shoulder on the way to the living room. "This daddy's not gonna drive today! Hey there, Julian."

I grinned and turned to Zane, who was rolling his eyes.

"The kids are with his folks. God knows what's going to happen today," he drawled. "He's complaining that we don't get out as much anymore, yet he's the one canceling plans and refusing to let anyone watch our children unless it's our parents."

And their parents lived out here, so when they were in New York…they were shit outta luck?

Asher chuckled. "So basically, either he's gonna get shit-faced, or he's going to worry himself sick about the kids."

"Pretty much," Zane laughed. "Let the party begin."

We all went outside to get some grub, and it was nice to have a day for just us guys. Shame Tennyson couldn't make it, but he was living his own daddy life up in Mendocino now. They both tried to be there as much as possible when Kayden and Ivy had school, though sometimes it was impossible.

"I don't think you want that one." Julian smiled slyly at the sandwich I'd grabbed for myself.

I unwrapped it and saw bacon everywhere, to which I grimaced. "Yeah, no shit. Thanks, baby."

He handed me one with mozzarella, pesto, and sundried tomatoes instead, and then we dove into a conversation about Asher being disgruntled because his eldest had just gotten a job in modeling. She'd graduated from college with good grades; I didn't see what was so wrong with testing it out. Zane, being a former model, had a lot to say.

"Noah," Julian whispered.

I didn't know why he was keeping his voice so low, but I leaned in and asked what was up.

He showed me his phone. "I just got this. Should I open it?"

I squinted at the display and saw it was an email. *Shit.* From his grandparents.

"That's up to you," I murmured.

We hadn't heard from the Hartleys even once. To be honest, I had hoped to get some kind of reaction after our interview had been published last Christmas. We'd even debated sending them an advanced copy but had eventually decided against it, mainly because Julian and I had made the cover along with another Hollywood couple. We'd been kinda hard to miss that month.

Julian opened the email and said it was from his grandfather. Then he got quiet as he read, and I only saw it was a fairly long letter.

"He's being cordial, at least." Julian scrolled down a little. "They read the article about us."

"That's good." I rubbed his neck gently, sensing the tension in him. Turning to the others, I acted as if nothing was wrong and did my best to contribute to the conversation. "Ash, before you put your foot in your mouth and have to face your daughter's wrath, ask yourself if you're against this because she's your baby girl or if it's the profession."

"Don't come here and give me logic, Collins," he bitched.

Daniel laughed.

"Technically, you came to him," Zane pointed out with a smirk.

They continued bantering—though Asher probably didn't

find it funny at all—and I refocused on Julian.

"They want to have dinner with us," he said quietly, and that revelation was a surprise. "He says he wants to give us the benefit of the doubt… Christ. I don't know whether to tell him off or just give him a chance."

I could relate there. They'd given us the doubt long before the benefit, I reckoned. That said, they were Julian's family; everyone fucked up here and there.

"If there's a chance they wanna reconcile and apologize, I think we should accept." I kept my voice low and pressed my lips to his hair. "We don't wanna live with regrets or what-ifs."

He sighed and rubbed his forehead, a crease between his brows. "I suppose you're right. But they have to fly out to us. I'm not going to Pittsburgh."

"That's fair. Did he say anything else?"

"He liked the trailer for the film." He gave me an uncertain smile. "Wouldn't that mean they're keeping track of what's happening?"

Given that the trailer was released yesterday, I'd say yes.

"Sounds like it." I hugged him to me. "That's good." He seemed to relax a bit, which made me happy, too. "Tell them we're happy to take them out for dinner if they decide to come out here. After Cannes, maybe."

The festival was only a couple weeks away.

"Okay. Yes." He nodded and got to typing.

Thankfully, we had a packed day ahead of us, so once he got that out of the way, we were all distracted for hours. Music blared out of our new surround sound system, and we assembled furniture and drank beer to rock legends.

Around lunch, we all ruled out a barbecue for dinner 'cause we were sweaty and tired already. After a quick dip in the pool to cool off, we were back at it and decided to order pizza for dinner later.

The funniest part of the day was without a fucking doubt when Asher, Daniel, and Julian struggled to carry our new pool table upstairs. We were lucky the stairs were wide, but it was a close call at the first landing where they had to flip the table in an upright position to pass. Then they got their own laugh when Zane and I almost dropped the flat screen going in the man cave.

I had to admit, that shit nearly gave me a heart attack.

"Are you okay?" Julian snickered at me.

I blew out a breath. "I will be. Fuck."

That made him crack up, and I lifted my T-shirt to wipe some sweat off my forehead.

"Jesus Christ, love." He eyed my abs.

I smirked. "Not to quote this fuckawesome song or anything, but you wanna pour some sugar on me?"

"Maybe…" He drew a finger down my stomach.

Asher felt the need to ruin the moment as he passed us with a box of movies. "Forget about it, you two. Make yourselves useful and call for pizza. We're starving."

Checking the time, I saw it'd gotten pretty late, and I was hungry, too.

I headed downstairs again and ordered some pies, and then I surveyed the living room, now empty of boxes and trash. We only had the desks left, and Julian and I could do that later. I'd hit a wall and didn't feel like being productive anymore.

To Julian, I showed my manliest goddamn pout, and he snorted and took pity on me.

"I suppose we can call it a day." He pinched my ass.

Daniel shook his head at Julian. "You're so whipped."

"Don't you mean smart?" Julian countered and tapped his temple. "You old folks need rest, or I'll have to go without sex tonight."

I widened my eyes. "You absolute *shit*."

He and Zane laughed their asses off while Daniel and I ignored them and went to the kitchen to get plates and whatnot. The cooler outside needed refilling with ice and beer, too.

"How about we turn this into a poker night?" Asher suggested as he joined us.

"Hell yeah." I nodded and grabbed a stack of napkins. "A heads-up, though. Julian plays innocent, but he's got game. Don't fall for his act."

I'd learned that the hard way.

The doorbell rang at that point, so Daniel took what was in my hands so I could get the door. On the way, I pulled out my wallet, noticing I didn't have much cash. Julian's wallet was in the hallway, though, so I snatched a couple bills from him.

Then I opened the door, and I kinda froze. Fuck me twice. It was Nicky. Fucking *Nicky*. Maybe hysteria got ahold of me for a beat because I laughed. *Hard.* Part of me felt like a complete prick, but fuck it, this was karma.

His expression hardened. He stood there with our pizzas, glaring, seething, and I couldn't stop laughing.

"I'm sorry, kid," I wheezed out. "Goddamn, this is too much."

It was evident he'd had no clue we lived here or that he was delivering to us. I did my best to smother some of my amusement as I handed over the cash and took the pies, and I made a mental note to never order from that place again. Next time, he'd undoubtedly spit in our food.

"You ruined my career," he gritted out.

"That was the fucking point," I said, down to chuckles. "Lord, Nicky. You just made my day. I can't wait to tell Julian."

"Go to hell, Collins." He stuffed the money into his pocket and turned away.

"Hey!" I called. He didn't face me, but he paused. "Unlike you, you scheming little asshole, I'm not a douche. I believe in making amends. But until then…" I walked over to him and stuck five bucks into his jacket pocket. "I always tip my waiter. Or delivery guy. Now, fuck off."

I closed the door in his face and chuckled to myself as I walked through the house and out to the deck.

Asher, Julian, Daniel, and Zane looked at me quizzically.

That made me laugh all over again. "You're never gonna believe this…"

*

Two weeks later

"We should hurry, Noah…" He writhed under me and gripped my arms as he pushed back and met my thrusts. "Fuck! Please stop teasing me, at least. I'm so close!"

I chuckled, out of breath. "But I love teasing you." Stroking his cock firmly, I spread the pre-come seeping out of his sensitive head and drove into his tight ass over and over. "*God…*" I groaned and closed my eyes, dipping down to kiss him deeply.

My body took over, and I fucked him harder and faster. The bed frame banged against the wall, Julian's gasps became shallower, and his begging drove me crazy with lust.

I cursed as I peered down between us. My cock was slick with lube, and the sight of it pushing in and out of him was almost more than I could take. He was a vision. His abs contracted, his thighs firm with muscle caged me between him, and his long fingers clawed at my back.

"You're gonna leave marks."

"Good." He panted and fisted my hair, pulling me down for a sloppy kiss. Tongues and teeth, heavy breaths. "I want to mark you. I want—" He let out a moan when I slammed in. "Fuck. I want you to be marked underneath your tux today."

"Dirty little boy," I growled. "I love it."

Staying inside him, I swiveled my hips to reach deeper, and he cried out. The look on his face did me in. As he trembled and began coming, I gnashed my teeth together, buried myself balls deep, and let go.

A surge of euphoria shot through me, leaving ripples of pleasure that made me shiver and tremor until the high slowly came to an end. My cock pulsed inside Julian, his ass clenching as if it wanted every fucking drop I had.

"I need a nap," I groaned.

Julian laughed breathlessly. "Too bad we don't have time."

It was. And I guessed I couldn't miss my first major premiere of a film I'd directed.

*

An hour later, Julian and I were dressed to the nines, and we met up with Tennyson and Asher in the hotel bar.

"How do ya fuckin' do, Wright brothers?" I grinned and slapped my hand to Asher's in a firm shake.

"Used and abused, Collins." He chuckled and motioned for a line of glasses of whiskey. "A drink while we wait for the ladies to make us late?"

"Cheers." I extended a glass to Julian and took a sip. "The cardio making you feel used and abused, or…?"

Tennyson laughed.

Ash rolled his eyes. "No, it's all Tennyson. I've taken his meetings this morning."

I lifted a brow. "I take it they went as expected."

"Why do you think I let Ash handle them?" Tennyson smiled wryly. "So far, only offers I can refuse."

I didn't need to ask further. *Catching Stars* had a big buzz going on, and studios had been making offers since we found out the film had been accepted at Cannes. With some strategically leaked clips and one official trailer, Tennyson was set to make bank. But yeah, before the actual viewing, the studios played hard to get, even when they were desperate to distribute the first Tennyson Wright Production.

It was funny.

"Fuck me," Tennyson muttered into his glass. He was looking at something behind me, so I turned and saw Sophie and Brooklyn approaching. They were stunning, and I reckoned their dresses alone could bring a third world country outta poverty. I wouldn't even speculate about the jewelry.

"We ready to go?" I emptied my glass and set it down on the bartop. Then I grabbed Julian's hand and kissed it. "I have a nervous boyfriend who's about to see his name in the credits for the first time."

Sophie beamed at him as Tennyson kissed her temple. "You've done an amazing job, Julian. I hope we'll work together again."

"Thank you, you too." Julian nodded and adjusted his bow tie. Maybe he was more than nervous. Hell, I was anxious as fuck, and I'd been around this life for two decades.

We exited the hotel together and ignored the paps that had flown in from all over the world for the festival. We had a limo waiting, and I sat down next to Julian as the rest piled in.

"Just wait 'til award season." Asher winked at Julian.

"Oh, God. I'm not sure I can take it." Julian slumped back and blew out a heavy breath. "If I didn't adore your wife, Tennyson, I might've caused you some serious harm for this."

"Nonsense." Tennyson slid him an easy smile. "It's your score. We give credit where it's due."

I agreed.

Julian had gone from being an inspiration of sorts to taking over. He hadn't merely set the tone with a few songs; he'd ended up composing all music. He disliked being the center of attention something fierce, so Tennyson and I had handled the hiring of an orchestra, artists, and a studio, and Julian had been the silent genius behind it all.

"What about you, Noah?" Sophie asked. "Nervous?"

I let out a breathy laugh after Tennyson sent me a knowing smirk.

"I'll take that as a yes," Brooklyn snickered.

Good call.

We drove through a buzzing Cannes that was packed with stars and the finest Hollywood had to offer. Festivals were a melting pot of music, fashion, film, and launches of brands. Everyone who belonged on the red carpet was a billboard, sponsored by whatever company and fashion house that had something to show off.

"Noah." Julian nudged me.

"Yeah?"

"From Grandma and Grandpa." He revealed his phone.

We wish you two good luck today. We are proud, no matter what.

That was nice.

We hadn't seen them yet, but Julian had been emailing them a lot, and as of a few days ago, he'd been on the phone with them. It wasn't as strained anymore, and though they definitely found our relationship a bit *too* unconventional, they were trying.

We couldn't ask for more than that. They were of another generation and had their own sets of beliefs. So it wasn't about handing out an ultimatum of "It's all or nothing." It was about meeting halfway and accepting each other, even when we didn't agree.

"You okay—" I was cut off by the sound of people cheering, and I looked out to see we were passing the fan area for our theater. Press and crew filled the sidewalks, and we had officially arrived. The line of limos didn't seem too long, so it would be our turn soon.

"Ask me tonight," Julian said nervously, peering out the window. The text message and previous topic were already forgotten, so I assumed he was okay. "Don't forget to keep your promise."

"Of course." I squeezed his hand. "Junk food in bed and shutting out the world."

Sophie evidently heard that, and she nodded in approval. "Oh my God, us too. Tennyson was out this morning to get us all the snacks we'd want for a lazy night under the covers. My feet are already killing me."

Well, what did she expect with six-inch shit-kickers?

"I'm taking my stunner out for a romantic dinner on a yacht," Asher said and kissed the top of Brooklyn's hand. She smiled brilliantly, and I knew they were looking forward to their vacation after today.

"I just want hot wings," Sophie said.

Tennyson smiled. "I just want you naked, so it works out great for me."

I chuckled and scooted forward in my seat, since we were next. An assistant was approaching our vehicle, speaking rapidly into her headset. Asher sat closest to the door, so he opened it and stepped out first.

Immediately, the background noise of the crowd morphed into a loud cacophony.

I stepped out too and extended my hand to Julian. Fingers wove together. A firm grip. His hand a little clammy.

"Before I forget," he said, squinting in the sunlight, "I'm so proud of you."

I grinned and kissed his hand. "Right back at'cha, baby. We make a good team."

"The best."

In-fucking-deed, and now it was time to hit the red carpet.

*

Julian became at ease halfway through the movie. He relaxed visibly, and I could tell seeing our creation helped. He believed in the project. He was satisfied with his own work.

I was satisfied with my work as well, but I knew I wouldn't relax until all was said and done. Until the audience had said its piece. Until Tennyson had gotten an offer he couldn't refuse.

Maybe he was sensing how high-strung I was, 'cause Julian put a hand on my leg and stroked it soothingly as the final scene began on the screen.

Light poured into the window of the art studio where April painted. It gave off an oddly warm and romantic vibe, a contrast to the sad reality of her not being able to live her life.

April's son watched her, his discomfort as clear as his love for his mother. He missed her, hated her fate and that there was nothing he could do about it.

She began humming quietly, and Julian's piano followed, along with more sunlight as the camera zoomed out to include a better shot of both of them.

"Don't worry, dear boy… Mommy can shelter you well. Don't worry, dear boy, Mommy can catch you stars." A few violins joined Julian's piano, and it was enough to give me goose bumps. *"Don't worry, dear boy, Mommy can keep you safe. Don't worry, dear boy, Mommy can catch you stars."*

I grabbed Julian's hand.

Dust particles danced in the light.

As the camera went behind Brad, filming over his shoulder, he let out a breath. April never noticed him.

"I believe you, Mom," he whispered.

Then he slowly turned around and walked down the darkened

corridor, and the music grew louder, including the recorded lyrics of April's lullaby.

"Directed by Noah Collins" appeared on the screen, which was a total mindfuck. *I did this.* I drew in a deep breath and waited. "A Tennyson Wright Picture" followed, and then I felt a ton of weight sliding off my shoulders as the audience gave us a standing ovation.

Oh, thank fuck.

The credits started rolling, and I stood up with my friends, never letting go of Julian's hand. Sweet mother of Christ, I was almost shaking.

"So fucking proud. I love you." He reached up and kissed my cheek. *To hell with that*, I thought, and gave him a hard kiss. He grinned. "I want to see that name at the top many times. But…in your passport…?"

I raised a brow, confused. And a bit too overwhelmed to decipher what he was saying.

"I think Hartley-Collins sounds good for us," he said.

Fuck me.

Unable to speak, I kissed him again, and I managed a firm nod before I had an audience to face. What a motherfucking release of emotion and stress. From the moment we'd started, when Tennyson gave me this script, to now. The most prestigious film festival in the world. And Julian had been there with me for every step of the way.

I shook hands with Tennyson, both of us relieved and excited, and I hugged Sophie and Brooklyn.

"I was right," Tennyson told me. "I knew you could do this."

"I had a great mentor." I shook his hand again, and then we were called up to the stage for a Q&A I couldn't say I wanted to sit through. But it came with the job.

The applause grew louder, and we reached the front when Julian's name rolled past in the credits.

Fuck yeah, Hartley-Collins sounded perfect.

FOR MORE, VISIT

www.caradeewrites.com

CARA ON SOCIAL MEDIA

FACEBOOK.COM/CARADEEWRITES

@CARADEEWRITES

@CARAWRITES

Made in the USA
Lexington, KY
17 May 2017